# HACKETTE

♦

## J KEMP

PublishAmerica
Baltimore

ISBN: 1-4241-2455-7
PUBLISHED BY PUBLISHAMERICA, LLLP
www.publishamerica.com
Baltimore

Printed in the United States of America

# CHAPTER ONE

O K, it looks a little seedy, Billie thought, but everyone starts somewhere. She was standing under a hanging metal sign decorated with a grin and the words "The Cheshire Cat", at the entrance to an alley off Fleet Street.

Next door to the pub was a grimy black door and a row of bells, the bottom one marked World Wide News/ Pics.

Her first job in journalism, a trial shift at a news agency. A humble beginning maybe but fast-forwarding a few years, Billie saw herself among excited friends in a crowded banqueting hall. An announcement: "The Pulitzer prize for her work on uncovering corruption in high places goes to Billie Wilson!"

After all, hadn't she been top of her year group at journalism college and won the silver cup for best all round student? That had to mean something. Recalling the motto engraved on the cup: "Truth, freedom and the defence of democracy" Billie pushed the bell.

No-one spoke through the microphone. The door buzzed immediately and she walked through. Inside, off a narrow hall was a medium sized room crammed with desks, terminals, newspapers, piles of paper and people, almost all on the phone, some holding two receivers, one to each ear. There was a whiteboard on the wall at the opposite end of the room with a black marker tied to it. It was divided into two halves and scored across into several sections. A large man with a red face and a brightly coloured bow tie was scrawling names on the right hand side, matching them to what appeared to be jobs on the left hand side. The list read: "Death Knock, Death Watch, Ind Ass, Cricklewood Doorstep, Machete Murder, Bow St, Snaresbrook, Woburn Sex D, Toast (off)."

After a moment, a tall, slim woman walked over and gave her a friendly smile.

"Are you the new scribe?"

"Yes, I'm Billie Wilson."

"Hi, I'm Sorrel," she said. She pointed over to the red-faced man: "That's Felix, he owns the business. I'm the office manager, I soothe the savage beast and try to stop him from devouring the staff - metaphorically speaking - not." She grinned.

"Are you all prepared? Let me get you a notebook and pencil - getting stationery out of Felix is like getting juice out of a sucked orange and never let him catch you wasting sellotape. It makes him lose all reason. Which, to be frank, is easily done."

Taking a key out of her pocket, she walked over to a large cupboard, opened it and got out two notebooks and a handful of biros which she handed over with the air of a fairy godmother. Then she gestured over to Felix, who was talking on the phone.

Billie had a knot of nervousness in her stomach. She sat down at a desk, noticing a slick of spilled coffee in which floated an elastic band.

Felix put the phone down. "You must be Billie Wilson. I thought you were coming tomorrow. I've got your CV somewhere." He looked round at the mountains of paper.

She tried to help. "Well, I've recently finished a post graduate course in journalism. I've done work experience at the Guardian and a couple of locals too, so I think I know the score."

"To be frank, Billie, we don't do a lot for the Guardian. We work to a slightly different agenda. But we do stuff for some of the other nationals." Felix looked at the board. "I don't know what I can send you on today, it's all death knocks and doorsteps. Tell you what, you can help Barmy. He's the picture editor. Barmy!" he shouted. A scowling man stuck his head out from a small room off the main office. "Yeah?"

"You've been complaining so much about that assignment I've decided to give you an assistant. This is Billie." He turned to her. "Sorry about this," he said "It's a pretty ridiculous job but unfortunately we can't afford to turn it down."

Barmy nodded. "You better come here."

"Sure." Billie wanted to appear keen. Hanging her beloved black leather coat carefully on an overloaded coat stand, she walked over to the side room, a small kitchenette with sink, fridge, microwave and toaster. A swing bin in the corner was marked with yellow streaks caused by carelessly-thrown tea bags.

Barmy was standing by the work surface surrounded by white, sliced bread.

"I get the real plum jobs," he said. "It's the sodding psychic toast. The Sunday fucking Spurt are running a story about one of their self styled 'readers' whose toast supposedly pops up on the morning of the League cup final with the fucking *score* inscribed on it. So of course he goes to the bookies, puts on a bet and wins a bastard fortune. And *I'm* taking the pictures."

"But the League cup final's not until Saturday."

Barmy narrowed his eyes. "I know that. We can't do it after the score's announced. That's not the Spurt way. We have to make toast with every possible cup final score inscribed on it and photograph it popping out of the toaster, see?" he said. "So, as Gary Gilmour said, let's do it."

She spent the rest of the morning painstakingly making toast and carefully cutting the scores into it with a blunt potato peeler. Eventually they carted the first batch and the toaster down to the basement where there was a small photographic studio and set up some shots.

"Haven't you finished yet?" Felix came in to ask at one point. "What are you doing, eating all the evidence? Hey d'you suppose if you eat psychic toast, you get psychic shit?"

"Don't suggest that to the wankers at the Spurt," Barmy said, unsmiling.

At lunch time, Billie was sent out with a complicated sandwich and tea order.

After lunch the office was quiet and Billie was given the job of phoning a long list of numbers - police headquarters, fire stations, coast guards, court offices across the south of England. Another reporter was doing the same thing and she carefully reproduced the form of words.

"Hi, I'm Billie Wilson from World Wide News and Pictures. Anything doing?"

Scotland Yard Press Bureau was at the top and bottom of the list. The first time a cross-sounding woman answered.

"Phone the tape," she said.

"I'm sorry?"

"The tape," she said, her tone making "You moron", unnecessary.

"Sorry, I'm new."

"You have to phone the press tape."

"What's that number?"

Felix looked over, tuning into the call: "Tell them the effing press tape hasn't been updated since 9am."

Billie ended the call and tried Scotland Yard again later. This time she got a much friendlier-sounding male voice.

"Hi, are you new? I haven't heard you before. I'm Theodore, we'll be talking a lot probably - we're just about to update the tape. We've got a dead body, a young woman found in a vehicle in Canterbury Gardens N 4."

"Wow thanks." she put the phone down, walked over and told Felix, who jumped to his feet.

"Get there, just get there," he shouted. "Sorrel! Get over here, ring round dead girl in a car? What kind of car? What kind of girl? How killed? Who found her?"

"Sorry, I didn't ask"

"You didn't ask?"

"There wasn't time," she said, picking up her jacket and the notebooks and pens Sorrel had given her. She slipped into a desk next to Felix and picked up a phone. "Hi, is that the Current? Hi Nigel, Sorrel Hayes here from Worldwide - we've had a tip the dead body of a young girl has been found in North London - you want cover? Yes we've got someone on the way, arriving any moment, OK thanks." With her left hand she waved Billie towards the door.

Billie ran to the station and flung herself onto a north-bound tube, hoping to be the first on the scene of the crime. One change and a ten minute walk later, she found a small cul de sac blocked by blue and white police tape and behind that a large white police mobile unit which blocked the view. A constable stood on guard at the tape and on the other side was a guy clutching a notebook. Damn, she had been beaten to the story.

Her rival was about her age, in his early 20s, with shoulder-length wavy, brown hair, slightly messy. He had a slightly crumpled suit on under a floppy brown coat and was carrying a canvas bag over one shoulder.

He said something and both he and the policeman laughed. Billie walked up to them and they both looked at her in silence.

"I'm Billie Wilson from Worldwide News and Pictures. Hi."

"Hi. I'm Rick Ansell from Global."

The young man stuck out his hand and Billie took it. His touch was light and brief.

"So," he said. "Are you friend or foe?"

"I come to steal your watch. Sorry," she explained to his puzzled look. "It's a quote from Shakespeare. Hamlet Act One, Scene One, 'The sentry says Halt who goes there, and the reply is, I come to steal your watch."

" A literary babe. My favourite. My watch isn't worth much I'm afraid. Are you new?"

"Comparatively," Billie admitted.

7

"You seem unusually friendly for a Worldwide scribe. Obviously you aren't aware that you and I are the hack equivalent of Capulets and Montagues at the moment."

"Why?"

"One of our girls went to spec out the industrial tribunal court, to see if there were any tasty cases. She had a quick whiz round, nothing caught her eye, you lot seemed to have been and gone, she left saying nothing doing but your bloke had seen her come in and hid in the broom cupboard!" Rick broke off and made an expression of distaste. "She never expected that. Anyway, your lot ended up getting a real Carry On sex discrim all to yourselves. Lots of fnarr fnarr jokes: The boss remarks on how his PA obviously likes a big banana in the afternoon, he claims later it's a totally innocent remark, stuff like that, the papers ate it up. You can imagine, news, comment, editorials about it. And we missed it. How d'you think that went down with our boss?"

"I can't imagine."

"The rest of us took cover under the desks, there was so much stuff flying across the room. It was just like the blitz. We're now under strict instructions not to fraternise with the enemy. You."

"Well I'm glad you're talking to me at least."

He grinned. "I'm a born rebel."

" Well I think I can promise not to behave like that. Relax. You can trust me."

"I've heard that one somewhere before. Trust me, I'm a journalist."

Billie smiled. "Any news about the dead girl then?"

"I don't know—they won't tell me anything until the press officer gets here, but it's a definite murder or at least suspicious circs. The trouble is, I don't know what kind of car it is."

"Do we need to?"

"You are new. It makes a hell of a lot of difference to the story. Like a beautiful blonde found stabbed in a Merc is going to make the front page, while some old scrubber in a Skoda is a page 17 filler. Get the picture? That's newspapers."

"OK. Any other tips?"

Rick looked at the policeman who had walked away a few yards to talk to a colleague emerging from the police van.

"Never use your own mobile to file copy. They don't pay you back. We call back on a free number. How about we go to the phones, fill the desks in and stop for a coffee on the way back. This weather is freezing my balls off."

"OK, But what if something happens while we're away?"

"Probably not much is going to happen in the next half hour, and as long as there's no-one here to see it, even if something does happen, it didn't happen, if you see what I mean?"

"OK," Billie said. "I get it. If a tree falls in the forest and no-one hears it, it didn't happen. It is a bit cold to be standing around."

Rick beckoned the police constable over. "We're just off to grab a cuppa? Be a mate, don't solve the crime until we get back, OK?"

"I'll do my best. Can't promise."

They set off towards the main road and a couple of phone boxes. One was occupied by two teenage girls. With mock gallantry, Rick opened the door of the other one for Billie.

"I'm probably supposed to race you to them. But I guess I'm not going to make Scoop of the Year, not this year anyway." Billie went into the phone box and Rick came in after her and shut the door. "You can listen to me file my copy, if you like," he said, grinning. "That's how much I trust you. Bit of a tight squeeze in here, isn't it. But at least it's warm."

He put his arm around Billie to lift the receiver, dialed and said: "Wotcher, Kev, it's Rick. First copy from the murder scene. Call it carkill one. I haven't got much yet. The corpse of a woman believed murdered was found in an abandoned car in North London today. Point. Par. Cap P police were desperately searching for clues to the identity of the murder victim after a passer-by made the grisly discovery shortly after 12pm. Point. Par. Cap F forensic experts in masks and white overalls were searching the car, comma, looking for initial caps DNA traces which might help to solve the baffling crime. Point. Par. Cap T the man leading the investigation, initial caps,

Detective Chief Inspector Ronald Bennet, two Ns one T, is expected to make a statement this afternoon. Point. Cap M meanwhile, anyone who saw or heard anything suspicious in the quiet, residential area where the body was found, comma, initial caps Canterbury Gardens in Tottenham, comma North London, comma is urged to contact police. Point. More follows. OK? I'd better go. Bennet is getting here soon."

Billie was impressed. "Was that all off the top of your head? You didn't write it down?"

"No, there's no time usually. Anyway I even dream in journalese these days. Your turn."

He went outside, leaving Billie to stumble through her copy alone. Felix sounded tetchy.

"So you're there. What's the story?"

She tried to sound crisp and on top of the situation. "We don't know much yet."

He didn't like it. "That's no good. Tell me what you do know."

"Forensics are there, in their overalls. The man in charge, that's DCI Bennet, one n two ts, is making a statement this afternoon. The body was discovered by a passer by just after 12 noon…"

In the background, computer keys were being bashed.

"You need to do better than that. The kind of car? Age of woman? How killed? Descriptions? Who found her? Any clues?"

"I don't have any of that yet I'm afraid."

Felix sighed. "Describe the scene. The area."

"It's a quiet, residential area, the street is a cul de sac cordoned off with police tape. There's a police van there."

"We need more as soon as. Call us in an hour, or before if anything else happens. Who else is there?"

"Global."

"Watch your back. That Global reporter will try to stitch you up. Keep clear of her but watch what she's up to - Understand?"

"Yes, boss."

"One more thing - Benett? One n two ts?"

She thought for a moment. "Actually no, I meant to say one t two ns."

Felix laughed, a loud, shouty laugh which Billie found vaguely alarming. Rick was waiting for her outside the phone box, leaning against a wall reading a newspaper, folded over to display the sports pages. They set off up the road towards a greasy spoon. The tea was a rich, invigorating brew poured from a brown china teapot standing warming by the grill plate, topped up with hot water. The bacon was fried in oil and folded between slices of white bread, absorbent as kitchen paper. They sat facing each other over a formica table on which stood brown and red sauce bottles and a squat round sugar shaker with a steel funnel.

"It's nice to be inside," Rick said, pouring a stream of sugar into his tea and stirring it. "I'm glad I persuaded you to come here. If you'd been Ms Keen I couldn't have come either and I'm starving. All I've had for breakfast is a packet of Fisherman's Friends to take away the smell of last night's booze. And I was freezing out there. I ended up staying on a friend's sofa after a night out last night."

"I thought you looked as if you'd slept in that suit."

"You are obviously a trained observer. Things are looking up for Worldwide. The last one of yours I met was more of a train observer."

Rick opened his sandwich and squirted in both brown sauce and tomato ketchup. "You wouldn't think it, but they're good together."

"I'll take your word for it. Where d'you go last night then?"

"D'you know Theo from Scotland Yard?" he asked.

"I've spoken to him."

"He's a great bloke, a real laugh. He had a few of us round to his new place for dinner last night. We had a few gallons of wine and most of us just crashed out there. Most of the crack reporting team of Global News and Pictures have got wicked hangovers today."

"And he's a copper?"

"No. Press officers are civilian staff. He's a Brixton boy - he's a laugh. He was smoking spliff last night and everything. But keep that to yourself mind. Hey Dr Watson," he said. "I've got an idea - shall we take a gander round the back of the crime scene? See if we can see what kind of car it is? That would be a bit of a scoop. Just five minutes?"

Billie thought about it briefly. It didn't feel like she was doing so great on her trial at Worldwide. She had one day to show them what she could do and this was no time for hanging back and avoiding opportunities. Finding out what kind of car it was could be her first scoop.

"OK", she said.

They left the cafe and looked around. A railway line ran at right angles to the main road along a low metal bridge which crossed the road between Canterbury Gardens and the cafe. The murder scene cul de sac backed on to the railway. Walking up the road away from the murder scene, they found that an identical cul-de-sac abutted the other side of the railway line.

There was a high wire-link fence blocking the end and behind it rose a steep embankment covered with young, bright green nettles. They reminded Billie of her mother Marina who picked them for nettle soup and pie. Marina and her partner Lotty were lesbians who as well as eating nettles, really hugged trees. Billie's brother Oscar had christened them the Moomins after a Scandinavian children's programme.

Among the nettles were glimpses of brightly coloured drinks cartons and bottles and the remains of plastic bags flew like streamers from bramble bushes further up.

A house on either side of the road backed onto the embankment, each with a garden wall ending at the fence. There was a smell of mingled damp earth and something sour and vaguely sulphurous.

Rick hopped up onto one of the walls which put him head and shoulders above the fence. "Climb up here and I'll help you over the fence," he said.

Billie took a deep breath and climbed up. Then she bent down and unzipped her boots and chucked them over one at a time. "Got to get over now," she said, "I love those boots. Right, give us a leg up."

Rick bent his right leg forward so that she could step on it. She planted her stockinged foot firmly on his thigh and put all her weight on it. She was heavier than she looked, Rick told her, but she managed to haul herself onto the top of the fence, hauling her skirt up to the top of her thighs for ease of movement.

"Oh help, I think I'm stuck." she said at one point. But she lowered herself down onto her arms, hung for a moment and dropped down onto the ground. Rick followed her over easily. Billie was sitting on the ground, zipping up her boots when he jumped down beside her.

"Next time I'll wear my commando gear," she said.

It had rained the night before and the ground was still muddy and slippy, obscured by thick undergrowth. At the top was a low stone wall, then the railway and then another low wall. They got over the first wall and walked across the track.

"I reckon Canterbury Gardens is over that wall. Let's walk along a bit before going over. We don't want to be spotted," Rick said.

They started to walk along by the line when they heard the rumour of a train. A second later the noise was a hundred times louder. It was coming fast. They ran towards the wall but Billie caught her heel, stumbled and almost tripped. Rick managed to catch her arm and steady her as she fell, then gave her a helpful shove over the wall at that side. They both rolled over the top and landed, shaken, in a heap on the grass at the other side as the train roared by.

"Hey, thanks pardner," Billie said, breathing out hard. She sat up and pushed her hair out of her eyes.

Their backs pressed against the wall, they looked down through the undergrowth. They could just see over it down to the side of a house with an overgrown back garden. Looking right, they could see what was almost certainly the very end of Canterbury Gardens, a chain-link fence, a small patch of road, a front garden and a doorway.

"We need to crawl along a bit to see better. Keep your head down," Rick said. Then paused. Something occurred to him. "Listen. D'you think we should be doing this? Interfering with the police investigation?"

Billie thought for a moment. "We're not interfering, really. We're just having a little peek. We simply want to know what kind of car it was. Come on."

She began to crawl along the top of the bank. Rick followed her, close behind. She stopped and he almost bumped right into her bum. She lay down and carried on commando-style on knees and elbows. Then she stopped again and somehow wriggled round so that he could see her face. There faces were very close together and they found themselves whispering…

"I think that's close enough," Billie said.

They peered though the grass and weeds down straight onto Canterbury Gardens. The long incident van was visible at the other end of the cul de sac . Behind it was the cordon of police tape. In front were other vehicles and vans including an ambulance. And right at their end of the cul de sac, centre stage, parked slightly askew was a white Rolls Royce.

"Wow," Rick said, "Result!" In the driver's seat they could see the figure of a woman, dark, glossy hair, a head tipped back above a white dress that was stained with blood. As they watched, some men in white overalls bent into the car and wrapped the lifeless body in a large white plastic sheet. She was lifted out and placed on a trolley which was then rolled into an ambulance waiting between the Roller and the incident van. They lay in silence, watching.

"Yeeuch," Rick said, "Hovis.You know, brown bread. Dead."

# CHAPTER TWO

That evening after dinner Billie told her fiance: "I saw a dead body today. And I met a guy. I think he fancied me." She was working on the theory that it's good to keep men on their toes. Antony raised his eyebrows. She certainly had all his attention.

They were sitting at the dining table in the window of his north London flat, looking out at the lights of the city below and eating a meal Antony had cooked, strips of white fish stir fried with mange tout and a bottle of black bean sauce, served with boiled rice.

Technically, it was Billie's flat too as she had moved in a few months earlier and was paying something towards the mortgage. But it was still his space.

"Tell me about your first day. Who was the corpse? And who's the guy?" He poured them each a second glass of Pouilly Fuisse, still cold from the fridge.

"It was a completely crazy day - he's OK - a journalist from a rival news organisation. Not particularly nice-looking, but a good laugh."

"The guy I suppose, not the stiff?" Antony smiled. "Yeah," Billie said, admiring Antony's perfect teeth, white against his ski-tanned skin. Tall and muscular, with long black hair, Antony was approaching 40, fifteen years older than Billie, but to her, he looked like the lead singer of a boy band.

"He was a bit mad actually. I got sent to this murder scene and I just tagged along after him because he looked like he knew what he was doing. We clambered round the back and saw a dead woman in a white Roller."

"I heard about that. Intriguing story. It was on the news just before you came in. Who was she?"

"I don't think they've id-ed her yet." Billie consciously used the journo slang that she'd picked up on the murder scene that afternoon. "I was there till nearly 8pm and they hadn't, but let's watch the news just in case there's been a development. It was absolutely bloody freezing. I was standing in the street for nearly ten hours until they got someone to relieve me, stamping to keep my toes from going numb and shouting stupid questions at anyone who looked important. A journalist from the Sun let me sit in his car for a bit but other than that, brrrr. "

"From the Sun? Your mother wouldn't like that."

Billie thought about that. Marina with her left-wing politics and her job teaching feminist literary criticism at Sussex University seemed to inhabit another planet from her. She regarded reporters from the Sun in the light that others regarded the legions of the undead.

"That's true. My mother's not from the Sun, she's from Moomin Valley. But actually he was really nice and it was bloody freezing. Turned out he was at Oxford with Oscar. Anyway, let's turn on the news. I want to see what they say."

They moved on to the sofa and turned on the TV. The news had already started.

*"The body of a woman, believed to be singer Rebelle Fernandez, the wife of flamboyant financier Xavier Fernandez, was discovered in a white Rolls Royce in a London street earlier today. Our reporter Mark Bland is at the scene."*

"Wow, it's Rebelle," Billie said. "God I thought she looked familiar. I was so into her when I was about 19."

The picture shifted to show a man in a dark suit holding a microphone standing in what Billie recognised as Canterbury Gardens. Over his shoulder, a crowd of reporters waited at the police tape.

*"Behind me you can see the scenes here as dozens of tabloid reporters bay for the latest on how - or why - the beautiful Annabelle Fernandez who was better known as Rebelle, the singer and songwriter, could have met her death. Her horrifically mutilated body was discovered in a white Rolls Royce registered in the name of her husband in this quiet north London street earlier today. Police have spent the day combing the area for clues. They are anxious to interview an individual seen fleeing through neighbouring gardens shortly before the body was discovered."*

"That's outrageous!"

"I know, what a disgusting crime. Nobody's safe, are they really."

"Not the murder, Bland! You should see what's behind him - The scenes were hardly caused by tabloid reporters. The BBC, Sky and ITV links vans turned up, they're like enormous lorries with 40 foot poles coming out of them, and there was another van with loads of cables coming out of it, and a noisy generator and about a dozen technicians all yelling across the street, things like 'Oy Bill have you got me spanner,' and then they phoned up for pizzas so there were three pizza delivery bikes as well, all causing a great deal more disruption than a few tabloid reporters quietly sitting in their cars, using nothing noisier than a propelling pencil." Billie stopped. There was a photofit of the suspect on the screen, a young face with a straight nose, dark hair and eyebrows.

"You know," Antony said, "That looks rather like you but not as pretty."

"Do you think so?" The face on screen did look vaguely like the one Billie saw in the mirror.

"Where were you on the night of March the 12th?" Antony raised his eyebrows again.

"I was here, with you, except of course you were out late, with your family because you went for a meal to talk about the wedding, didn't you?"

"Yes," Antony said, going over to the table and picking up the plates and cutlery. "And by the way I hope you're remembering the wedding meeting tomorrow. It's really important, we've got so much to discuss. We haven't had a meeting for more than a fortnight."

"But Antony, the wedding isn't for another four months and I'm doing something."

"What?"

"I can't remember, but I'm sure I was doing something - oh OK." Billie said, giving in gracefully. "I'll be there." She hated arguments, especially with Antony. He could stay angry for ages.

"Good, it's at my parents' house and all the ushers are coming. The bridesmaids are coming too, have you forgotten? It'll be fun, we're having lunch afterwards. I suppose Oscar's a no-show. Again."

"Sorry, you know he can't make Saturdays."

"Well, he is giving you away. It would be nice if he would show some interest." He went into the kitchen and started washing up.

Billie sat staring blankly at the screen, remembering the morning. After lying on the embankment for a few minutes, Rick and she had decided to get out before they were spotted. After crawling back through the long grass to the railway wall, Billie raised her head above it and quickly ducked down again. Two policemen were making their way along each side of the track, obviously searching for evidence. Much as she might have said to Rick she thought what they were doing was fine, there was no way Billie wanted to be explaining herself to the murder squad.

"Shotty," she called in a low voice. "The cops are coming!"

Rick wrinkled his brow. "Better go that way." He pointed down the embankment.

Below was a row of back gardens through which they should be able to reach the main road. They slid as quickly as possible down the bank and Rick helped to shove Billie over the wire-link fence before climbing over himself. But as Billie dropped down on the other side, a face appeared at the window by the garden and she found herself looking into a pair of fierce blue eyes. She flung herself over a wooden fence and ran through the next two gardens, then stepped over a low wall onto the street, brushed herself down and, heart still rattling like a train over points, attempted to saunter back to the police tape. A few minutes later, Rick rushed up, with grass sticking out of his hair.

"What happened? Was it something I said? You legged it as if you were a zebra and I was a lion who'd missed lunch."

Billie looked around at the pack of journalists and photographers who had now gathered. "Shh" she mouthed. Then, taking his arm she moved him to the edge of the crowd.

"Someone saw me," she said. "It was horrible. Can we forget that ever happened? Please?"

"Definitely," he said. "After we've filed."

Felix had let out a whoop of delight when Billie told him what she had seen. Then he backtracked. "Better watch it though mate, I don't want you overstepping the mark. Whoa, back, keep your enthusiasm in check. But that's great. They'll announce it soon anyway but first is what we want to be. Has anyone else got it?"

"I think the Global reporter might have snuck round the back too - he saw me coming back."

"Not so good."

"Is there anything else you want to know?"

"Was she a looker?"

"It's kind of hard to say, Felix. I was some distance way and she was - well - dead."

"Right, get the picture. Congratulations though mate. You did well."

"Anything else?"

"One more thing. You're hired. See you tomorrow, same time, same place."Billie had put the phone down feeling good. But what if the person who saw her had described her to the cops and they were now hunting for her?

No. it couldn't be. The time factor would be completely wrong. It must be a coincidence... Billie filed it away in her mind, with the unopened letters from her bank which she was somewhere dimly aware were completely jamming her drawer of the desk in the bedroom.She shivered.

"What's the matter, darling?" Antony asked.

"I think the cold just got into my bones, I still feel it."

"Come here and let me warm you up," Antony said from the sofa. Billie slipped gratefully into his embrace.

The wedding meeting the next day was as tedious as Billie had expected. It wasn't that she didn't want to help but she felt nostalgic for the lazy, carefree Saturday mornings they had enjoyed before getting engaged, scrambled eggs and fried mushrooms, Saturday papers and leisurely mornings in bed. Antony was a busy guy and there wasn't a lot of time for just hanging out in his schedule.

Seeing that Billie was sulking, he let her drive his car, a nippy BMW sports model, too fast all the way. They set off after breakfast and arrived a few minutes after 11 am in the gravel drive outside the parents' grand redbrick mansion on the outskirts of Henley. Antony's mother Sara rushed out to greet them.

"Hi darlings. I hope you're feeling full of frisk. We've got lots of terrifically important things to discuss."

Sara was a smart, confident woman in her sixties with weapons of mass destruction concealed behind a fearsomely jolly manner. Billie kissed her cheek and allowed her to take her hand with fake affection and lead her into the house. Billie found Sara slightly scarey and rather perplexing. When Antony had announced their engagement after only six months of dating, she had seemed at first a little crestfallen before deciding to be absolutely thrilled.

Billie's own parents could not have been less interested in the wedding. Her mother was vaguely opposed to the whole concept of marriage, which she regarded as a bourgeois institution created to oppress women and her father lived in California where he had remarried for a third time and, with two children under ten, a busy job and low holiday entitlement, it wasn't clear he would even be there.

So Antony's family, who felt they understood what was needed on these occasions, having married off two daughters, had stepped into the breach and set themselves up as the wedding committee.

Billie was grateful to Sara for all her hard work and genuinely tried to be fond of her, but secretly she felt that Sara was a little under-impressed with Antony's choice although glad that at almost 40, he was finally settling down. Antony said that it was all nonsense, Sara thought that she was charming but just had trouble coming round to the idea that anyone could be quite good enough for her only son. Billie expected he was probably right and that Sara would get used to her in time.

Sara lead them into the formal sitting room which was decorated like the third act set of a Noel Coward play. Billie constantly expected Antony's father Simon to appear in a quilted dressing gown but as usual he was hovering around in M and S casuals holding a tray of drinks. Two of Antony's sisters, Rose and Marguerite, Rose's husband John, her toddler daughter Fern and Antony's best man Frank were sitting in armchairs that had been arranged in a semicircle in front of a small table with a laptop on it.

"What will you have to spark up the grey cells? Coffee?"Sara asked Billie."A beer would be nice," she said, rather mischievously.

Sara looked quickly at Simon, a look which meant "Oh dear, alcohol at 11 am. Can she be a nice girl?" But the drink was provided and they got down rapidly to business.

Sara, an inveterate organiser who in civilian life worked as office manager at an advertising agency, kicked off the meeting.

She opened the laptop. "I've prepared a short PowerPoint presentation which I hope will focus our minds. Can everyone see?" Everyone nodded.

"By the way before I start I'd just like to ask if Oscar could be present at our next little get together. He is giving you away after all. He has missed a lot of meetings and I do feel it's important to have some input from him. What does everyone else feel?" There was a general murmur that sounded like assent and Sara made a note in the pad in front of her.

"I'll ask him but Saturdays are a bit difficult for Oscar as you know," Billie said thinking how impossible it would be to drag Oscar along to one of these events. Probably just as well, if she did bring him he would probably do something outrageous like demand that all the women at the ceremony wear the hijab in accordance with Sharia law. Billie's brother, who had converted to Islam, was, she felt, an amazing guy with great spiritual qualities but it might be best to keep him out of the spotlight as much as possible until the day.

"Now." Sara clicked the mouse and a picture appeared of Antony as a child with curly blond hair looking impossibly angelic on a swing. Superimposed on a cloud above him was a snapshot of Billie, taken unexpectedly on her last visit with a mobile phone. She had arrived with a hangover and no makeup on, and was captured grimacing into the phone, wearing a surprised expression. The shot was captioned *"Dreaming of His True Love."*

"That's just to get us in the mood."

"Aw," said Rose, holding up Fern to show her.

"Moving on." Sara clicked the mouse again.

The next page was headed *"The Importance of Organisation"*. Under it were five bullet points. *'Poor Organisation Leads To Confusion and Stress.'* read the first one. Sara started to expand on the negative effects confusion and stress could have on the wedding as a whole.

Billie looked round the room. Marguerite, Antony's youngest sister, was playing with her hair. She caught Billie's eye, winked and mimed being sick behind her chair. Billie put her fingers over her mouth to stop herself from giggling.

Billie looked out of the window and observed that it was a beautiful spring day. There were several things she would rather be doing in the pale March sunshine than planning an event that was scheduled for late July. Perhaps they could escape for a walk through the muddy lanes to a pleasant country pub where there might be cold beer and a warm fire. She looked at her watch. No chance. Sara didn't look like winding up too soon and then there was lunch. This was going to go on until it was dark.

Simon had taken an easy chair slightly turned away from his wife and appeared to have fallen asleep. Billie suppressed a sigh. Sara stopped.

"Wake up and smell the coffee, Billie," she said, with a light sarcasm that reminded her of her maths teacher at school. "What do you think?"

She looked at the power point presentation. Superimposed over an image of people in evening dress laughing hysterically was a screen entitled. *'The Marquee'* and underneath were bullet points: *"Lay Out, Installation, Furniture, Decoration, Removal"*.

Sara drummed her fingers on the desk in front of her in an irritated way. "We're on point three," she said. "The decorative trim round the marquee. We are selecting from the McSween tartans in honour of Antony's maternal grandmother who was a McSween before she married." She clicked and a sub-screen appeared showing various tartan ribbons. "There. What do you think? We can have the McSween, the Hunting McSween or the Antique McSween."

"The Hunting McSween definitely. That's a really lovely one."

"Are you sure? I think I prefer the Antique McSween," Antony said.

"In that case, Antique McSween it shall be, my lord and master." Everyone smiled. Billie felt forgiven and relaxed again.

"Great," said Sara. "Now I'm sure you are all getting hungry so just one more thing before we eat, I've some quotes for the helicopter here. They came in last night."

"The helicopter?" Billie said.

Antony sighed. "I'm sure I told you about that. We thought that instead of a car bringing us to the ceremony it would be fun if we came by helicopter. Don't you think?"

"Wouldn't it be great if we just like, parachuted in for the ceremony?" Billie said, with a touch of sarcasm.

But when she looked round, everyone was nodding enthusiastically.

"Woa, that would be cool," Frank said. "That would certainly get it into the gossip pages."

"I think you're really onto something there, Billie, for once. It will certainly help Antony's profile to have a nice spread on this in Chatter and that could be the hook that brings them in. Nice to have that journalistic brain on the case," Sara smiled over at her. "Log that into the minutes, please Rose." Rose made a businesslike note in her book.

Later that afternoon, Billie got a call on her mobile from Sorrel asking if she could work that night. She complimented her warmly on her work on Friday and said they really needed someone for an unexpected shift that evening. Pleased to be asked, Billie said she would be there in two hours.

"Don't come to the agency," Sorrel said. "I'm going to lock up and go home. We don't usually work on Saturday night but we have orders from about four papers for cover on the Fernandez murder, to doorstep the husband."

"Right, what does that entail?"

"Just go there, hang around, wait and see if anything happens. He's with the cops and for some reason they haven't put him up for a press conference yet. But there's just a chance he might speak when he comes home. I've got the address here, it's in Richmond, 250 Richmond Hill. OK? I'm going to give you my home number. Call me around midnight and I'll see if I can get you called off."

Antony drove home as Billie had had too much of the Pinot Noir Simon had served with the roast duck at lunch. He dropped her at a tube station and she made her way across London. It was already dark when she left Richmond station and the temperature had fallen to freezing levels. She was dressed in black jeans, a tight, black T-shirt and Antony's black Berghaus fleece jacket which he had loaned her to keep her warm. Hopefully, someone would offer her a seat in their car or she was going to be hypothermic by midnight, she thought. After buying a bucket of cappuccino and a roll to stick in her pocket for later, she made her way up Richmond Hill.

Number 250 was one of the multi-million pound houses right at the top with panoramic views spreading out across the Thames Valley, noticeable because of the group of warmly-dressed men with cameras slung round their necks who were standing outside it. There were about half a dozen photographers. One was much younger than the others, a skinny, black lad of about 19 whom she had seen in the Worldwide office. Standing close to them was a woman in a smart white mac and high-heeled shoes holding a notebook. She was talking to two men in suits one of whom had a pen behind his ear. The reporters. From the fact that the cars parked illegally on the yellow line beside them were empty, Billie deduced that something either had happened or might be about to happen, accelerated her pace and arrived at the knot of reporters a little out of breath.

"Hi," she said in a friendly tone. They broke off their conversation to stare at her coldly. At the same time, a man walking his dog tried to make his way through. "What's happening here?" he asked, interested.

"Nothing much," one of the reporters said in a conversation-killing monotone.

"Oh". The man gave up and walked off.

Billie tried. "Hi, I'm a reporter, from Worldwide."

"Great." The woman in white opened her handbag to slide her notebook into it. "That's me off then. I'm Lisa from the Star, you're on for us."

"And us. You're on for the News, aren't you?" The younger of the two men, wearing a smart dark blue suit and a wildly-decorated tie, looked at her, in a more friendly way. "We need some copy on this - we're hoping Fernandez will come back here and talk. That's your job." He turned to the woman. "Fancy a quickie then, Lisa?"

"Fnarr, fnarr, I 'm panting for one. What about you Beattie?'"

The third member of the trio was a stocky man with a bald head in his 40s. He looked at Billie meaningfully. "All right with you if I go off for half an hour?" He had a strong Glasgow accent.

"Sure." Billie shrugged, with absolutely no idea why this man would be asking her permission to go to the pub.

He looked at her harder. "What I mean is," he said, talking slowly and clearly as if to a non-English speaker, "I'm going to that hostelry

along there." He pointed to a pub a hundred yards away. "I'll be there
if it all goes off. Here's my mobile number." He handed her a card
reading Ned Beatson, reporter, News of the Week and some
numbers. "And if you try and stitch me up, I'll be hinging you out tae
dry on Glasgow Green. All right?" He smiled genially.

Billie was unsure whether to smile back or to run away, but
decided to smile, took the card and placed it in her jeans pocket. The
others walked off. She obviously had to stay put in case something
happened but she had just realised she didn't have a notebook. At
least she had a pen, even if it was a chewed up biro fished out of the
lining of her bag. The tools of the trade. Billie looked at it a little
forlornly.

This was living the dream but it wasn't quite living up to the hype.
It had always been her ambition to travel around the world, earning
a living with her pen but this was the rough end of the business,
intruding on the privacy and grief of the famous.

The idiocy in the office with the toast had been quite funny. Then
the murder scene had been exciting and she had been a little carried
away by it. Now, she had the feeling that hanging around in the street
hassling a murder victim's family might just be sad. The
photographers in their dark clothes looked a bit like vultures or
hyenas, waiting for the scraps the killer had left behind.

But this was her best chance to get into the business she had been
dreaming of for years. The letters she had sent out so hopefully to the
newspapers which her family and friends read had met with no reply.
Even the local paper where Antony lived had said they wouldn't take
her without experience.

Billie thought of jacking it in, going home to Antony. She
pictured him sitting with a glass of wine on the sofa and trying to
explain why she had left. Antony would understand and she loved
him for that. She thought gratefully of the warm bed waiting. London
could be a lonely place and for the first time, Billie was beginning to
feel she had a home in it, thanks to her relationship with Antony. But
apart from him, she had nothing. If she failed in her first job, what

would she do? Antony deserved better. She squared her chin and determined to stick to it.

Walking up the street a little, stamping her feet she took out her mobile to phone Sorrel. "Hi. Just checking in."

"Wonderful," Sorrel said, as if she really meant it. "Can you file some copy? Just to show we're there, some colour about the scene, the house, all that. The reporter who was there earlier saw the son arriving so we know there's someone in there. He didn't say anything, just let himself in with his own key - that's Xavier's son from his first marriage. His name is Carlo.

"We've got a snapper there called Mark - ask him to show you his clippings, he's got some pics of the family."

"Just a few pars. There's no hurry. Any time in the next two hours. Phone me and run it by me first if you like. I'm at home for the evening. It's just me and the telly and a takeaway curry."

"Oh?"

"Sad and lonely little me, boo-hoo. No actually I'm quite happy. I've had a knackering week and we've got the accountant in next week so that'll be fun, not. Anyway, speak to you later, Billie. Thanks for your help."

She passed the tedious waiting time by listening to the photographers arguing about whether the Kokan B7 flash gun was better or worse than either a) the Kokan B6 or b) the Pinnacle Definitive 3.

"No, how can you," one was saying in an angry voice, "How can you go out and actually spend money on a PD3 when you went through what we all went through with the PD2? Remember the Ryder Cup last year? I missed a couple of really good shots because it started to rain and it bloody well doesn't work in the rain. And I wasn't the only one."

The angry one's mobile phone went and he answered. "No," he said firmly. "No absolutely not. Yes I am scared. I know I've just come back from a war zone but I'm telling you I am not going anywhere near the fucking celebrity chef. And that's final." He clicked the phone off and explained proudly that he was refusing point blank to doorstep Fabrizio Garibaldi Smith.

"You're right. We should all refuse. You remember what happened to Mike. He was taking some pictures of the outside of his place for a restaurant guide and the mad bastard smashed his cameras."

"But he hates us because of the coverage of his marriage break - up. You can't blame him in a way," one of the younger photographers said. The others looked at him.

"Well, I'm just trying to see it from his point of view."

The angry one spoke. "If it wasn't for us, he wouldn't be a fucking celebrity chef living in a big fuck-off house and hobnobbing with the stars. He'd be a bad-tempered man selling overpriced food on big white plates. He'd be bankrupt in a week."

"Yeah, Doug, I guess you're right."

"I have sympathy for some people but not for him." Doug said. "What about this guy? Fernandez - d'you think he did it?"

"Naw. No way. A guy like Fernandez might kill his wife but I can't see him doing it like that. He'd flip out and wring her neck or maybe he'd pay someone to drive up on a motorbike, she opens the front door and blam - though I can't see him doing that. either. But he certainly wouldn't stab her 20 times, drive the car to some suburban street and run away. Can't see it."

"No," one of the other photographers said. " I've doorstepped him a few times- he was big news when he got together with Rebelle. I did the wedding a couple of years back…"

"Remember that? *So!* magazine had bought them up and they were driving around with a decoy bride in a Bentley. And they had an articulated lorry pretend to break down across the road to block us. The real bride arrived in an unmarked van which snuck round the back. Imagine letting a bunch of show biz hacks loose on your wedding like that."

"That's what the rich are like though - they'll do anything for money. *So!* paid them something like 100 grand for the worldwide rights."

"So! he's a money-grubber. But he's not a violent bloke. I can see him in Ford open prison for tax evasion. But not doing life for murder. He'd divorce her, he wouldn't kill her - he's got a couple of ex-wives already. No I reckon it's got to be a stalker. Some nutter who's been obsessed with her for years or something."

Remembering that she had to file some copy, Billie looked up at the house. It was a beautiful late-Georgian building, painted white, with pillars by the door and lots of handsome sash windows. It reminded her of the dolls-house Marina had painstakingly made for Oscar and Billie at her woodwork class. She had finally confiscated it after it had been attacked by dinosaurs one too many times and she got sick of mending the tiny furniture. Billie pictured what might be revealed if the hook were undone and the front swung open. A little dolls-house father in a coat with tails reading a paper while dolls house ladies in long dresses stood about in the drawing room, all completely unprepared for the horrors about to engulf them.

What could she write? And what could she write on? Taking the roll she had bought earlier out of her pocket, she smoothed out the paper bag it had been in. Best keep it short.

As she was thinking how to begin, her mobile rang. It was Felix.

"Hi there. You're on the Fernandez case for us, I believe. Thanks for doing that at such short notice. That's a good sign. I really think you've got what it takes and you'll certainly get a good training with us. Now, have you knocked at the door or rung the bell?"

"I think that others have tried that. I don't think there's anyone in."

"Actually I think you're wrong there, at least Carlo is in. Others have tried and they weren't answering but you never know. I want you to go and try. And if they don't answer I want you to put a note through the door saying that if they are interested in getting their point of view across then they should call us."

"Don't you think that we should kind of leave them alone?"

"No. Why?"

"In their grief and all that."

"Look at it this way, Billie. The more publicity there is about this case, the greater the chance of catching the killer. Ring that bell."

Billie nodded and put the phone back in her pocket, scribbled a note on the bag and with a sense of something that might have been shame, wandered up to the imposing front door and rang the bell. Silence. She was about to heave a sigh of relief and walk away again when the door opened. The photographers who had been watching silently started blasting away and the dimly lit street was brightened by a series of powerful flash guns.

She saw a young man of about her own age, 25, or a little older. He was shorter than she was with fair hair and a tearstained face. "Look," he said. "We're grieving here. I've lost someone I really loved and so has my Dad. He's at the police station helping the police but really trying to convince them that he had nothing to do with it, which of course, he didn't. The last thing I need is people hammering at the door wanting to ask me how I feel. D'you think you could, in the nicest possible way, just sod off?"

"OK," Billie nodded and went back up the path to the photographers. Her mobile rang again. It was Felix again.

"What's the story?"

"The stepson answered the door. He said, he was grieving for someone he really loved and the last thing he needed was people hassling him."

"Wow, fantastic." Felix sounded happy. "Great copy. File just what he said, quotes, description of how he looked and how the house looks. Just file it to me - I've got the intro here - *'The stepson of slain singing star Rebelle Fernandez spoke tonight about his deep grief for the woman who helped to bring him up'.*

"Open Quotes, hit me with it baby."

"Don't you want me to use the phone box?" Billie asked.

"Not this time. I'm waiting."

Afterwards, Billie went back to hanging round and feeling cold. She was trying to read a cutting about Carlo one of the snappers had leant her in the light of a lamp post when she looked up to see a very red faced and furious Ned Beatson lurching towards her. "Thanks for nothing, pal. You've made an enemy who'll not forget you the day."

# CHAPTER THREE

Billie found herself alone after that. Beatson stood smoking furiously and the snappers also seemed to be annoyed with her for some reason. She caught a couple of nasty looks in her direction. Hurt and cold, Billie stuck her hands in her pockets and paced up and down, stamping her freezing feet on the pavement. A police car arrived and a policeman and woman knocked and were let in through a narrowly opened door. Over the next hour or so several more reporters turned up. Billie overheard Beattie growling at one newcomer that "that silly wee cow", thumb pointing in her direction, had sent copy round after knocking on the door. "Dinnae believe all that tear-jerking tragedy. All your man really said was 'fuck off or I'll call the polis.' I was standing here and I heard him."

Billie saw the reporter look over at her scornfully. The copy which had been sent round must have made it look to Beatson's news desk as if he'd missed something. Perhaps they suspected he hadn't been on the scene and had given him a bollocking. Billie had obviously transgressed some code of reporters of which she had been unaware. Perhaps she should go up to Beatson and apologise but she wasn't sure how helpful that would be.

Cold and miserable, Billie felt a sudden lifting of the heart when a figure in a floppy, brown coat came up the hill towards them.

"Why do you always wear black? Are you in mourning for your life?" Rick asked her.

"Maybe," she said."

"How's it going? Are you OK? You look gloomy."

"I'm cold, hungry and a bit shell shocked."

"Shell-shocked? You mean you feel like you have seen an entire generation massacred in a futile, imperialist war?"

"Well, maybe not quite that bad. But bad all the same."

Rick walked over and sat on the low wall that ran in front of the next door house. Billie joined him and took the cigarette he offered. She didn't usually smoke but felt perhaps it would warm her up.

"I feel shit too," he said, lighting her cigarette and handing it to her. " If that helps. I'm moonlighting, doing a shift for the Post and it's so tough to get noticed there. I've got a feeling they're going to keep me here all night, just out of badness. And they're jittery because some wanker knocked on the door and worked up what was basically a nice fuck off into ten pars of tragedy."

"That was me."

"Really?" he looked at her almost respectfully.

An honest impulse made her add. "And Felix from Worldwide. Do you know him?"

"Only by reputation - or lack of it. Did he hassle you into hammering on the door till your knuckles bled?"

"Kind of."

"I always tell them I have broken three toes kicking it and they still aren't answering. But actually I go and have a swift pint."

"I would have done that too if I'd thought of it. I wish I had now. That Scottish bloke was in the pub and he thinks I tried to stitch him up."

"Beattie from News of the Screws?Oh - oh. He won't like that."

"No, he doesn't. I didn't realise."

"You're pretty new aren't you?" Rick asked, stubbing his cigarette out on the wall and throwing it into the basement area of the house they were sitting outside.

"Today is my second shift. How long have you been doing this?"

"Two years. And I'm so sick of it. I never thought it would be like this. I get paid shit. I work longer hours than a junior doctor, but people aren't nearly as pleased to see me. When I started I was full of idealism and I thought I would be like a better looking version of Robert Redford in "All the President's Men". But then came the day when I lost my integrity."

"Oh yeah? How was it for you?"

He shrugged. "It was over so quickly - it was a sex discrim. The boss said the woman who was claiming it was being vindictive because they had had an affair and he had ended it because she smelled, you know, down there. They had an order from the Sport and they wanted me to go and ask her about it. I actually went to her house. Then I saw sense, pretended to ring the bell phoned the office and said she wasn't in."

"D'you get a lot of that sort of thing?"

"Death knocks, doorsteps and sex discrims, all the things the staffers don't want to do."

"What's a death knock?"

"That's like this, when someone has died and you go to try and get a reaction from the family."

"It's a pretty horrible thing to do."

"I know. And I've found it pretty hard to get out of that—Its hard to take the next step up the ladder. You have to do shifts for the papers. They're always at night or weekends when you're tired—unless you go sick spelled s-h-i-f-t from your agency job. And then when you're the shifter on a big paper you really have to shine to get offered a contract. They say the life of a shifter on the Post is shorter than a Battle of Britain fighter pilot. If I don't get a story soon, like tonight, then I can forget a contract."

"And is that what you want?"

"I think so. It would be nice to have a fifty grand a year job on a national newspaper. I'd feel I'd made a success of it then, made it to Fleet Street. There's a lot who don't. But then, quite a lot of the time, I feel like I don't really give a toss. Then I fantasize about someone coming to take me away from all this. What about you?"

"I'm spoken for," she said. "What do you want, if you don't want money?"

"I don't know. The usual things. Glory. Love. But right now, I'd settle for a ham sandwich and a pint of Guinness. What do you say we go to the pub down there?" He pointed to where a semi circle of golden light fell onto the pavement from the pub's open door. It looked like Paradise.

"I don't know," Billie said. "It's my second day and shit as it may be, I don't want to lose my job."

Rick looked at her. "OK," he said. "Cover for me and I'll go and see if I can score us a takeaway."

He stood up to walk away. Billie called his name. He turned round and she held up both hands in the shape of guns and made shooting noises.

"Cover for me?" Billie said.

While he was away, Sorrel phoned on the mobile. "I'm really sorry. I just can't get you called off. The papers have got an idea something might happen and we aren't getting a thing from the cops on this story. The desks are just baying for blood on this one."

She asked Billie to stay until someone could relieve her the next morning, offering to pay a double shift to make up for it. She agreed, not particularly reluctantly.

Eventually Rick reappeared with a clinking white plastic bag and some brown paper parcels of fish and chips. By this time they were the only people left on the street. Most of the reporters had come and gone. Those who remained had taken refuge in their cars. There were four that Billie could see with people in them. The nearest one was a white Renault whose occupant was sitting with his head back, snoring with his mouth open. There was a note on the windscreen. Curious, she went over to read it. It said "If happen, please wake up". The window was slightly open and she could hear radio voices talking earnestly.

In silence, Billie and Rick sat on the wall and ate fish and chips and drank beer.

"I used to be really into Rebelle, when I was about 19," Billie said.

"Me too. She was phat." Rick opened another bottle of beer. "D'you remember that one 'Baby I don't really want to try ...oh-oh,

I just don't want to live it all again, oh-oh-oh, and feel that pain tomorrow…"

Billie joined in and they sang the chorus again, twice.

"D'you know what," Rick said. "This is just shit. I feel like I'm pissing on the grave of my childhood hero. I'm going to phone the Post night news editor, who, by the way is a complete jerk, who pretends to be shouting at people on the phone whenever the management walk past his desk because he thinks it'll get him promoted, and tell him to stuff his contract."

"Is that wise?"

"No."

"Let's just phone him up and sing him a song. Lend me your phone so he doesn't recognise the number." Rick grabbed Billie's phone which was lying on the wall and dialled. Then he started to sing itto it. "Join in," he hissed at Billie. She obliged in a half-hearted mumble.

"Baby, oh-oh, I just don't want to feel this pain tomorrow, Oh oh," Rick sang. Billie could hear a male voice coming out of the receiver. "Hello, hello? Who is this?" Rick changed song to another of Rebelle's haunting melodies. "Walking through the woods, changing moods, glaad to be maaad," and then cut off the call.

They both collapsed in laughter which they had to stifle when Rick's phone rang a moment later. He took a deep breath and answered it "Really? God, that's so weird. I suppose she had a lot of fans. Yes, yes I will, yes I'm right outside, freezing my bollocks off. Yeah, yeah, they're like frozen peas. I know, I've knocked, and rung the bell. No not excessively. Yes, I do know I'm representing the Post tonight and not some two-bit news agency. OK, soon as."

After that not much happened for a while. They were getting so cold they had to stomp up and down the pavement to keep warm. Then Mark from Worldwide appeared.

"Hi, you're doing this for us aren't you?" he asked and smiled at Billie. "Do you guys want to come and sit in my van? It's a bit warmer than it is out here."

"Cheers," she said. "What a lifesaver. My feet are beginning to go numb."

They passed the next few hours sitting in the front seat of Mark's battered VW van, occasionally getting out to stroll up and down the street . The lights went out in the Fernandez house at about one am. Other than that, nothing happened. Every hour the sound of the World Service time signal could be heard coming from the reporters' cars and then a few bars of the familiar tune and a precise English voice saying: "This. Is. London."

They dozed a little in the van, too wired to sleep, while the clock limped slowly round the hours until morning. At 6 am, Billie walked down the street feeling stiff and gritty and got tea and rolls for everyone in a cafe. Rick's shift ended then and he went off home. Mark and Billie chatted and listened to music until 9 am when the relief appeared. It was 10 am by the time she got home, showered and fell into bed, pink-eyed and damp-haired in a lacey white nightie. Antony reached for her and tenderly wound a lock of hair behind her ear.

"Hi darling. Were you really sitting outside that house all night? I'm not sure I like you having a job. I preferred it when you were hanging round the house and cooking me nice meals."

"I know. So knacked. Gotta sleep," was all Billie managed to say before unconsciousness hit her like a Japanese bullet train.

On Monday morning, Billie jumped out of bed with the most enthusiasm for work she had ever felt. Most of the Sunday papers had used what Felix and she had filed the night before on the front page. The quotes from Carlo were the only new take but the story was still big enough to be splashed across the fronts. The story may not actually have her name on it but she felt amazing. Nine national newspaper front page splashes on her second day in the job.

On the way to work, she grabbed a Post from a news stall. "Secret Sadness of Rebelle's Last Song" was the splash. According to the story, the singer's last album which was yet to be released contained a song that was dedicated to the child she had had as a teenager and given up for adoption. The paper had discovered, it didn't say how, that Rebelle had kept the child's existence a secret all her life, but recently she had been reunited with the girl who had contacted her after turning eighteen.

"Wow, dynamite," Billie thought and wondered which newspaper would be first to track down the daughter.

When she arrived at the office, Felix was sitting with the newspapers spread out in front of him eating a sausage roll and talking to Sorrel. He looked up, a large flake of pastry clinging to his lower lip and said, with his mouth full of sausage.

"Hey, we did well on Sunday."

Billie grinned and nodded.

"Have you seen this?" Felix pointed to the Post. "We were just talking about where to go next with it."

"What are Scotland Yard Press Office doing on this story? Are they on strike or something?" Sorrel said. "They haven't put anyone up yet, except for Bennet denying that he's baffled as usual."

"I know. It's odd. In a sense they don't have to. Normally they're fighting to keep it on the front pages as long as they can to get witnesses to come forward. As soon as it fades into the Nibs column, the chances of finding the killer are probably reduced. But this one is going to be on the front pages whatever. So there's that."

"But there's still the news management angle. If they put Fernandez up at a presser then there wouldn't be people on his doorstep the whole time."

"Mm-mm. Maybe he's refused. It worked out well for us, anyway. The thing now is to find the girl." Felix jabbed a greasy finger at the Post front page. "What we want to do is find her and buy her up."

"She probably won't need money though. She'll be loaded now surely?"

"I don't know, perhaps not if Rebelle hasn't left a will. I don't think adopted children have inheritance rights from birth parents. But that's irrelevant. She's eighteen, nineteen years old, what does she know? It should be possible to convince her that if she gets into bed with us we'll protect her from the rest."

"Yeah," Sorrel nodded thoughtfully. "It'll need to be a smooth operation."

"Billie," Felix turned to Billie. "We need to find this girl. I want you to start at St Catherine's House."

A short time later, she walked through the glass doors of the records office at the bottom of High Holborn where she had been instructed to start by looking for Rebelle's marriage certificate to verify her real name and date of birth. Her age according to her publicity material was 33, but Billie was to take that as more of a loose starting point than a chronological record.

The marriage records were kept in enormous, heavy black books, one for each quarter. First, Billie looked up the wedding date, which was in the clippings Felix had printed out from newspaper archives he accessed on the computer. They had been married four years before in a London hotel.

She thought about what the photographers had said about the wedding as she looked it up, remembering seeing the pictures in the magazine. It had been big news at the time.

Once she had verified the date and place, she filled in a form at the desk and got a copy of the marriage certificate. It didn't take too long to get the certificate. This showed that they were legally married, Xavier Fernandez, divorced, profession company director and Karen Jane Broadbent, spinster, profession singer. He was 52, she was 37.

She wrote down Rebelle's correct birth date and moved through to the birth records. They were stored in big green books, again by quarter. When she found the right book, she laid it on a table, leafing through the thick pages with their neatly written ink entries to B. Broadbent. There had been four born in that particular quarter, but only one Karen Jane, in Catford. She wrote down the details and went to the front desk to order a copy of the birth certificate, paid the £5 and got a receipt. They said it would be ready in a couple of hours.

Those details might help to search for the daughter but in the meantime she took down the book for the third quarter of the year Karen Jane turned 14. The sparse entries in the book were little enough to go on. Luckily there were comparatively few Broadbents in each quarter. In the quarter Karen Jane turned 19, she came across one in Catford, a boy, Ian John. She ordered that birth certificate too. Perhaps the Post was wrong about it being a girl. She knew from Rebelle's publicity material that her parents had split up, that her father was dead and her mother lived in the highlands of Scotland but there was a good chance she might have still been in Catford when the baby was born.

Billie made a long list of all the Broadbent babies born in the UK in the relevant period, names and places. Then she went out to find something to eat, found a sandwich bar near Holborn tube station and ordered a plate of minestrone and a cheese ciabatta. The minestrone had a film of grease floating on the top but it tasted OK.

As she ate the sandwich, she flicked through the cafe's copy of the Bulletin and found an obituary interview about Rebelle by the record producer she had worked with most often, Mark Cannon, as told to a reporter.

*Rebelle. She was special. That word is used a lot in the world we lived in but she really was. She had this tremendous energy, you could really feel her presence when she came into a room. I remember her arriving at the studio for rehearsals. She was always on time, but she'd act like she was late, she'd come bursting in, her long black hair loose and flying behind her and say 'Have you started yet?' As if we were going to start without her. I mean, she was the star, and she wrote all the music.*

*"She had a phenomenal work rate, she wrote a real lot of stuff, and she threw away a lot of it too. She was the biggest critic of her own work. When she came to the studio, she always seemed to have a wicker bag, like a basket, with sheets of new music in. I think she wrote a lot at night, she had terrible trouble sleeping and when she was up in the middle of the night she told me that she would pace around the living room singing to herself and then go into the kitchen and drink herb tea and write down the songs that came to her. She said that was when she did her best work, about 3 or 4am when everyone was asleep.*

*"That was how she worked in her later years, after she was married. I think she was happy in her marriage, I really do. She seemed to settle down a lot and her work became much more mature and thoughtful. But she always had a difficult side as well. She would get ideas in her head and you couldn't challenge them.*

*"To her fans, she seemed such a strong, confident person, she was such a powerful performer, but in private she was a real worrier, a nervous person. She carried a lot of guilt. She stressed out about a lot of things that she couldn't do anything about. If anything went wrong with the relationships with the other musicians we were working with, she would blame herself. I might say, look Rebelle that is nothing to do with you, but she couldn't take it on board. She wanted everyone to be happy all the time and she thought it was her job to make that happen.*

*"Rebelle and I went way back, I produced her second album and when she was younger she was much wilder. She was a real wild child in those days, popping pills and partying and getting involved with some really dodgy guys, but even then, writing, writing all of the time. I think that way of living actually took its toll on her, on her mental health. She wasn't as strong mentally as she seemed, she could be quite eccentric on occasion.*

*"But she was a beautiful, brilliant woman, a wonderful songwriter and a fantastic musician and I know I'm really going to miss her."*

After lunch, Billie went back to the records office and picked up the birth certificate. Now she could tell Felix that when her baby was born Karen Jane had been living at an address in Plum Tree Lane in Catford, south London. "Go there," Felix said.

"Go there?" She was surprised.

"Yeah, I know it was a long time ago but we don't know when Mum left there. You might find a neighbour who knows something. Worth a try.

"Meanwhile, I will stay here in the office and look at cuttings and maybe on the electoral roll CD to see if we can find Mum. It'd be good to find her, though the chances are that someone already has and she ain't talking. But I'll give it a shot anyway. That's how we operate."

It took nearly two hours to get to the address. Catford was a long way into the hinterland of south London. The bus trundled past depressed-looking housing schemes decorated with tags and BNP graffiti. But Plum Tree Lane, which Billie reached after a long walk along a bleak main road with high rise blocks of flats on either side, looked different. It was a row of small neat houses off the main road, which looked as if it were struggling to dissociate itself from the surrounding squalor.

There were builders working in one of the houses and a few well polished cars were parked along the pavement, in contrast to the empty car parking areas that surrounded the high rises. There was a small park on one side of the street, its tufty grass looking rough and unkempt and probably full of dogshit, but nevertheless it was a patch of green. There was a small play area there with a couple of swings and a young woman was carefully helping a toddler into one. The child's chubby body looked too heavy for his skinny young mother to lift. Billie noticed that she was underdressed in a thin jacket and her legs were bare and goose bumped, but the child was warmly wrapped in a padded, red coat with a hood. Billie smiled and the girl smiled back, her thin, sharp features pink with the cold wind.

She was probably five years younger than Billie. She might not even know who Rebelle was. There was certainly little point in asking her if she knew the people who lived here before she was born, Billie thought.

These houses might have been new when the Broadbents moved in and started their family. Seven had white curtains at the window and a brightly painted green front door. It was a small house, but it had its own tiny patch of front garden and two floors, and no doubt a minute square of garden at the back, the English nirvana. The English aren't really city lovers, Billie thought .They have no apartments like the ones in Paris, built round a pleasant courtyard, quiet even in the centre of town, or like the Edinburgh tenements round a back green where she had lived as a student. She pressed the bell and heard it ring but the house stood silent. No doubt the family were at work. Streets like this were often empty during the day.

The house on the left, number nine, looked promising. The window ledges were painted a sort of chocolate brown and hadn't been washed any time recently and the hedge that lined the font garden was overgrown. When Billie rang the bell, it played 'The Red Flag'. Silence. She pressed again but this time the bell played a different tune. She was trying to name it when the door opened. As it moved, a fat, ginger cat came out and walked between her legs and down the path.

"Hello, how can I help you?" A very old, very thin black man in a frayed cardigan and carpet slippers was standing there.

"I'm sorry to trouble you. I'm looking for the people who used to live next door.'

"Debt collector are you?"

"Certainly not," Billie stopped, unsure how to proceed. "Actually," she confessed looking at the man's bright brown eyes. "I'm a journalist."

"A what?"

"A JOURNALIST!"

"We don't often get those round here. You better come in."

"Thanks." She followed the man as he shuffled slowly and painfully into the living room and let himself down into an armchair.

"Sit yourself down. Would you like a cup of tea? If you do you'll need to make it yourself you know. My rheumaticals very bad this morning."

"I'm OK, but would you like one?"

"You what?"

"Would you like a cup of tea?" she bellowed.

The man fiddled with the volume control of his hearing aid. "I wouldn't say no. If you don't mind making it."

"Sure", she disappeared into the galley kitchen, which was tidy but smelled musty and damp as did the rest of the house, where she found two blue china mugs in a cupboard. A tea caddy stood on the work top next to a large plastic bottle of Grant's whisky but there was nothing in the fridge except a carton of milk and a half-used can of cat food.

Billie carried the mugs through.

"Thank you. It's nice to have a mug of tea made for me and a bit of company. I don't see many people these days. Sometimes I wonder if my vocal chords have seized up, it's been so long since I used them. Tell me about yourself. Why is a journalist, looking for my old neighbour David Taylor?"

"Em, I'm not actually looking for him. It's a family who lived next door. It may have been some time ago. The Broadbents."

"The Broadbents." The man considered this for a while. Then he said, "Yes I do remember them, but you are going back some. That must be 15, 20 years back. Maybe more."

"Is it?"

"You were not even born when they left here, most probably."

"I'm older than I look. How long have you lived here?'

"A time. I came to this country from the West Indies in 1955. Then I met my wife Carol and we moved to this house soon after we married. So I've been here a few years now. My wife would have been the one to ask about the neighbours but sadly she is gone. She died five years ago this November. She was always chatting to the neighbours. She would tell me this and that about them but as she was always saying to me 'Dennis, Dennis, you don't listen to a thing I say.'"

Billie mumbled something about being sorry to hear that.

"The Broadbents. That would have been Bill and Susan, am I right?"

Billie nodded, holding her breath. The man sighed. "It's a real sad shame my wife isn't here. She would be able to tell you all about them. I mean, everything, what was the colour of their knickers to how much money they had in the bank. Now me, I don't remember much. They had a little girl, called Claire or some such name. She was a pretty little thing. Our daughter Josephine was a year or two younger but they were good friends. Yes I can see them now sitting in the apple tree in our garden, laughing together. I built them a tree house up there and they spent years up there." He smiled at the memory. Then he came back to the present and looked at her sharply. "So why are you looking for them then? It was just an ordinary family, nothing to interest a journalist. Now wait a minute, she became a singer didn't she, is it something to do with that?"

Billie felt a sinking of the heart. Now she was going to have to break the news that his daughter's playmate had been brutally murdered. She rushed the story a bit and consequently had to repeat it twice, eventually bellowing "She's dead" and miming a throat cutting motion.

Eventually Dennis seemed to grasp the story although the gloss Billie had put on of how any new information would help the investigation and details of Rebelle's past might lead to the killer might not have got through.

Dennis seemed to go into himself after he understood, slumping in his chair and staring across the room as if at something Billie couldn't see. She sat sipping her tea for a minute or two. Questions were forming in her mind but she discarded them as being too complicated or too brutal.

"What was she like?" she settled on. "WHAT WAS SHE LIKE?" she repeated.

"Don't shout." Dennis gestured towards a dresser in the corner of the room. "Look in there," he said. "There's a box of pictures in there. I think there are some of her."

Trying not to look as excited as she felt, Billie rushed over to the dresser and hauled out a big old cardboard box. It was filled with photographs. She took them out one by one and piled them up on the faded brown and gold carpet. The most recent ones were at the top. "This your wife?" she asked, showing one of Dennis standing next to a dumpy little woman with stringy blonde hair and pale blue eyes. "That's her," Dennis said, smiling.

"She looks lovely."

"She was, she was a real nice lady."

Billie quickly flicked through the pictures, occasionally asking Dennis a question. There were very few since Carol had died. Most at the top were scenes involving grandchildren, then further down grown up children who got younger as she went through the box. Often there were just family in the pictures, then there would be a series of photographs taken at parties, picnics and so on featuring friends. But none of them looked like Rebelle. About half way down the box, Billie found a picture of two little girls sitting on a picnic rug. One was Josephine, the other had dark hair and a little pointed chin like a pixie. Dennis nodded. "Yes, that's her. Karen, that's right. Pretty little thing she was."

Further down, Billie came across a group of pictures of the two girls, some in the apple tree, some sharing a pair of roller skates, each wearing one skate and obviously larking around posing for the camera. "These are good." She put them on Dennis' knee. Dennis looked at them, his old eyes watery.

"They grow up too quick," he said. "It all goes by too quick. I've been lucky, I've got a lot of memories." He stroked the photograph. "They were good kids, all of them. Great kids. And they've got their own now. But It's all over for me, weddings, parties, baptisms, graduations. All the happy times are over. It's all over for me except the dying."

"I know what you mean," she said, checking through the rest of the box, feeling an urge to phone Felix. "CAN I USE YOUR LOO?" Billie shouted, flushed with triumph. Having achieved permission and directions she found the toilet, small and damp with a lime green toilet suite, locked the door and got her mobile out of her pocket.

"Good stuff. Get the pictures, take them away so no-one else can find them. Tell him you have to take them away to get them copied and you'll send them back. Give him a card. Make sure you get them all, they'll go down well with the tabs, previously unseen pictures of Rebelle's happy childhood. Well done. Does he know anything about the baby?"

"I don't think so. I haven't asked him yet. He's pretty deaf."

"Well ask him. Ask him if he knows where the mother moved on to. He might still have a change of address card lurking around. you know what old people are like, never throw anything away."

45

"Cheers."

Billie went back and asked if she could take the pictures away to be copied. It was surprisingly easy. "You promise you'll bring them back? Josephine might want them."

"Cross my heart. Thanks mate, see you," she said, before rushing off. Her heart was thumping and she was too excited to pursue any more questions.

She thrust the pictures inside her notebook into her bag and started on the long trek back to the center of town, the thrill of her first scoop vying with unease. Was she turning into an ace reporter or a horrible foot in the door hack? She wasn't quite sure.

# CHAPTER FOUR

When she got back to the office, Barmy was waiting to grab the pictures. They had already been sold to a Sunday paper, he said.

Sorrel sidled by and spoke close to Billie's ear. "Make sure you get a bonus from him. I don't know how much he and Barmy got for those pictures but he must be feeling flush because there are two rolls of sellotape, count them, two, openly lying on his desk and not under lock and key."

"Sit down," Felix said. "You seem to be on a bit of a roll at the moment. Here's some more valuable information." He pushed a pile of cuttings over.

"I think we might have found the kid. I looked up the cuttings and found that the mother remarried and her name is Susan Paton. She married a man named Fraser Paton and they live in Perthshire. But she owns some kind of horse sanctuary in the Highlands. I found out where that was from cuts and then just on a whim, I looked up the horse sanctuary on the electoral roll and I found this." He waved a print-out. At the top it said "Bogmillo Horse and Donkey Trust, The Mains, Bogmillo". Below were half a dozen names. The last read Ian John Ford, 19.

"I reckon it's got to be him. Perhaps he was never adopted at all. Grandma brought him up, and nobody else has found him - yet. We don't know exactly."

"Sounds convincing. So what happens next?"

"It's been your story so far, mate, and you've handled it well. I want you to go up there and check him out, see if you can sign him up. This could be a biggie. We've got a flight for you in the morning."

Later that evening, Antony and Billie sat waiting for Marina, who was in London attending a conference and had offered to buy them dinner in an Indian cafe which was a favourite of hers. She was late as usual and they had worked their way through several popadoms and a steel dish of mango chutney by the time she came through the door, slightly out of breath and carrying an enormous black leather satchel with papers sticking out of the top.

"Hi," she called, with an enormous grin and a wave. She came and sat down opposite them on the hard bench.

Billie felt rather than saw Antony looking at Marina's salt and pepper hair which was, as usual, escaping from a half-hearted pony tail and was conscious of a wish that she would try to look a little smarter. Her Moomin-like figure was not disguised either by the rather low cut figure-hugging purple T shirt she was wearing.

"Sorry I'm late," she said. "Some batty woman from the Feminists for Islam group was spouting some terrible nonsense and I'm afraid I got in a bit of a row with her. Well a discussion I suppose."

"I'm sure you gave her what for Mar."

"I was wasting my time really because she was mad as a spoon but I felt some of her ideas needed to be taken on. How about you? How's the job?"

"Wicked," Billie said. "I'm really enjoying myself. I think I'm learning a lot too."

"Good, good. And how's you Antony?"

"Well, thanks. Very busy of course, planning the wedding." Billie was aware that Antony thought Marina's attitude to her daughter's wedding deplorably unsupportive but cast him a pleading look which meant "Please don't start a row".

The waiter came by for their order and Marina ordered a Masala Dosa Deluxe and a bottle of Kingfisher lager without consulting the menu. Antony knowledgeably ordered a selection of dishes for himself and Billie.

While waiting, Marina scrabbled around in her bag like a hamster in its food store for several minutes before triumphantly pulling out a book jacket. "Look," she said. "At last, we have agreed on a cover for the new book."

She took the glossy paper. On the front was a picture of a tampon and in red ink the words *Bloody Women: Menstruation in Literature* On the back was a picture of an unusually tidy Marina and a blurb which told the reader that Marina, a lecturer in feminist textuality at Sussex University, was the author of several books including the classic *Down With Men* and the more recent: *Talking About Men.*

"Gosh, it's cool."

"At least it's not a used one." Antony held the jacket by the very edge as if it actually were a soiled sanitary article. "How very," he said, handing it back.

"We thought that might be going a bit far," Marina said, "although we did consider it."

Antony made a face. Billie looked at Marina and decided she was being mischievous.

"You're having a laugh, aren't you Mar?"

"Perhaps a little tongue in cheek. Although I do think too much fuss is made over menstrual blood. It's not really different from any other kind of blood. And did you know how much the average woman loses during her monthly cycle?"

Billie shook her head.

"A tablespoon. Isn't that fascinating?"

" I do not consider myself at all closed-minded and I am very happy to discuss this business at some other time. But I can see the waiter approaching with our food and if you don't mind I would really rather not discuss it at the dinner table." Antony said.

"Sure, I can see that." Marina picked up her knife and fork and began to tuck into her meal, which was an enormous pancake rolled into a strip perhaps two feet wide. Antony, who was watching his weight, was using a teaspoon to eat from a small steel dish.

"Although," Marina went on. "I really did discover some amazing stuff writing this book. When I started I wasn't sure if I'd find enough to make it more than a pamphlet but in the end the publishers were trying to get me to cut it back to 200,000 words. I think the material we dug up from 16th century Italy is particularly valuable."

"Would you like to hear about your only daughter's wedding?" Antony asked. "We're going to start having meetings weekly instead of fortnightly. There's just so much to do. Mother said to tell you that you're very welcome to come along. In fact it would be great to have you involved. You might even enjoy it."

There was a pause as Marina finished a large mouthful of food. "It's not really my bag. You must be aware of my views on marriage."

"Not really."

"If you read my book *Down With Men*, you would. But I'll save you a trip to your local leftie bookshop by telling you that it's not really something I'm into. As far as I'm concerned, marriage is a bourgeois institution created to oppress women. Why don't you just live together?" She pointed her fork at Billie.

Billie shrugged and answered: "Love and romance?"

"Rubbish," Marina said, warming to the subject. "What's romantic about a ceremony which is essentially registering the change of ownership of a woman from one man to another? What do you think Antony?"

Antony frowned. "To be honest I think that's just a little bit, kind of, last century."

"What is marriage to you Antony? A deed of property?"

"I wouldn't say that at all. It's a ritual, a rite of passage if you like. But I do certainty see it as - well, an organisational challenge involving a whole family. It is a big picture." Antony waved his teaspoon expansively to illustrate his point.

Marina blocked it with her fork. Billie said: "Oh please, let's not spar. We've been over this ground before haven't we?"

"OK I don't want to be like Banquo's ghost at the feast, so let's just leave it there. But I'm not sure I could really be involved in organising it - if you don't mind. But how about I give you some money towards your holiday, or honeymoon, whatever you want to call it? Or your new flat, I just sorted out my advance."

"That'd be great, Mar, thanks." Billie was keen to get off the subject and moved the conversation onto the Rebelle murder and made a funny story of how she accidentally stitched up one of the most experienced reporters in the business.

After dinner, she went with Marina to her car to pick up a proof copy of her book. It was a weighty hardback, the sort of thing that would cause serious damage if you dropped it on your foot. "Take two copies," she said. "One for each of you."

"Thanks," she said, hesitating. "Mum. Do you like Antony?"

"I don't dislike him. I've got nothing against him at all. But. " Marina got into her dented and scratched old Ford Escort and handed the books through the window. "Put it this way. I wouldn't want to spend a whole weekend with him."

She started the engine. Billie leapt out of the way as she accidentally put the car into reverse and then jerked forwards with a crunch of gears.

"God Mar," Billie said, to the disappearing car. "That is so bitchy."

Piling the two books on top of each other, she carried them along to where Antony was waiting in the driver's seat of the BMW.

"She gave me two copies," she explained. "One's for you."

"Oh *goody*. I'll save my copy for the beach - not." He took his copy and threw it violently out of the window. There was a distant crash and scream. Billie, who had been brought up to treat books, particularly those by her mother, with the utmost respect, felt an appalled thrill at the rebelliousness of this.

"Good god, I hope you haven't killed someone."

"Billie, I think your Mum is getting worse. She is odd."

"D'you think?" Billie had always assumed that her mother represented normality, while Antony's family with their obsession for matching accessories were strange. Apparently, he saw it the other way around.

"I'm certain of it. By the way, she is coming to the wedding isn't she?" Billie nodded.

"I hope she's not going to come in fancy dress. We don't want her wrecking the photographs."

The instructions were clear enough - fly to Inverness airport and then pick up a hire car and drive to Tomintoul. It was a beautifully sunny, if cold, spring morning and the countryside was a fresh, pale green. Traces of snow lay at the edges of the road and clumps of it remained in the dips of fields. The surrounding hills were still topped by white caps and the burns and rivers were swollen with melting snow. At the same time, a few early lambs were wobbling by their mothers and the leaf buds on the trees were unfurling. Billie passed by a village with a decent looking pub and stopped for something to eat, pausing long enough to take a short stroll to stretch her legs. After London, the air was as fresh and invigorating as toothpaste.

The road to Tomintoul was marked as the Devil's Elbow on the map - it was a switchback of a road, heading steeply up and down across the hilltops. Although it had been cleared, snow was still banked steeply at either side, coming several feet up the high poles which marked the edges of the road. There was a sign to the Lecht Ski Centre and it looked as though a couple of ski runs were still functioning as a few figures were skiing down a distant hillside and there was a straggly queue waiting for a chair lift.

Once Billie had to stop, rounding a corner as there was a sheep lying in the middle of the road. She pulled up and hooted the horn and the sheep looked at her with reproach, got heavily to her feet and started to walk along the road with the car following at a crawl. "I'm sorry madam," Billie said, hooting the horn again. Finally she waddled onto the verge.

Further down the road Billie could see two black shapes hovering in the air, large birds with the characteristic glide of birds of prey. Buzzards perhaps, too small for eagles. They were circling above the road where a rabbit had been killed by a car.

Tomintoul was not unexpectedly pretty, more pretty in an unexpected way, a collection of cottages around a village green. It looked like the idealised version of a peasant village that you might find in a Dracula film. Sorrel had booked her into a bed and breakfast - the agency didn't run to hotels - a trim little cottage off the main street with a neat garden. After dumping her bag on the yellow counterpane of the little room, she went downstairs and was served a cup of tea by the owner, a middle-aged Englishwoman who introduced herself as Helen. She was very friendly. "You don't need to sit in solitary splendour in the dining room if you don't want to," she said. "You can come and chat to me in the kitchen if you like."

So Billie took the little tin tray with its red metal teapot and blue patterned mug into the kitchen and sat at the oak table while Helen pottered about putting things away and the black cat slept in front of the range.

Unfortunately however, Helen asked as many questions as she answered. Aware of the fact that she was supposed to avoid attention and certainly not to let slip she was a journalist, Billie mumbled something unsatisfactory about wanting to get away from London for a few days. Helen looked unconvinced. "I see," she said.

Billie drank her tea as quickly as possible after that. As she left the cottage, she looked back and saw Helen peering out of the living room window at her, talking to someone on the phone.

From the map, the horse sanctuary at Bogmillo looked as if it was less than a mile out of the village, so she decided to enjoy the fresh air and walk. The village green and the main street were almost deserted. No cars moved but one elderly inhabitant slowly walked over a zebra crossing in front of the village shop.

Billie set off briskly to keep the cold out. As her ears became attuned to the lack of cars, she became aware of the canopy of country sounds: birds, water gushing, the wind in the trees.

Soon she came to a sign to Bogmillo and turned off the main road along the top of a small valley, bathed in sunshine. Below was grass pasture and then farmland. Through a copse of birches on the other side of the small glen she could see the white-topped hills. In the field below were around twenty horses and donkeys. Most of them were elderly, slow-moving bays, chomping at the grass. A few lifted their heads as Billie walked by, whistling, but most carried on with lunch.

At the end of the road was a stone-built two storey house with a glass porch. Some dogs somewhere started to bark. There was no bell so she lifted the old-fashioned iron letter box and let it clang shut a couple of times. There was the sound of footsteps, then the door opened a fraction.

"What do you want?" asked a hoarse voice through the crack. Billie tried to peer through but the hall was in shadow and she could not see the face.

"I was looking for Ian Ford."

"Well he's not here - he's gone away indefinitely."

"Oh? And may I ask, who are you?"

"A family friend," the voice said and the door was pushed shut.

Billie felt a surge of disappointment. All this way for that. She started back as she had come. There was no signal on the mobile so she would have to wait and call Felix from the telephone boxes on the green at Tomintoul.

"Sounds a bit dodgy, don't you think?" Felix said. "Hang around, ask questions. Go back. You want to see the kid himself. Don't be fobbed off. OK? Nobody fobs off Worldwide News."

It was only mid-afternoon but it was already getting dark. Back to the B and B, then feeling restless, Billie picked up the day's papers and went to the pub on the green for something to eat. Only a few people were in there, obviously local. The barman seemed friendly and she thought she would definitely go up and try and ask him subtly about the sanctuary after her meal. But for now, Billie felt tired of asking questions of strangers and took her roll and crisps, which was all the pub offered, to a seat in the corner.

She was just about to take a bite when she saw a familiar face. It was Beattie, looking much the same as he had in London, dressed in a dark suit with a shirt open at the neck above a loosely knotted tie, standing at the bar while the barman poured him a pint. Billie returned the roll to the plate and sat motionless like a rabbit paralysed by a stoat. Beattie, waiting for his drink, casually glanced around the room. His eyes fell on her and stopped. Then he smiled.

The big man picked up his pint and walked over to the corner table. "Hello there," he said and lowered himself onto a bar stool, legs apart, his suit trousers pulled tight against his crotch. "Barrie, isn't it?"

"Billie, actually. Billie Wilson."

"I'm Ned Beatson but the lads all cry me 'Beattie'. What brings you to God's holiday park?"

"This and that. Just wanted to get away from the hustle and bustle."

"Me too. Sometimes you've just got to get hame." To the tune of 'Fly Me To The Moon', he sang softly: 'Fly me to Dunoon and let me hang around in bars' Sometimes you just need to unwind and relax after a hard shift at the coal face of truth."

"You know that time in London…I wasn't trying to stitch you up or anything. It was kind of an accident. I'm new to the job and…"

"Lass, lass." Beattie slapped her hard on the back with a strong, square hand. "Dinnae fash yersel, as my auld mither used to say. No, no. Not at all. Listen, to show there's no hard feelings, can I get you a drink?"

"No,no." she said, hand in pocket. "Let me get you one"

"I insist. What'll you have?"

"Right, OK. A lemonade shandy please."

Beattie went to the bar, bought her a drink with a whisky for himself and brought them back to the table. He drained his in one. "That's good, the vin du pays, as they call it." He put his hand in his pocket and pulled out his mobile phone. "No reception in this bloody wee dump though. Listen. I've just to nip out to the phone box and call my girlfriend. I said I'd speak to her this afternoon and she'll not be very pleased if I don't. You know what some women are like. But just sit here and wait, I'll be right back."

Beattie left and Billie sat for a moment or two, thinking. It was pretty clear that he was not here for the hiking. After a few minutes, she left the pub. Sure enough, the phone box was empty.

She went in and dialled the office.

"Hello, Worldwide News and Pictures," an Australian voice answered.

"Hi, it's Billie."

"It sure is chilly."

"No, no. Billie Wilson the reporter."

"I'm sorry, he's not here."

"No, no. I am she. I am Billie."

"Oh, geez, why didn't you say? Hi, Billie. How are you going?"

"Fine. Em…Is Felix there?"

"No, I'm glad to say he's finally torn himself away from this dump and gone home to his screaming nippers in Fulham. I'm Lou, the night news editor. What are you doing? I can see your name on the board here. You're in Scotland right? Is it as beautiful as they say? How's the weather?"

"Uh-huh, I'm chasing this guy the son of Rebelle, I went round to his address earlier and there was a guy in a suit who wouldn't let me through the door. Now I've just met a News of the Week reporter in the local pub."

"Right."

"What should I do?"

"Search me. What do you think you should do?"

"Go back and check it out?"

"That sounds like a cool idea, why don't you do that?"

"OK." Cursing at the waste of time, she ran back to the bed and breakfast, jumped in the hire car and drove round to the sanctuary.

As Billie reached the narrow road up to the house, she saw approaching headlamps and had to stop to let the other vehicle pass safely. The headlights illuminated the inside of the car and she saw: Rick in the driver's seat and Beattie holding a map sitting next to him. There was a third figure, in the rear seat. As the car shot by, she caught a brief glimpse of startled eyes in a young face. Presumably, it was Ian John. Beattie and Rick had cut some deal with the boy and were taking him off somewhere.

Struggling with a sense of betrayal so strong it made her eyes sting, Billie thrust the car into reverse, forced it up onto the verge, swung round to face the other way and put her foot on the accelerator, hanging on to the tail lights disappearing towards Tomintoul. How could Rick be stitching her up like that after being so friendly to her? She felt that they had come to an arrangement, informally at least, that they would pool their information and just pretend to their bosses that they were rivals. What a bastard! Perhaps he had been simply gaining her confidence so that he could trick her in the future, when the stakes were high enough. Well he wasn't going to find it as easy as he had thought. She put the hurt to one side and focused her heart and soul on staying in the race, pushing her foot down and taking the corners on the incredibly steep and winding road at a dangerous pace.

She had caught up with the car by the time it reached the Devil's Elbow, staying close behind as it accelerated round a series of corkscrew bends at breakneck speed. It was personal now.

At one point, they met a car coming the other way on the one lane road and only just managed to avoid a smash as it swerved onto the verge.

The chase continued for 15 minutes and then, at a lay-by marked with a passing place sign, the car in front indicated it was pulling over. Rick waved for Billie to stop too.

Beattie was getting out as she pulled up and he held up a hand to indicate that she should remain in the car. He smiled into the headlights and walked round to her window. Billie pressed a button and it whirred down.

Beattie spoke through the window. "Lass," he said. "You're smarter than you look. This is a buy-up. We've cut a deal with our client there and we are taking him away, to a place of safety if you like. And I know you can follow us and I know that you can make life hard for us. You've already done that to me once. You've proved yourself. You can beat me." He met her eyes with his. They were a deep blue and looked hauntingly sad.

"Look doll. It's a hard life being a reporter at any age, let alone when you're pushing 50. Let's face it, I'm a has-been. You're only as good as your last story in this business and I'm at the kind of age where they'd be happy to bin me for someone younger, cheaper and keener. Someone like yourself in fact. You're young, you've got your life ahead of you. I'm coming to the end of my career but there's no sanctuary for tired old hacks and I've an old mother in Glasgow depending on me. Think about it, doll."

He looked and Billie looked back, uncertain and off guard. As she looked, Beattie's broad hand slid into the car. Before Billie knew what was happening, he had grabbed the two ignition keys on their metal ring, twisted and pulled them out of the steering column.

"Fuck," she shouted.

With a flick of his arm, Beattie chucked the keys way across the snowy wastes of the Lecht.

He looked back at her.

"It's a dog eat dog business." He smiled, showing white, false - looking teeth, jumped back in the car and drove off.

A dense cloud cover meant that there was no light at all, not even star light. And it was utterly freezing. She tried to roll the window up but it was no good, they were electric. Billie turned on the hazard lights. Luckily, they came on. In the flashing red beam, she could see something white. A fine, soft snow had started to fall. She shivered, laid her head on her arms folded over the steering wheel and began to cry.

# CHAPTER FIVE

Time passed. Surely someone would come by soon. It wasn't that late. But what if they didn't? It was an unpleasant situation and the options were stark. She could stay where she was or start walking. How far was it back to the village? Four miles? Six? If the snow kept on it would feel like a long, long way. Surely someone would come by. Surely it was best to stay where she was. But the time went by slowly. She couldn't even listen to the radio without the car keys and there was no food or drink to keep her going. Snow was piling up on the windscreen and she was starting to shiver.

Then, she was aware of brightness filling the car. Headlights shone in from behind and Billie heard voices. The driver's door was pulled open and a figure leaned in and shook her.

"We're in time," a man's voice called. "She's still alive. Just." The man turned to her. "Come on, my quine. You're just a daft lassie. It's not as bad as all that." He lifted the newspaper off and helped Billie, stiff with cold, to get out of the car.

Together they walked back towards the beam where the landlady Helen was leaning out the driver's window, calling "Oh, dear, is she all right?"

"A bit cold but otherwise unharmed."

" Oh why do they do this? And why do they do it here? Can they not stay at home?"

The man shook his head. "Search me."

"Right," said Helen. "Get in the car and we'll take you back. I'm afraid we'll have to get the doctor out and the policeman too. This is not the place to do this you know. I had a suspicion as soon as I saw you that this is what you'd come for. You're the third in a year."

What was she talking about, Billie wondered hazily.

Helen's male companion unscrewed the top of a flask and was about to offer her a drink but Helen stopped him with a shake of the head. "Best not. Don't give her anything until the doctor's seen her, she might have, you know, taken something."

They drove back in silence to Helen's pretty cottage. A plump young woman with curly hair emerged from the doorway, wearing a parka over a frilly polka dotted dress and carrying a notebook.

"Bloody hell, that's all we need,' Helen got out of the car. "Thanks Duncan, you're a good neighbour." she said to her companion. "I can manage now."

"Good evening Mrs Page, I'm Angela Dryburgh from the Central Highland Despatch, you probably remember me."

"I do."

" I hear you found another person in trouble. Quite a local angel you are turning out to be. Mother Theresa of Tomintoul, we are planning to call you in the next issue."

"I'm afraid I'm not going to talk to you. I really don't want another story like the last one."

"Can I talk to your guest?"

"Certainly not, she's…extremely tired."

Billie cleared her throat. "No, it's OK, Helen. I don't mind talking to her. But what about?"

"Maybe later then," Helen said, putting her key into the front door and opening it. She virtually pulled Billie into the living room and slammed the door firmly before the reporter could come in.

A second later, the doorbell rang.

Helen sighed, "Just ignore her."

The doorbell rang again, hard, as if someone had placed a heavy thumb on it.

"I'll go and speak to her," Billie said.

"If you don't mind, I'd rather you didn't, at least until the doctor's been. I suppose what you do after that is your own business."

"OK, I'll go and get rid of her then."

She walked into the hall and opened the door.

"Oh, it's you." Angela seemed taken aback and flicked back her hair, nervously.

"Well?" Billie waited.

"So what happened? In your own words?"

She parried for time, not sure exactly how much Angela knew. "I can't talk to you now, I've got to wait for the doctor. Do you want to speak to me later? "

Angela hesitated. "What about tomorrow?"

"Sure."

Angela seemed to reconsider. "Actually no, best make it tonight. Who knows what might happen by tomorrow? I'll wait in my car." She pointed to a white Renault Clio parked by the gate.

"OK." A car turned into the dark street.

"That'll be the doc," Angela turned and went back to her car, whistling *If Tomorrow Never Comes*.

The doctor was a small but muscular looking woman in her 30s, who wore a plaid jacket and walking boots. She waved a friendly hand at Angela as she passed.

Billie let her in and they walked back to the living room.

"Thanks so much for coming, Fiona, this is the patient." Helen pointed at Billie.

"That's fine Helen, I was up anyway. I did a bit of cragging this evening and then went for a pint with the boys and I was just in the door when you called. Just grabbed the old black bag and whizzed round. Don't worry about it."

"I'll leave you two together."

"Take a seat," Fiona said firmly, pointing to an easy chair and pulled a straight back one up to sit beside Billie. "Have you taken an overdose of paracetemol or anything else?"

"No."

"Ah. You weren't proposing to commit suicide by exposure were you? That could take a long time even at this time of year."

"No, I wasn't. Not at all," Billie was perplexed. "Is that what Helen thought? That I was trying to kill myself?"

"Yes. Weren't you?"

"No."

"Well what were you doing on your own sitting in a parked car on the Lecht on a freezing cold night?"

"Em...well it's difficult to explain."

"Try me."

Billie thought hard, not wanting to blow her cover completely. "I, em, I'm very interested in cosmology."

"Cosmology?"

"Yes, you know the stars. The sky looked so amazing, I stopped the car to get out and have a better look at,em, Orion's Bat and when I was out in the dark, I dropped the car keys and I couldn't find them again."

"I see, what a silly misunderstanding." The doctor sounded as if she was talking to a child. "Well, let's just have a look at you, shall we and check that you are none the worse for wear."

"You don't believe me, do you?"

"What makes you say that?"

"Well you obviously don't believe me."

"And is there a reason why I shouldn't believe you?"

"Yes," Billie said. "I mean, no."

The doctor reached over to take her pulse.

"Incidentally the study of the stars is astronomy not cosmology."

The doorbell rang again. Billie heard voices and then feet. There was a light rap at the living room door and Helen peered round. " The police are here."

"Could you ask them to wait a moment until I have finished my examination," Fiona said. "Pulse, normal," she added and started to check Billie's blood pressure.

After a few moments she tried again. "Now, would you like to tell me if you have taken any pills or drugs of any kind."

"Honestly, really, NO."

Fiona looked hard at Billie, who looked back into her pale, slightly washed-out blue eyes, seeing a face which was kind, tanned, a little weather-beaten and clear of make up under cropped, brown hair. Fiona smiled.

"OK," she said. "I don't know what you were doing out there but you seem fit enough. Forgive us if we seem paranoid. We do get a lot of it. You Londoners are the worst. Townies. They come up here to commit suicide because they think way up here in the wilderness no-one will notice. Actually the opposite is true. And it's upsetting for the villagers. They're permanently on the look out for would-be suicides now."

"I see."

"We've had quite a few, that's why a reporter from the Despatch is sitting outside wanting to talk to you."

"Well I'm not a suicide tourist I assure you. Thanks for coming out anyway."

"Don't mention it." Fiona stuck out her hand to shake the other woman's. Billie took it and had to curb the desire to wince, so firm was her grip.

"Thanks again."

"Helen will let me out." She paused to have a word with the policemen on her way.

There were two of them, standing in the hall, looking awkward in their hats and coats. "You'll have to move the car," one of them said. "That's a potential hazard there."

"The doctor says you lost the keys," the other said.

"That's right."

"You'll need to call out a roadside rescue patrol."

Billie went up to the bedroom to get the papers she had collected with the car and call the breakdown number. Finally, she got through on the phone and a patrol was organised from Inverness. She borrowed an extra-thick jacket from Helen who seemed even more suspicious now and the police took Billie back down to the car to wait with it.

Back in the car, she sat wondering what to do next and how to break the news to Felix. The car would be taken to Inverness and he would have to pay a penalty for losing the keys and the call out. She would be stuck in Tomintoul with no transport and even worse, no story. Shit.

While she was sitting a car came by and pulled up ahead of her. It was the white Renault Clio. Angela got out and came over.

Billie pushed open the passenger door. "Get in if you like". Angela did.

"I'm sorry to disappoint you, Angela. I'm no suicide tourist. My car has simply broken down and I'm waiting for the recovery lorry."

"Broken down eh? Then why don't you turn the heater on?"

"I can't find the keys actually. It's a simple if embarrassing tale, I got out to admire the stars, dropped the keys in the mud, it started to snow, can't find them anywhere."

"Are you sure you're not thinking of harming yourself?" Angela asked.

"Sorry mate. Can't help you there. I'm thinking what a long time it is until breakfast actually. Sausage, bacon, potato scones, egg. Can't wait."

"Black pudding."

"Maybe."

"Shame about the story though," Angela said. "It means I have to go back to Plan B for the front page exclusive this week."

"What's Plan B?"

"Dead buzzard was pregnant, police reveal."

"Eh?"

"Well it's either that or 'Battle for new pedestrian crossing on more-or-less totally empty stretch of road'. We've got a picture of kids from the riding school trying to cross the road on ponies and there's like one car waiting but the rest of the road is completely empty, as far as the eye can see."

"I'd go for the dead buzzard if I were you."

"Yeah, that is pretty good actually. Buzzard found poisoned two weeks ago, now the wildlife liaison officer tells me they found out she was expecting an egg. Development."

"The plot thickens."

"Exactly."

"Who killed cock robin?"

"Well I do bloody well know that actually. It was the gamie on Lord Lowdie's estate but you can't say that of course. No evidence."

"Frustrating."

"Tell me about it." Angela looked out across the hillside. "Run this by me again, you got out to look at the stars, dropped the keys. Do you want me to help you have another look for them?"

"That's nice of you. Don't you have to get off and write your story?"

"Hell, no, that won't take too long. It writes itself a story like that."

"Well, OK, it might be worth having another look."

Angela got a large torch out of her boot and together they went across to the hillside. Angela shone the powerful beam onto the area where Billie pointed and started walking around kicking at the snow with her feet.

"What are you doing here, anyway?" she asked. "You're not a climber or a walker are you?"

"How do you know?"

"Without being too personal you don't have, you know, the build for it. Or the gear. You're not a twitcher, due to lack to emotion at hideous murder of bird of prey, so why are you here?"

Billie decided to take a risk. "I'm an undercover journalist," and caught a quick, bright look from Angela, who then tried to seem bored.

"Oh yeah? Who for? What's the story?"

"Well I might as well tell you. I didn't want to fess up to the civilians but I was here looking for a young guy who we think is related to Rebelle."

"That singer who got killed?"

"Yes."

"Wow,"

"I know but it looks like he's been bought up by the Screws. I just missed him, bummer." While she was telling the story, Angela carried on circling around kicking the snow and towards the end of the story bent down to pick something up.

"Eureka!" she said, holding up the keys.

"Oh fantastic," Billie said. Angela chucked them to her.

"What do you want to do now then? Chase them?"

She shook her head. "There's not much point in that. they could be anywhere. They could be in Glasgow by now. What do you know about the stables? Is there anyone there who could help, who might know something about Ian John or where he's gone?"

Angela thought a minute. "You do realise that if I get anything there I will want to use it for the Despatch?

"Uh-huh. When are you coming out?"

"Thursday. Two days."

"So if we get anything I could file it on say Wednesday night, so it wouldn't steal your thunder but be out at the same time?"

"I suppose. But how do I know you won't stitch me up?"

"C'mon." Billie grinned at Angela. "You can trust me. I'm a journalist."

They sat in the car, arguing the toss for a while.

"I trusted you first," she said.

"You didn't have a lot to lose. The guy's gone. I can't print anything without some more evidence. Your best chance is to tag along with me."

"True. But if you ditch me you don't know what I might get up to. I could get something good - on your patch. How's that going to look to your editor?"

Angela shrugged. "I doubt it. And the story is coming from somewhere else anyway. But OK. I concede we can help each other. This could be big. This could be my passport out of here and on to a real newspaper. I'm going into the office to search the cuttings file. Coming?"

She nodded. "Let's go by the house first."

Angela got back into her own car and they drove back up to Bogmillo in convoy. Billie pulled over in the drive, some distance from the house and Angela stopped behind. A faint column of grey smoke was still rising from the chimney but the lights were out. A dog barked.

"No point in waking them up I suppose."

"No. Probably not the best way to get a printable quote. Follow me to the office," Angela said. "We'll try them first thing tomorrow."

"Where is your office?"

"It's about half an hour from here.'

As she drove along the dark country roads, following Angela's tail lights, Billie's mobile rang.

Fishing it out of her jacket, she saw it was her home number.

"Great, finally we have a signal!"

"Is that what was happening?" Antony's voice was surprisingly clear.

"Yeah, there's hardly any coverage up here."

"There are such things as land lines. I don't like not knowing what's going on. I've been calling all day."

"Sorry darling, I haven't been able to get through either, but I've been thinking about you. What are you doing right now?"

"Well, I'm sitting drinking some very nice wine working on the agenda for the next wedding meeting. We really need to get the invitations sent out so I'm just sorting out some addresses, post codes things like that. I thought you could help me."

"Can't quite hear you, I'm afraid," Billie made a noise into the phone which she hoped sounded like crackling. Holding her mouth away from the phone, she shouted. "You're breaking up darling, I can't hear you. Call you lat..." and switched the phone off.

Angela was slowing down coming into what looked like a small market town. Driving along the main street, she indicated left and turned into a supermarket car park. Billie pulled up next to her.

"This is the best place to park, we're back on the High Street."

They walked through an archway and onto a pedestrian section of the High Street. Posters in a dingy window in front of a broken Venetian blind announced that it was the office of the "Central Highland Despatch".

Inside the hall was a booth into a cupboard like room marked "Advertising". Behind it was an open plan room with a big table and four chairs and under the windows a couple of desks with old looking computer terminals. A galley kitchen was visible.

"I live up there," Angela pointed at some stairs with a door at the top. "Fancy coming up for a quick dram before we start on the cuttings?"

The flat upstairs had a small kitchen living area with a table at the window overlooking the street. They sat at it and Angela uncorked a bottle of whisky.

"It's a Speyside malt," Angela said. "I prefer them to the Island whiskies. What about yourself?"

"I haven't drunk much whisky."

"Oh well you'll like this. Just add a touch of water. Good isn't it?"

Billie thought it tasted like mouthwash but didn't say so. "Um." But persevering, she discovered it was drinkable - just.

"What's it like living above the office?"

"I like it. If it's quiet we sit downstairs and play poker until someone comes in and tells us something interesting. It's a laugh. The editor owes me about seven grand."

"Who's the editor?"

"His name's Danny. He's 23 and he lives with his girlfriend – who used to be his English teacher - in the middle of nowhere. He comes from down south too actually, the Wirral. There's a part time photographer called Mark and Jane who does the ads and admin and stuff. She only works mornings. I'm the only one who lives here at the moment. The pay of course is absolute shite."

Angela pointed to a sofa in the corner of the kitchen. "You can kip on that if you like. Save you going back to Helen's. I've got a sleeping bag."

"Cheers."

Taking the bottle and two glasses, they went downstairs and started hunting through the back copies of the paper which were tied together with string into big books. A walk-in cupboard off the newsroom was full of weekly issues going back at least ten years. As well, there was a filing cabinet with specific cardboard files of paper cuttings on different subjects.

Searches for "Rebelle" and "Bogmillo" elicited nothing but in the file for "Highland Games" they trawled up a yellowed picture of Rebelle attending the Games ten years before, when she was just becoming well known. The caption said simply: "Singer songwriter Rebelle who is visiting friends in the area was among the crowds enjoying the sunshine at the Games on Saturday."

"Hm. Interesting," Billie said. "It kind of proves we're on the right track but it doesn't take us any further."

"No. But the Despatch can reproduce it if we can track down the original. You know - dead pop star's happy Highland holiday remembered. Might be able to work up some line about the police searching into her life for clues to her mysterious end. Anyone who knows anything to come forward."

After that they went upstairs again. Billie sat on the sofa and drank another whisky, diluted with plenty of water. She rolled it round her mouth meditatively. "You know this stuff's actually not bad when you get used to it." She lurched to her feet. "Well, I'm off to bed then. See you tomorrow."

"You go to sofa," Angela said. "You can crash out right here. I'm going to bed."

Billie woke up the next morning, with a dry mouth and an aching head, lying fully clothed on the sofa covered with a chenille bedspread. Even after a shower and a restorative fried egg roll cooked by a surprisingly cheerful Angela, she felt as if her head was in danger of falling off, so they set off back to Bogmillo in Angela's car. The sun shone, the air was full of bird song and the landscape was lush with the beauty of spring.

"It's nice round here," Billie said.

"Sure is. I grew up here and I do love it. Nowhere to beat it when the sun is out. Although to be honest it isn't, most of the time."

But the movement of the car as Angela accelerated round the hairpin bends with one hand on the wheel started to make her feel incredibly nauseous so she closed her eyes and lay back in her seat concentrating on calming her turbulent stomach.

Opening her eyes as they slowed to enter the drive to the horse sanctuary, they saw a girl standing at the entrance to the field by the road with a bridle in one hand and a carrot in the other, about to open the gate. Angela pulled over and got out to go and talk to her. Billie followed.

She turned towards them. Her hair was tied tightly back and she was wearing jodhpurs. She didn't smile. "Och no, more reporters."

Billie nodded.

"Well there's no point in coming here. He's gone and we're not supposed to talk to anyone now." She looked more closely at Angela.

"Don't I know you? Angela Dryburgh?"

"Yes."

"Angela Dryburgh on Rocket." She smiled. "Remember me? Pony Club Gymkhana, a few years ago now. You beat me for the Best All Round Competitor Cup. By two points. I cried for weeks. That cup should have been mine."

"That wasn't yesterday. I must have been 13. You've got a good memory."

"Yes I have. Are you here about Ian?"

"Yup, I work for the Central Highland Despatch now. Any chance of a cup of tea and a wee chat? At least can you fill us in on what's happened with the other journalists? Pretty please? For old time's sake?"

Smiling slightly, she looked at her watch. "I suppose. Hang on till I get Myrtle, cos the vet's coming to look at her this morning. Go along to the house and I'll be with you shortly."

After parking the car in the yard, Angela and Billie waited by the house door.

"Result." Billie said

"God yeah. I suppose there is an upside. Sometimes I feel a bit trapped you know. The only trouble with working where you grew up is that sometimes it seems like there's no escape from the Pony Club. "She's improved a lot. I vaguely remember some really pushy little squirt who complained to the judges that I shouldn't have won because my mount wasn't properly groomed. I hadn't plaited his nose hair or something. We lived on a farm and we had a couple of old horses. Rocket was more experienced than I was, he had done so many competitions with my sisters. All you had to do was sit there and hold on. He was a star."

After a few minutes, the girl appeared leading an old donkey. She patted the animal firmly on the flank, expertly led her into a stall and closed the door.

"OK. Come in - just for a minute."

The house was bright and freshly painted. A wooden-floored living area lead into a large conservatory with views across the large garden and on to the valley beyond. A huge vase of daffodils sat on a coffee table between two big, floral patterned sofas. An archway led into an old-fashioned farm kitchen, without fitted units,where the dog's basket lay in front of an Aga.

The dog came towards them, growling. "Oh shut up, Pericles." The girl pushed him away and went into the kitchen where she moved a big, steel kettle from the edge of the ring on the Aga into the middle.

"Beautiful morning, isn't it," Angela said.

"Yes. But how can I help you? I really don't have long. The vet is due any minute."

"What do you know about Ian John?"

"Not much actually. How's Rocket? Is he still around?"

"Sadly no. But he was a great horse. I cried troughfulls of tears when he died. I was fifteen."

"Poor you. It's so sad when you lose a favourite horse."

The kettle was already boiling and she made some tea. "The sugar's over there," she said, handing them each a mug.

Billie decided to try. "What happened with the other journalists?"

"All I know is that these two chaps in suits arrived yesterday when I was out exercising some of the horses. When I got back, they were in here with Ian and one of them told me not to come into the living room because they were having an important meeting. They were with him for ages, then one of them went off, then he came back and they dragged Ian off with them."

"Against his will?"

"Oh no. He said something to me about having signed a contract with a newspaper. But Ian's quite - how can I put it - sort of dopey and laid back. He really goes with the flow and I think he was doing what seemed easiest."

"OK thanks."

Angela moved back in. "Have you worked here long?"

"A couple of years."

"And what about Ian?"

"He's been here about a year."

"He's the owner's grandson isn't he? Does she come here much?"

"Yes she comes quite a bit. She loves the horses and donkeys and she brings people to see them, rich friends and so on. She raises money for the place. It costs a fortune to run. Ian's a real animal lover too, I think the plan is he's going to run this some day."

"And did you know that Rebelle was Ian's mother?"

Billie tried not to shoot Angela an admiring look, impressed by the deft way the question was slipped in.

"Well, it wasn't a total secret. Most of us knew or guessed, but she didn't talk about it in interviews or anything, because Susan and Ian valued their privacy. They weren't - aren't - limelight kind of people. They're really not performers, which Rebelle is - was. Susan's had a lot of strain I know since Rebelle was murdered and you lot hanging around like a load of vultures has not helped. She puts up with it because she wants to find the killer. And I suppose the press have only just found out about Ian. I must say I think he was a bit mad going off with these guys. Where do you think they will have taken him?"

"I wish I knew," Billie said. "Do you think we could look at his room?"

"No you bloody well cannot." The girl looked annoyed. Pericles ran to the door and started to bark. "That'll be the vet. You better go." The doorbell rang and the girl ushered them out before greeting the vet.

"Sorry," Billie said to Angela. "I'm not feeling too good."

"That wasn't exactly what you call finesse. Och well."

After walking back to the car, Billie decided it was time to phone the office. Angela drove her to the call box on the green in the village. Heart sinking, she dialled the number.

Felix answered with an angry bark. "Billie? Where have you been? You've been out of contact for fourteen hours."

"I'm sorry there's no signal here and I've been busy."

"Yeah? What's the story? Spit it out."

"It's a buy-up."

"Shit."

"These two guys from the Screws had bought him up before I even got here. They've taken him off somewhere."

"What did you get?"

"I spoke to a family friend who confirmed that Ian John is Rebelle's son. She said behind the scenes it wasn't a secret but she never, ever talked about him publicly or even acknowledged his existence. Her family are very into privacy.He was raised by her Mum and she never had that much to do with him, reading between the lines."

"OK. What's the friend's name?"

She leaned out of the phone box and hissed the question at Angela, but she only shrugged.

"I'm sorry, I don't have it."

"Well bloody screwing go and get it, you half-assed amateur," Felix was furious. "With no name it's worthless. I can't afford to be sending out any made up rubbish to the news desks.We sell truth, and that comes with names attached,"he added, Billie thought, rather pompously.

"OK. Sorry. Call you back in a minute." Billie put the phone down.

"Angela, what's her name?"

"That's what I'm telling you. I can't remember. I think it was something like Cindy or Lundy. I didn't like to ask because she remembered mine. I was embarrassed."

"Well fuck, go along and get it now."

"Who me? No way. You go. And can I just remind you that according to our deal, you are not supposed to file any of that until this evening."

Billie thought. "Anything new. That's hardly new. All I've got is what I already knew, that Ian John is Rebelle's son and he's been bought up."

"You've got confirmation of it. OK." Angela waved her hand. "Forget it I'll go" . She jumped back in the car and disappeared.

"Hope she doesn't get an exclusive interview," Billie thought. She wished now she had gone along.

But Angela was back in a few minutes.

"She wouldn't say."

"Come on."

"No, honestly, she wouldn't. I said 'How do you spell your name?' and she said "How d'you think?' I thought it was Lucinda so I tried that but obviously not. She just gave me a filthy look and walked away. Probably annoyed because I couldn't remember it. I mean I guess I can find out but it'll take a little while and I've got to go, I've got a front page deadline this morning."

Billie went into the phone box again.

"Look," Felix said, as soon as he heard her voice. "Will you stop wasting time? I don't know if you've noticed but you are not exactly at the epicenter of the story. Or any story."

"But I thought I could get some people to talk about Ian John."

"We are not interested in Ian John now. He has been bought up by the Screws."

"I know that."

"Well the other papers won't want to talk up what a great scoop their rival has got. All they will do is get the first editions of the News of the Week on Sunday and rip off the best bits into a smaller story. That's all they are going to want. So if it's not too much trouble and if you aren't otherwise engaged could you please GET BACK HERE NOW!"

"Ow." Billie replaced the receiver and rubbed her ear. Her head felt even worse now.

Angela kindly took her round to Helen's to pick up her stuff and pay the bill and then she took her back to the Despatch office to pick up the car.

"Thanks," she said to Angela in the car park, scribbling her number and address on a piece of paper. "It's been a gas. When you come to London to seek your fortune, we've got a sofa you can definitely sleep on. Give us a call."

# CHAPTER SIX

The first couple of days back in London, it seemed like everyone was pissed off with Billie. Antony was annoyed because she hadn't called and because he felt she wasn't taking enough interest in the wedding.

She herself was miserable. Sorrel took her to one side and explained that Felix' bark was worse than his bite and that he was very sorry for having yelled at her. Billie accepted that. She had never really had a boss before and they obviously were a rather terrifying breed. But that was only part of the problem. She felt deeply betrayed by Rick. In the whole unfriendly world of journalism it seemed like there had been at least one friendly face, one colleague she thought she might be able to trust. But he had stitched her up, like a kipper, she said to herself.

They drove to the meeting in silence that Saturday morning. It was a smaller crowd that day, Frank and Millie having cried off because the twins were teething and Marguerite because she had to take her cat to the vet's, so it was only Antony's parents and the efficient minute-taker Rose who made little effort to hide the fact that she found Billie disorganized and annoying.

Sara went though the agenda as usual. "Now this week," she said. "I thought we could tackle a rather knotty problem."

"What's that?" Antony asked.

"The top table."

"What's difficult about that?" Billie asked, playing with her ring. She looked up to find that all four Ternshaws were looking at her with exactly the same rather pitying expression, their heads tipped to the right side. "What though?"

"You haven't been to that many weddings, Billie, let alone organised them I know but I'm sure you are familiar with the top table line up. It is - almost invariably, I think you'll find- the bride, the groom, the chief bridesmaid, the best man and the four parents. That is what the rules of tradition and good taste dictate," Sara said.

"So?"

"Well, on the groom's side that will be absolutely fine. But not on the bride's side."Billie shook her head.

""I don't get it."Sara mouthed the word "Lotty".

"Oh, Lotty. Well, as my dad probably isn't coming, on my side, I'll just have Marina and Lotty. That'll make the numbers work OK won't it."

Sara sighed and put her fingers together. "Well, Billie dear, this is rather a difficult subject for me to broach and I think it is something you and Antony perhaps need to discuss in private. But have you thought that through? Remember it is Antony's day as well as your own. We, his close family, of course know about your mother's relationship with...uh. But it is even in this day and age quite controversial and remember - although we are very open minded about that sort of thing, the same can't be said for everyone in the village. Also some of Antony's employers and so on will be there and it will cause a certain amount of gossip you know. Of course, also Antony has wider audiences to impress. You know. Oh Billie, you are slow today. Selection committees. After all, we do want him to get that safe seat next time."

Billie scrunched up her face in disbelief. "Oh come on." She looked around. "Oh come on, you can't be serious. Oh my God, you are serious. Antony?" She waved her fingers in front of his face.

He smiled. "Can we just make a note of that one, Mum," he said. "Em Billie and I will tackle that one between the two of us." Turning away from his mother he winked at Billie and mimed a cutting throat motion.

After lunch, driving back to London, Billie was silent.

Antony cleared his throat. "Look Billie, I know you were a bit upset about my Mum you know broaching the whole top table thing."

"A bit upset? I'm furious."

"I know and thanks for not making a scene. That was great. The thing that you have to remember is that Mum's from a completely different generation and she has kind of old-fashioned views."

"Yes but I can't believe you let her go on like that without challenging them. I mean, this is my Mum we're talking about. I can't tell her that Lotty can't sit at the top table!"

"Well, if you feel like that you can't, but actually I've been to lots of weddings and divorced parent's partners don't usually sit at the top table."

"I can't believe this."

"Don't get all het up, Billie. We can sort it out. I promise you." Antony stroked her back. "Calm down, pussy cat."

"You know what? I am so sick of this wedding. The thing seems to have taken over our life together. In my mind, it's like a huge triffid, like the man eating plant in Little Shop of Horrors which is devouring more and more of our relationship."

"Oh, it'll be over soon enough. We'll have a fantastic wedding you'll see, and then we can get on with the rest of our lives, have kids, settle down. it'll be great."

"I don't know Ant, I just don't feel great about that."

"Well, if you feel that strongly we'll make it happen. But do me a favour first - sound out Lotty because she may not expect to sit at the top table - she may not even want to."

"Oh, OK."

Billie gave into what she knew was a reasonable request, but she felt resentful and misunderstood nevertheless.

Going into the office, Billie discovered there were problems there too.

"He's not too pleased," Sorrel said when she came through the door. Annoyed, Billie had to restrain an impulse to be rude.

"I worked hard but we were just a little too late."

"I know. It's not fair. Luck of the draw. Anyway, you're our woman on the doorstep again today."

Looking over at the white board, Billie saw her name at the bottom of the list of reporters, scribbled next to the words "Fernandez doorstep".

"That means I go and sit outside again?"

"Fraid so," Sorrel said sympathetically. "You'll find it's a bit quieter there today."

Sure enough, Billie was the only one there for most of the day, just sitting watching. It was tedious and uncomfortable on her own as she didn't have a car to sit in. She sat on the same low wall as before. Nothing happened. No-one came or went. Eventually, she phoned in and got Sorrel.

"Nothing seems to be happening."

"No. I don't think they're even there. But we have a couple of orders to sit it out so stay put, please," she said.

The day unrolled with incredible slowness and she felt doubly pissed off when she was sent there again on Friday.

It was another long, boring day. Towards evening, Felix called. It was the first time that he had spoken to Billie since she returned from the Highlands.

"I've got a job for you, for the Sunday Parrot," he said. "It's undercover. Could be good experience. But it's this evening, can you make it?"

She accepted the assignment. Antony was going for drinks with a bunch of his political friends. Normally, Billie might have gone and enjoyed herself as they were an interesting and lively crowd but she was still smarting from the row about Lotty and decided she would prefer to work.

"OK, I'll do it."

"Good girl. By the way, lose the jeans. It says here, you're to dress for a party."

Looking in her wardrobe at home, Billie settled on a short, red dress with a pleated skirt that came half way down her slender thighs, fawn stockings and boots. She wriggled into the dress, blow-dried her hair loose and stuck a silk flower in it. To complete the outfit she wore a fawn wool coat. Arriving at the barracks-like building which was the office of the Sunday Parrot and other newspapers, the security guard smilingly came out of his glass box to usher her to a chair in the lobby.

Once in the reception area, Billie picked a newspaper out of the display rack and went to sit in front on an enormous TV where the receptionist told her to wait. She was expecting another reporter to pick her up and drive her to the job, which Felix had said, was to infiltrate a secret group operating behind the scenes at a bar in Bexley Heath. Terrorism? Race fixing? A royal connection?

A recognisable figure came though the glass door. It was Rick, wearing his floppy coat over a dark suit and carrying a set of car keys in his hand.

"Cor blimey guv'nor, strike me blind with any old iron," he said. "You scrub up a treat. I was hoping it would be you. Come on then. My car's round the back."

"No thanks" Billie said. "If it's you they can go hang. There are some people I don't trust enough to work with." She got up and stalked out, so furious she was almost shaking.

She was half way down the drive when he caught up with her.

"I came back for you."

She kept walking, refusing to meet his gaze. He dodged in font of her.

"Come on talk to me. I called and your phone was switched off or something so I sneaked out of the hotel after we arrived and drove back to see if you were OK but you were gone. So I realized you must have found the keys. I wasn't surprised, I knew you would be OK."

"It was a lousy trick."

"Actually the car keys thing wasn't my idea and to be honest I was quite pissed off about it but what could I do? You must see that there was nothing I could do? We bought the guy up for a load of cash, I couldn't say to Beattie, hey, my mate's just arrived, can we let her in on the story please. I mean, he would have thought that was idiotic. Wouldn't he?"

"There's absolutely no excuse for leaving someone who's supposed to be a mate stranded in the middle of a blizzard. Whatever the job you don't run out on mates like that. I could have died."

"Yes, but like I said, I came back for you."

"Oh." Billie chewed her lip. "Did you? How did you explain that?"

"I didn't. I just hoped he would think I had gone to crash out."

"Oh.""Forgive me? Pax?"Billie sighed. "That does change things a bit I suppose. I'll think about it."

"Thanks. You going to do this job then?"

"I suppose."

"Good. Let's go then. The car park's this way." He indicated a path leading to the back of the building."What, where, why?" Billie asked, following."You've been sent to chum me on this undercover job, haven't you?""Yeah, I think so.""I'm shifting here and there wasn't a female reporter available. I told them to phone Worldwide and ask for you. I'm glad you said you'd do it. Nice to have some immoral support."

They found the car, a dark green Vauxhall Astra.

"It's a pool car. Do you want to drive or navigate?" Rick asked.

"Drive." They got in and Billie took her coat off, slinging it into the back.

"Wow," said Rick fanning himself. "It suddenly feels very hot in here. I hope I can fight them off - I suddenly feel quite selfish. I'm not sure if I want to share."

"What are you talking about? Felix told me to dress for a party."

"Well you could put it like that. Didn't they tell you? It's a wife swapping club. Yeah I know, real seedy tabloid territory you are in now. But don't worry, we'll make our excuses and leave. Before it gets too racy."

" I didn't think that kind of thing still went on. That's so retro. Am I supposed to be your wife?"

"Yep. This is my lucky night. I wasn't sure if you were still at Worldwide. I hadn't bumped into you for a while and nor had anyone else so I thought maybe we had put you off and you had decided on a career change."

"Funnily enough, not really."

"Good. Sometimes it seems like a stupid game. The reason they didn't have a staffer to go with me tonight is because they're going crazy in there because some supermodel has had a row with her boyfriend. I mean, she's a typical surly teen and her idea of a conversation is 'Yes, no, can I have an ice lolly'. So she's fallen out with some idiotic schoolboy and all these ruthless, hard bitten middle-aged hacks are sort of flinging themselves at the story, desperate to find out what the row was about. Is that sad?"

"I guess. D'you think you could look at the map? Maybe I took a wrong turning."

"Oh sorry." Rick scrabbled around looking for the map which he had put down when he was talking.

"Bingo!" he pulled it out from under his seat and began to flick through it. "Bugger, where are we?"

"Here's a sign coming up"

"Left...er,, OK.How did we end up here?"

"You're navigating."

"I was distracted by your legs. No man could be expected to concentrate sitting next to you in that dress."

Rick began to concentrate on looking at the map and after a complicated detour they got to Bexley Heath.

The bar was easy enough to find, brightly lit on a dark, residential street. It looked more or less empty.

"The club's downstairs," Rick hissed into Billie's ear and taking her hand led her down the steps into the basement. There was a thick door at the bottom with a grille in it. Rick rapped twice and the shutter opened, half-revealing a face.'

"I'm sorry, this is a private members' club," said a voice.

"Yes, we're new members. We joined on the Net. Our number is 1152."

"Hold on a minute." The face disappeared and moments later the door swung open. The woman who opened it was in her late 40s or early 50s and wearing thick make up, over a studded dog collar and tight leather cat suit. In her hand she carried a small whip.

"Hello," she said, smiling broadly. "Do come into my parlour." Rick who was still holding Billie's hand, moved a little closer. She giggled nervously.

The woman waved a hand and they walked into a windowless hall. It was decorated with flocked red wallpaper and there was a long bar at one side with some tall bar stools at it.

"Would you like a drink?" asked the woman moving behind the bar. "Take a seat. You're just in time for our little party. It's supposed to begin at ten, but they can hang on for a few minutes. What would you like? Gin, beer, wine? Sherry?"

"A beer, please," Rick said.

Billie shook her head. "Something soft please, I'm driving."

"Oh too bad. It's a shame you're not going to have any of the - hard stuff tonight." She poured a coke and passed it to her. "Tell me about yourselves.? Are you local? It's nice to really get to know the neighbours." She gave Rick a meaningful look.

"Yes," he said. "Round the corner actually."

"Oh really? Why didn't you walk here?"

"Oh we would have." Billie stepped in. "It's just that we're going on somewhere else afterwards."

"I see. I'm Julie. What are your names?"

"Rick and Billie," Billie said.

"Have you been married long?"

"Oh we're not married yet. We just live together. Maybe one day."

"I see you're engaged. What a beautiful ring, my dear. I love emeralds. Why don't you come to the aid of the party now? Bring your drinks."

They followed her into another room where a few couples were sitting on low sofas or velvet cushions that littered the floor. Even in the dim lighting from uplighters on the wall which were tuned down very low, Billie noticed that they were all at least a decade older than she and Rick and some more like two. Some had their arms round each other, some were holding glasses and chatting.

Julie clapped her hands together.

"Hi everyone. This delightful couple are Rick and Billie. Aren't they cute? Now don't eat them up, remember this is their first visit. Take a seat guys," she gestured to a pile of cushions.

"Now let's just relax and listen to some music. " She went over to the stereo and turned on some rock music, before coming into the room and dancing a little, gyrating her sharp, bony looking hips. Then she went and sat down beside a rather plump man in tight leather trousers who had been sitting on his own near the door.

Billie shivered. Rick placed a comforting arm round her shoulders. She curved into him. "I'm scared," she mouthed in his ear.

"So am I" he mouthed back.

Julie turned to her partner and they began to kiss deeply. After a few minutes, they stood up and wandered hand in hand over to another couple. Julie grabbed the hand of the other man and lead him out of the party room.

This seemed to be some kind of cue. The other couples started to kiss and touch each other.

Rick put his mouth next to Billie's ear. "Oh-oh," he said. "What do we do now."

"Play for time," said Billie and slid onto his knee. He put his arms round her and for a moment rested his chin on the top of her head. His hands were warm on her bare arms.

Playfully, she touched his lips with her finger. Rick laid a hand on Billie's thigh and his fingers found the bare skin at the top of her stocking and caressed it gently.

Then Billie found another hand on her arm and looked up to see a hard faced man in his mid 40s standing with a woman of about the same age.

"Want to swap?" said the man.

"No." Rick said.

"Oh.' The pair seemed taken aback and walked away quickly.

Billie and Rick kissed. They slid off the sofa onto a pile of cushions in an embrace.

Another couple came up to try to swap and were turned away. "Piss off and leave us alone. Can't you see we're busy," Rick said. They walked away, sounding annoyed. "What the hell are they on?" Billie heard the man say say. "How very selfish. It's really not on. I will speak to…" the woman replied, her voice fading as they walked away.

"Phew," Billie said, breaking away after a few minutes."D'you think we ought to get going while we can? This place is giving me the creeps."

"If you say so."

They looked around the room. Apart from the last couple they had rejected who were sitting on a sofa looking angrily at them, the sofas were full of gyrating couples in various states of undress. They got up and went wandering along the corridor. The first door they came to was shut. Rick put a finger to his lips and gently turned the handle and pushed it open a crack. Peeping through, he put his hand over his mouth. Looking over his shoulder, Billie saw a water bed on which three or four naked bodies were wriggling together, a little like a net full of fish emptied onto the deck of a trawler.

Rick shut the door again and carried on along the corridor.

"D'you think we can get out this way?"

"I dunno."

They came to a flight of stairs and a fire door.

"That looks like it's alarmed," Rick said.

"I know how it feels," Billie said.

"Hello, can I help you?" It was the man in tight leather trousers, zipping up his fly as he strode along the corridor towards them, looking angry and suspicious.

"Actually, d'you know what, we're looking for the way out."

"I'm sorry to hear that. Are you sure we can't encourage you to stay a little longer and join in the fun? Come with me? Reich! Durkheim!" he called and two large Alsations came bounding up to him. "Why don't you consider staying a little longer? We normally ask our new members to fill in a couple of forms and so on."

"Hm. Fine," Rick said, looking at the dogs.

The man lead them back along the corridor and opened the door of another room with a water bed.

"Why don't you just slip off you clothes and relax on that. Maybe some others could join you."

"Maybe next time," Rick said. "We really do need to go, You see my wife suffers from asthma and we've just realised she has forgotten her inhaler."

Billie found that her breath was coming in shallow bursts and leaned against Rick, flopping her head down onto his shoulder.

"It's actually a pretty serious condition. It's mainly caused by over-excitement. She's taken.Viagra you know, just to get her a bit tingly. She's been really looking forward to this, it's been a fantasy for her for a long time. You see, normally she has a bit of a problem getting turned on. But this scene is really exciting for her. So she really would love to stay. But she is also on medication for mental health problems and perhaps all taken together…I wouldn't like you to have the embarrassment, I mean calling an ambulance might…"

The man looked at Billie carefully and seemed to weigh up the situation. "Yes she does look unwell. Perhaps it is best if you leave. I hope you will be able to enter into the spirit of things next week." He smiled meaningfully at Billie. She lifted a hand wanly and leaned harder on Rick's shoulder…

The man lead them to the door with the grille, took out a key and opened it.

Rick put his arm around Billie and half carried out the steps. "Hey," he said at the top. "It's all right. Were you acting or was that for real."

"I just put it on for the cameras." Billie said, pulling away from Rick and walking on ahead.

"You can stop shaking now then," Rick laughed, catching up and walking along beside her, his hands in his pockets.

"Thanks for making out that I am a class A nut."

"Oh come, on, you wanted to get the hell out, didn't you. Although I was enjoying your...role-play."

Billie blushed. "Er.That was em purely professional."

"Extremely professional.""I didn't mean that.""I know what you meant." Rick answered. "Let's hit the road baby, and file that story. Wife swapping in Bexleyheath, eh? I reckon we might get a page lead out of that - on page 32."

They headed back to the office, in silence that felt a little awkward.

"Seems to have gone pretty quiet on the Fernandez case. I've been sitting on the doorstep the last couple of days and it has been dead," Billie said, into the silence."They're not there. They're at an undisclosed location. You sitting there is just belt and braces and buttons as well. But the word on the street is that they think the old man knows more than he's letting on. He's under some heavy pressure apparently. " Rick answered. "By the way did you see Crimewatch the other night?"

Billie shook her head.

"I must say the chief suspect identikit looks a bit like you."

"Yeah, someone else said that."

" I'm a bit worried that the old man who saw you at the murder scene described you to the cops."

"But the timing was completely wrong."

"I know, but maybe he didn't know the time. Maybe he said it was early in the morning or something. Who knows? Maybe he went back to bed until the police knocked on his door, that afternoon. D'you think we ought to tell them?"

"Surely it can't be me. That would be too mad. No, shit, I'd rather not. I might get charged with something nasty."

"Better than getting stuck with a murder rap."

"True."

"You going to come into the office and help me write this up?"

"Definitely."

They returned the pool car to the newspaper car park and headed into the building. it was brightly lit and there seemed to be plenty of people about despite the late hour. The air was full of a low buzzing noise from the machines and lighting and people, some in uniform scurried here and there on urgent errands. It felt a bit like the HQ of an international villain out of a Bond film, Billie thought.

They shot up to a top floor office in a fast glass lift and Billie followed Rick into a large open plan office.

At the front was a large island made of desks pushed together. Only one was occupied. "The night news editor," he said. "He's OK. Unusually. Hi, George. This is Billie from Worldwide. She was the one who came with me."

"Uh-uh. Any joy?"

"Yes. we didn't come, but we did see and conquer, made our excuses and leave."

"Any celebs of any description."

"Fraid not."

"But the woman Julie was there. She's a drama teacher remember."

"Mm. Pity she's not a head or something. That would make it a bit stronger. OK, you'll have to go on secret vice act of Miss. Real life drama as sex scandal hits suburban secondary. But keep it shortish, 600 words. If it makes, it'll be a downpage lead. You know the kind of thing. Little did the residents of a leafy London suburb suspect that the dedicated drama teacher who directed their children in this year's performance of...Oliver or something...was involved behind the scenes in stage managing far less wholesome performances. As founder of a local wife swapping club, over the last year Miss X has drawn dozens of friends and neighbours into a sordid sex ring involving orgies at steamy sex parties in a hired room below a local nightclub..."

Rick had a pen out and was scribbling in shorthand into his notebook.

"Ta, George, that's me first par. Billie's going to add in some quotes, OK?"

"Sure."

They wandered over to a desk in a block near the newsdesk. Apart from a blowsy blonde woman seated on the other side, it was empty. Rick gestured for Billie to sit down next to the woman and took a small tape-recorder out of his pocket. "Hi Carol. Carol is the woman's editor. This is Billie. D'you want to start transcribing this? I'll grab us a coffee.Do you want one Carol?"

"Yes please love."

Billie opened a file and started playing the tape and typing it out. There was a lot of noise in the background so she had to turn it up to hear what the people were saying. After a few minutes Carol handed her some earphones. "Put these on," she said. "It's distracting," she said.

"Sorry." She put them on. Rick returned and put a coffee on her desk. He had forgotten the sugar and Billie went off to fetch some. When she returned, a middle-aged man had sat down where she had been and was talking to Carol.

Billie stood for a moment waiting but he didn't seem to see her.

"Excuse me," she said, keen to get on with her work. "I was sitting there."

The man broke off his conversation and stared hard at her. Then he stood up and stalked across the office, banging the door of an office on the other side of the newsroom behind him. Then the door opened again and he bellowed 'George!'

Rick clicked his tongue. "Oh-oh. That was Dick, the editor. I'm afraid he's not going to like being made to stand up like that."

Carol shook her head. "No. Dick's very big on authority I'm afraid. And he does get himself all worked up."

George came over.

"What did he say?" Rick asked.

"He said, tell her she's a blank and sack her. I didn't bother to explain she doesn't work here. There didn't seem to be much point. He'll have forgotten her next week."

"Oh dear," Carol turned to Billie. "I'm very down on Dick today. He has been a bit of a prick. But don't worry dear. He needs to be sat on by someone."

Billie was upset. "What should I do?"

"Head off home and don't give it a thought. Rick will finish the story."

"Yes" Rick agreed. "That's the best thing.Don't worry."

When she got home, Antony was waiting for her.

He sat up when Billie came sadly through the door. "Where have you been, darling? I was worried." Billie went to sit on the sofa next to him and he put an affectionate arm round her.

"I was out on a job, actually. An undercover assignment that came up late. Sorry I didn't let you know.""No I'm sorry. I really am. I feel terrible for upsetting you about Lotty and Marina. of course she can sit at the top table if it'll make you happy. This wedding business has been getting a touch out of hand. "So I've called off the meetings for a month or so. Mother isn't pleased, naturally. But it's your big day sweetheart, not hers. So, a month break and we'll have weekends like we used to.""That's a good idea, I really think it's starting to get out of hand. We've got months to go until the wedding anyway."

"Yes, I know. I just want you to have a splendid day that you'll remember all our lives, that's all." he stroked her arm. "Hey you do look stunning tonight. Why all the finery?"

"Em, well it was an undercover job and I had to infiltrate this wife-swapping club…"

"Hm, how seedy. I can't imagine why people go in for that sort of thing. They're obviously nowhere near as lucky as I am."

He took Billie in her arms and smiled down at her. What a handsome man he was, she thought, and how understanding. Just as well she had managed to wriggle out of that rather embarrassing situation with Rick earlier before it had gone too far." Or I," she said, and they kissed.

Getting up the next morning was difficult. Leaning over Antony, Billie turned off the alarm feeling like going back to sleep for a few hours, but it was already after nine and she had to open the office at 10 am as she was doing her first Sunday shift.

Clutching an egg roll and a coffee, she let herself in at quarter past. The phone was ringing and she ran into the office to pick it up.

"Hi?"

It was Felix.

"Hi, sorry I'm a bit late."

"Well you're here now. It said on the news that Rebelle's family was going to make a statement. They must be putting the husband up at a presser. Get on to it would you? Phone me back with the details I'll phone the Sundays from here and get some orders."

Billie phoned Scotland Yard Press Bureau and got Theo, who actually remembered her.

"Hey Billie. Yes, Mr Fernandez has kindly agreed to make an appeal for information about his wife's killer. Her stepson is appearing too. It'll be at twelve noon at Scotland Yard. Bring your press card."

"I don't have one yet."

"OK, ask for me."

The press conference was clearly big news. Link vans and camera crews were arriving in strength, there was even a Japanese crew. They filed past Billie through the double glass doors of the annexe where the press office was situated. Because she didn't have a police press card she had to go into the main office and wait, sitting on a sofa.

Eventually Theo, a slim black man in jeans and trainers came through found her and took her past the security into the conference.

"Cheers," She was very grateful. Theo lifted a thin hand.

"Don't worry about it. I'll see you later."

There must have been 150 people in the room. At the top was a table covered in a blue cloth. Behind it were three chairs and at each place was a microphone on a small stand, a glass of water and a folded card with a name typed on it. Billie looked for a seat and saw a hand moving among the people at the back of the room and picked out Rick. He waved her over. Momentarily, she hesitated, before going over to stand beside him.

"Hi," he whispered. "I saw Theo this morning I told him all about you know what."

"You what?" Billie was puzzled.

"You know, Canterbury Gardens."

"Oh fuck. Why?"

"It seemed like the best thing to do."

A middle-aged policeman in uniform came into the room and sat at the table.

"I am Detective Chief Inspector Bennet, the officer in charge of the investigation into the murder of Rebelle Fernandez. I have spoken to many of you in the past. Rebelle's husband, the financier Xavier Fernandez and her stepson Carlo are going to give a statement this morning. There is nothing unusual about this. I have had questions from some of you about why we are taking this step and it is routine in a murder enquiry such as this one. All that is happening is that we are trying to encourage witnesses to come forward who might not realise they have an important piece of information. Now, as all of you can imagine, this is an incredibly difficult ordeal for the family and can I ask you to respect their privacy and obey the rules. If you want to ask a question, raise your hand."

After he had spoken, the policeman left the room. He reappeared shortly afterwards, following Xavier and Carlo and a policewoman. They took their places at the table.

Xavier was a big, broad-shouldered handsome man with thick black hair which was combed back from his wide brow, pale but otherwise showing no trace of nervousness. "Hello," he said. "As you know, I am Xavier Fernandez. I don't think it's exaggerating to say that the last ten days have been hell for me. I loved my wife very much. She was a wonderful person, and she was loved by so many people outside her own family. As well as being my wife she was a creative spirit who in a sense belonged to all of us. A star that shone for the whole world has gone out."

He looked into the nearest camera." I am here today to ask any of you who has any piece of information no matter how small, no matter how trivial it may seem, which might help the police with their investigation, to come forward."

At that point, Fernandez seemed to break down. His big head fell into his broad hands and he hid his face from the crowd. The policewoman who was standing nearby put a hand on his shoulder and he stood up and left the room, looking straight ahead of him as if trying to prevent tears from running down his face.

Carlo spoke into his own mike. "I would just like to reinforce what my father has said. Rebelle was a lovely woman, a joy to have around and in the time that I knew her she enriched my life as she enriched the lives of so many with her music.

"The police don't have much to go on yet. We have a description of a woman seen fleeing from the scene shortly before she was found. If she had nothing to do with it, let her come forward to be eliminated. Thank you." Carlo stood up and walked out.

The policeman nodded.

" I'll take a few questions."

A TV reporter shoved her mike forward.

"Jane Green, Sky News. Is there any truth in the rumour that you have been questioning Xavier Fernandez about possible involvement in his wife's killing?"

"No," Bennet said.

"Ben Barber, CNN. Do you believe she was killed by hired assassins?"

"We can't say who killed her. But there is no reason to believe it was a contract killing."

"Sally Francis, News 24. Do you believe she was killed by someone who knew her?"

"She could have been".

"Carl Dunn, Post. Did she drive to Canterbury Gardens to meet her killer? Or do you think she was killed somewhere else and then her killer drove there and dumped the car."

"It's impossible to say for certain. But we believe it is possible that she was killed elsewhere and then driven to Canterbury Gardens. There is no evidence that supports the idea she was killed at the scene. No-one heard her scream, there is no blood, no sign of a murder weapon.

"The car was abandoned there in the early hours of March 12. Her killer must have left there on foot, either by road or scrambling across the railway line. This is our main line of inquiry. One more question."

A print journalist in a sharp blue suit took his pencil out of his mouth.

"Ian Andrews, Recorder. Do you have any indication as to what the murder weapon might have been?

"The early indications are that it may have been a large bladed implement, such as a very large kitchen knife or a machete."

There was a murmur from the crowd. Someone shouted something which Billie didn't hear.

"Yes, I suppose it could have been a Samurai sword. It was probably more likely to be a machete or even a large kitchen knife but it could have been a sword. Ladies, gentlemen." Inspector Bennet got up, nodded and left the room.

Rick turned to Billie. "Wow, dynamite," he said. "Samurai sword kills singing star. Big news."

She turned to the subject that was troubling her. "I wish you hadn't told Theo."

"I felt I had to. We might be screwing up their investigation. If that identikit is you, then they're barking up the wrong tree. Best tell them now really."

"I suppose you're right. They'll be furious."

"Bound to be. The real killer might have got away by now.

"Oh thanks, try and make me feel better why don't you?"

Theo came over.

"OK you two, walk this way. Chief Inspector Bennet wants to see you."

"Oh-oh," Rick said. "Are we in trouble?"

"Fraid so."

# CHAPTER SEVEN

They followed Theo in silence through a corridor and a couple of security doors, though the press office, which was empty and noisy with ringing phones and into a smaller office where he sat behind a desk.

"Pull up a couple of chairs," he said. "Now, tell me, what 's going on?"

"Er. Theo. I'm sorry but we really need to file our copy from the presser. Can we do that first please? Pretty please or we'll be in the shit ."

"OK," Theo said, "I know what you scribes are like with your deadlines."

Rick picked up the phone on his desk. "You don't mind do you? Is it nine for an outside line?" Flipping his notebook open, he began to file his copy, quoting chunks.

"There's no-one in my office so I'll have to file and send out when I get back," Billie explained. "Will this take long?"

"I hope not," Theo said. "Rick told me a bit about what happened. I just wanted to get it clear before I tell Bennet. You two went round the back and crossed the railway line, to get a look at the corpse, is that right? And then when you saw the representatives of the law you made your escape in a northerly direction across the back gardens?"

"Yes. We're really sorry. It sounds terrible but it was just an impulse thing, we didn't mean any harm, we were seeing what we could see from the other side and we …kind of went a bit far," Rick said. "We were carried away by enthusiasm for our jobs."

Billie didn't say anything.

"It was Billie's first day as a reporter," Rick said. "And so it was really my fault. I suggested it and she just tagged along."

"Now that has the ring of truth," Theo said, smiling. "That was a pretty stupid thing to do but I don't really see how it can affect anything. OK, I need to get back to help rescue him from the mob but give me your mobile numbers. I'll tell DCI Bennet. He's pretty busy but he may want to talk to you later."

Billie waited until they had left the building before turning to Rick. "Thanks for taking the rap for me. Looks like we've got away with it this time."

A sense of relief washed over her. That hadn't been so bad. Thank God it was over with. Back at the office, she rattled her account of the presser into the computer and pressed the send button. and then, as per instructions, locked up and went out to buy the entire range of papers except for the Guardian. As well, she bought a cappuccino, a salad from the sandwich shop and a large crumbly cake they sold there, the kind that Sorrel called a "chocolate orgasm" to take back to the office. Enjoying the feeling of being alone, she put her feet up on the desk and grabbed the Post on Sunday magazine *Night Night*.

While she ate, she read a profile of Xavier Fernandez by someone called Courgette Hollondaise.

*That punctuality is the politeness of kings has long been one of my favourite aphorisms and thus it was through no fault of my own but due to circumstances without my control, namely, the exigencies of the London transport system, that I was late to meet Xavier Fernandez.*

*The great man forgave me at once and welcomed me with a basket of fruit and delicious East Tibetan coffee at the hotel suite to which he has decamped from his sumptuous mansion in Richmond, from whence he has been compelled to flee, both from the memories of his dear wife Rebelle so recently horribly murdered in a London street, and the persistent tabloid reporters who also haunt him, he says like a dark hovering cloud of ghouls, set on picking white the bones of his wife's corpse.*

*Being a fair man as well as an extremely attractive one, Fernandez, although he hates the necessity of baring his innermost feelings, recognizes that the carbon monoxide of publicity may be what is needed to trap his wife's killer and for that reason he has taken it upon himself to face the cameras at a press conference organised at Scotland Yard today when he will again voice a heartfelt appeal for anyone who has any scrap of information which may help the police to come forward.*

*I have interviewed Fernandez more than once over the two decades of his business career in this country and so it is with genuine human sympathy that I condole with him on the tragic loss of his ringingly beautiful Belle. "Ah, she has gone and with her have gone all the sunshine and laughter of my house," he mourns.*

*Xavier's large bull-like frame shows every trace of the ordeal he has been through these last days and the shock of thick black hair I remember is turning rapidly grey.*

*As he paces up and down upon the diamond patterned "Allied" carpet of the oval room in which we are seated, he lets me into something of the torment he is suffering. "Sleep? How can I sleep? Every night I wake and see her face, there in front of me, bleeding and in pain. This is the hardest thing I have ever had to deal with - for me a problem is something that you can solve. But how can I ever solve this if I live to be a hundred?'*

*Solving problems is what the legendary businessman has excelled at throughout his life. Along with his tremendous drive and energy, this was what allowed him to pull himself by the sock suspenders from the Buenos Aires slum in which he was born, the youngest of nine children, to create a clothing empire, marry and divorce one of Argentina's most beautiful women, model Gisella Ramos, and then create a financial services empire headquartered in Britain.*

*Sadly, now, feeling himself a broken man, Xavier declares that all of this worldly success means nothing and that he would gladly exchange it for Rebelle to be returned to him once more.*

*He has lost interest in it all, he says and wishes when this situation is solved to hand it over to his son Carlos and return to live out the remainder of his days in the peace and solitude of the beautiful ranch he has built in the Argentinean countryside.*

*Fernandez has no clue, he says, as to what motive can have lain behind his wife's death. She had no enemies and if he did, they can have had no quarrel with his wife. Did he know everything about his wife's life? I ask, tentatively. Of course., he replies, scornfully. They were a couple deeply in love, "without secrets, completely without secrets".*

*Famed as a man not to cross in the world of business, if Rebelle had had a shameful secret, might she have held onto it, afraid to tell him? Again no, absolutely not. Xavier Fernandez may have been a lion abroad, but at home he was a simple, domestic mouse, he declares, so peaceable and amenable that his wishes were hardly ever taken into account. His wife, his son, they did what they pleased.*

*Business lion, domestic mouse, we leave him pacing the floor of the hotel suite, unable to settle to anything, mourning his wife with the faithful passion of the elephant.*

She had just finished reading when the phone rang. It was Theo. "Billie, Bennet wants to talk to you. He's going back to north London now."

"OK, sure. I'm busy today and tomorrow. Monday be any good?""I'm afraid not. He's going to send a car for you."

"A car?"

"A police car. It'll be there in about forty-five."

"Forty-five?"

"Minutes," Theo said patiently. "You're going to as we say, help the police with their enquiries."

"Shit. I'd better let Antony know," thought Billie. But when she phoned the flat the answer phone came on and his mobile was switched off.

Apart from anything, else, Billie worried that she was alone in the office. She called Felix. It was a difficult conversation.

"They're going to question you about what?"

"Well kind of about the Rebelle murder."

"Yeah?"

She felt forced to expand. "You remember when they found the body and Rick and I..."

"Rick?"

"Oh, sorry, hiccups. I... hic ...sneaked round the back."

"I didn't tell you to do that."

"No. Well They found out I did and they want to know if I saw anything suspicious really."

"How did they find out?"

"I'm not sure but they want to question me. I'm going to be helping police with their enquiries, they said."

"Oh that's a great... shame. Hang on in there I'll send someone round."

Thirty minutes later the bell rang. It was Barmy, the picture editor.

"Wotcher. 'as the Bill showed up yet?"

"Not yet."

"Good. I hear they're taking you in." He made a motion with his hand as if pouring something out of an imaginary jug.

Billie looked puzzled.

"Custard, innit. That's custody in monkey speak. Snappers, photographers. If someone gets sent down like, a reporter usually comes out of the court and makes that sign so the monkeys know there ain't going to be a photo opportunity.

"By the way Billie, have we taken any snaps of you, for, you know press card, office files, or anything?"

"No."

"Might as well just do those since we're here eh? Stand over there. OK fine, no don't smile, try and look natural, that's better, lovely." Barmy asked her to stand against the wall of the office and fired off a few frames.

"So the cops are going to talk to you?"

"Yeah but it's nothing serious. Just a chat. I'm going to, you know, help with their enquiries."

"Right, yeah. Just a few details for the press card then." Barmy had a notebook and pen out. "Age, address, phone number. Married, no."

"Engaged"

"Oh yeah? What's he like then, your bloke? Successful is he? Handsome?"

"Very." Billie fished her purse out of her pocket and showed Barmy the picture Antony had inserted in it when he gave it to her. It had been taken on a holiday to Ibiza and they were standing holding hands on a sunny beach with blue sea behind them in swimwear.

"Cor," said Barmy, "you do undress to advantage. Hey if he ever has any trouble keeping you satisfied, you can give me a ring. Tell you what, I'm hung like a donkey," he said conversationally.

"I 've got a man. I don't need a donkey."

Barmy laughed. He was holding the purse. Deftly, he flipped the picture out of its slot and, placing it on the desk held his camera above it and snapped the shutter.

"What d'you do that for?" Billie was suspicious now.

"It's just I've got a mate who's a spotter for a model agency. He's always on the look out for girls like you."

"Yeah but I don't want to be a model. I'm a journalist."

"What girl doesn't dream of being a model?" Barmy handed back the purse and Billie stuck it into her back pack.

Just then the sound of an engine in the alley outside the office silenced them.

"Cops?" Billie asked.

"Could be."

A low humming filled the air. Barmy went to the window. "It's a link van," he said. "There's a camera crew out there and about a dozen snappers. They've got ladders and everything. I reckon it's you they're after. Hell's biscuits, what are you going to do? You don't want your picture splashed all over the red tops do you?

Particularly with your fiance being a PR exec and all that. Might be embarrassing for him. Look, I know what. Stick something over your head".

"Stick something over my head?" Billie said.

"Yeah people do it all the time. You must have seen it on the telly, people being hauled in for questioning. They usually stick a blanket over their head or something."

"D'you think?" She was totally off balance now, unsure.

"I'm sure". Barmy's gaze swung around the office. "Hey this'll do the trick." he picked up the wastepaper basket and emptied the contents onto a desk. Upturning it, he shoved it over her head.

"But this must look ridiculous," she protested.

"A bit," said Barmy. "Better than seeing yourself on the ten o clock news though innit?"

"But I can't see a thing."

"No need. But OK," Barmy pulled the wastebasket off her head and jabbed two eyeholes with a pair of scissors.

The bell rang. "That must be the cops." Barmy ushered her towards the door and opened it. "'Ere she is," he said to the two policemen who stood there. "Best get going sharpish with this mob out here." There was a silence and Barmy spoke again. "Looking for Billie Wilson? This is her. Doesn't want her picture taken. You know how it is."

"Is that right?" one of the policemen asked.

"Yes, yes it is," Billie said.

"Speak up," Barmy said.

"YES," she shouted.

One officer took each of her elbows and they moved her towards the squad car. Billie could just see it through the slits in the waste basket. She thought about hauling it off her head but perhaps Barmy was right. After all, she didn't want the Moomins leaping out of their chairs in horror as she appeared on telly being led away between two cops. If it had been after a demo or even a riot, Marina would have been quite pleased but a murder investigation? She kept the basket on.

Even with limited vision she could see the flashes popping and hear the clipped voice of a famous TV reporter asking: "Are you arresting this woman?"

The policemen didn't answer. Billie felt a downward pressure on her shoulder and bent down to get into the squad car. It moved away slowly presumably because of the press of people.

Billie heard a familiar, amused voice. "You can take that thing off now. It's not Hallowe'en you know."

She took the wastepaper bin off and sitting on the black plastic upholstery of the back seat of a police car, next to her, was Rick.

"You're having a laugh aren't you?" he asked.

"No. Not really. I put that over my head because I didn't want my picture on the news."

"Don't think they would have risked a picture of you in this case. Even if you were the absolute red-handed chief suspect which, clearly, you're not. Sub judice. Or it might be. The lawyers wouldn't let a pic go by at this stage. "

"You're right," she said, trying to remember the law she had studied at journalism college. It was hard to apply the abstruse academic language of her law exam to the moment but he was right. "Identity might be an issue." .

"That was daft because now they can use pictures of you walking to the car on the news, because you can't be identified, because you've got a bin over your head. It actually makes better footage because it makes you look scarey. You've been monstered."

"Shit," Billie said.

"Who told you to wear that ridiculous thing?"

"My picture editor actually."

"Right. Presumably he's got a little exclusive picture package up his sleeve for later."

"Bastard." Billie wasn't sure whether she wanted to kick herself or Barmy. Antony's mother would chew her up like a raptor on the Atkins diet if that photo of Billie and her son ever made its way into the pages of a tabloid newspaper, she thought.

The two policemen in the front of the car were silent as they wound their way through the comparatively empty centre of town, before hitting the usual jams in the suburbs.

Eventually they reached the police station and they led them from the car park through a back door into a small windowless room with a table and four chairs. The air in it was stale, it felt stuffy and overheated. Billie could feel a familiar throbbing starting behind her eyes. She hoped she was not about to start a migraine. She rubbed her temples with her thumbs and Rick patted her shoulder.

"Sit down," said one of the policemen. "DCI Bennet will come and talk to you in a few minutes."

After sitting in silence for a few minutes, Rick turned to her, "I'm so sorry. I didn't forsee that this was going to happen. I should have realised there might be a bit of a feeding frenzy. It's such a huge story that anything, absolutely anything will make on it. I should have warned you.

"And the police don't really seem to have much of a clue, you know, as to motive or whatever. They seem to be suspecting everyone. Thank God they're not desperate enough yet to just try and pin it on a convenient nutter."

"Do they do that?"Billie asked.

"Oh yeah, everyone says so. There's so much pressure on them to get someone in a case like this, I think after a while they get so desperate they do. But they haven't reached that point yet. "

"So they won't try and get me for it. Thanks for those few words of comfort."

"It's OK, you big nutter".

The door opened and in came DCI Bennet, a big, beefy man with a reddish face and deep set blue eyes, dressed in a grey suit. With him was another man who looked like a younger, more streamlined version of himself.

"We meet again," he said. "I think I saw you at the press conference yesterday, standing at the back weren't you? I'm Charles Bennet as of course you know, and this is my colleague Jack Tierney.

By the way, Richard, your old man's been on the phone. I told him you were being most co-operative."

Billie looked over at Rick who smiled and nodded, a little ruefully.

They sat down at the opposite side of the table and Bennet asked them to run through the story they had told Theo.

"So you got up on the embankment. Is this what you saw?" He took a sheaf of pictures out of his briefcase and thrust them across the table at Billie.

Billie picked them up and made a face of disgust. The top one showed a close up of Rebelle, her face contorted into a scream, eyes bulging.

"That knife must have been pretty sharp," Billie said. It looked as if the killer had stabbed her many times, a pulp of bloody tissue below the still recognisably beautiful face. Looking up, she saw that Bennet was watching her closely and flicked quickly through the others before offering them to Rick. He shook his head. "No thanks. If that's OK. Not my scene."Bennet looked at him. "OK." Rick looked at the top picture and screwed up his face. "Yes, this is pretty much what we saw, but we weren't nearly as close."

"OK"

Bennet seemed particularly interested in the fact that it had been Billie's first day as a reporter. What had she been doing the previous night, he asked casually. Oh-oh, she thought. He looked over at Rick who rolled his eyes and lolled his tongue very slightly out of his mouth. "Nutter," he mouthed and Billie had to choke a hysterical laugh.

After a few minutes more chat, the police officers got up to leave.

"Would you mind hanging around for a bit longer?" Bennet said.

Billie was finding it hard to breathe and raised a hand to hide a half-yawn.

"Bit tired are we Billie? Would you like somewhere to lie down? I fink we can arrange some accommodation for a little lady such as yourself." Bennet and his colleague laughed loudly at their own wit. Rick gave a small pained smile.

"Only joking. You can go home now, Richard. It's just Billie that has to stay. There's something we might need her to do. Come with me and I'll let you out the front. By the way, thanks for being a good boy and telling Theo what you saw. But don't go doing that again, will you? The little matters of trespassing on the railway line and potentially wasting police time could be very serious. Next time you mightn't be fortunate enough to come across a nice, cuddly old school cop like me. Leave the detective work to us, stick to your own side of the tape, OK. That is, unless you want to see sense and join the family business?" Rick lifted a hand to wave at Billie as he was ushered out.

Soon she was left alone, staring at the walls. There were a few leaflets in a holder hanging up and she grabbed a handful, hoping to pass the time although not to cheer herself up "Stay Alive Don't Drink and Drive" showed a car smashing into a dummy pushing a pram. "Crime fighters" showed an elderly lady looking out of her window at two men kicking the head of a prone body.

Eventually, the door opened and a uniformed policeman came in.

"Come with me, please" he said and ushered Billie along a corridor, through a fire door and down a staircase. At the foot was a small, windowless hall where a policeman sat at a desk.

"This is the custody sergeant. You're going to have to wait in a cell for a bit."

"Am I under arrest?"

"Oh no, not exactly, just being held for questioning." The policeman turned to the custody sergeant. "Billie Wilson this is, can you just hang on to her here for a little while. We're busy up the stairs."

After confirming her full name and date of birth, Billie had to empty out her pockets and remove belt and boot laces. All of her things were put in a clear plastic bag and she was led along the corridor and put in a cell, the door clanging shut unpleasantly behind her.

It was small and bare with a bench upholstered in grey plastic and above that, a high window. A partition half hid a flushing toilet.

Standing on the bench, she could put her face to the window but was unable to see out through the frosted glass. A small grille in the heavy metal door was open but there was little to be seen through it, just a small section of corridor and another identical door almost opposite.

She sat on the bench, sighed and wished she had something to read other than the leaflet about crime prevention she had shoved in her pocket.

The minutes ticked slowly by. From time to time Billie would get up and walk round the cell, which she could do in a few paces, look through the grille in the door, trying to angle her face so that she could see along the corridor. The air felt thick and rancid and her head was starting to hurt. Obviously, the police had grounds to question her. She had been clearly identified by an eye witness at the scene of a murder acting suspiciously and an identifit of her face was on show all over the country. The gravity of the situation suddenly hit her and she sat on the bench sunk in despair. Rick had been joking about the convenient nutter idea but this was starting to feel quite scarey. She decided that if she was not let out soon she would ask for a phone call to Antony or Marina. They would get her out.

She could hear voices and shouted out once or twice, hoping that someone might fetch her an aspirin, a glass of water or let her use the phone. After what seemed like hours, she heard footsteps and then a flap was opened in the door and an elderly woman in civilian clothes looked through. "I've brought your tea," she said, handing her a covered tin plate, a plastic fork and a metal mug.

"Cheers," Billie said. "What time is it by the way? How long am I going to be here for? Can I make a phone call? Have you got anything to read?"

"It's five. And I don't know nothing about how long or what you can and can't do. What sort of thing d'you want to read?"

"Anything at all."

"I'll see what I can do." The woman clanged the door shut again and his footsteps and the wheels of a trolley could be heard, moving away a little and then stopping at the next occupied cell. Billie could hear the murmur of voices.

Lifting the cover off the tin plate, she found some mashed potato, an overcooked sausage and some baked beans. She didn't feel that hungry, in fact her head was throbbing and she felt a bit sick but she made herself eat some beans.

Some time later, the grille in the door flipped down to reveal a small window and she saw the old woman's face on the other side.

"Here, I brought you something to read," she said and pushed some stuff through. Leaping over, Billie found a copy of the Watchtower and a six month old copy of Police News. "Thanks, thanks a lot, " she called, picking them up.

She had nearly finished Police News and was trying to string out a report about a team of policemen who were competing in the London marathon when she looked up and saw a face at the grille.

"Oh, you still here then?" asked the policeman who had brought her down earlier. "I thought they'd let you out."

"No, I can assure you that they haven't."

"I just got a phone call from someone asking about you. I don't think Bennet knows you're still here. I'll try to get hold of him."

The face disappeared. Too strung out to read now, Billie went back to trying to peek along the corridor. Some time later, she heard a heavy footfall and the custody sergeant came and opened the door.

"You can go now." he said. "You have to sign a declaration that you will return for further questioning later but you're to go home tonight."

"Thank God," Billie said.

"It's not God's doing, it's someone more important than that. We got a phone call about you from the chief constable or else you might have been in 'til morning. I think that lot up there had forgotten they still had you to deal with. Things have been that busy. These are yours, aint they?" They were back at the desk and Billie replaced her belt and threaded her laces back in. After signing something to say she had received everything back and that she would come back for questioning later, a policewoman took her upstairs and let her out of a door into the public waiting area, where a woman in a sheepskin jacket was standing at the window pressing the bell for attention. The policewoman went behind the window to deal with her and Billie made her way out through the main door, under a Victorian style lantern that said "POLICE" in square blue letters, onto the empty street.

It was dark now and the sign was lit. Although it was freezing after the stuffy, overheated police station, she took a huge, breath of the clean, cold air. Then, dizzy, she leaned against the wall for a moment to recover. Her head was still hurting and it felt like her brain was being squeezed inside her skull. But as the fresh, cold air coursed through her, the pain lessened a bit.

She had never been so happy to see such a plain old street, busy with early evening traffic, headlights reflected off the dark road which was wet from an earlier shower of rain. At a bus stop 100 yards away, a queue of people waiting wore macs and carried umbrellas.

Across the road a man who was leaning against the wall, straightened up, took his hands out of his pockets and crossed the road towards her. It was Rick.

"Thank goodness. I thought they'd lost you in the system."

"They pretty much did. Someone called, I don't know who...Have you been waiting outside here all this time?"

"Yeah. I didn't like to run out and leave a mate in trouble."

"Thanks"

"That's OK. Fancy a drink?"

Billie thought. She wanted to go home, have a bath take two painkillers and climb into her comfy bed next to Ant. He might be worried about her. But Rick had waited out here for ages and she was very thirsty.

Nearby was the lighted window of a pub called "The Slammer". They went in and Rick ordered a pint of lime and soda and a packet of crisps for Billie...

A TV stood above the bar, and Billie gazed at it nervously. It looked like the end of the local news. The sound was so far turned down that she couldn't hear it but it was clearly an item about a long running West End show musical "Hats!", which seemed to be closing after dozens of years. Billie was nervously awaiting the moment when the presenter recapped the headlines. Would a picture of herself with a bucket over her head feature?

The headlines. First up was a photo of Rebelle, then a picture not of Billie, but of Carlo, closely followed by Carlo and Xavier at the press conference and then a picture of a press pack surrounding DCI Bennet. Bennet appeared to be outside, there was a dark sky behind him. Then a cut away shot of an airfield. What had happened? Anyway, there was absolutely nothing about Billie so, thankful for that, she let out a big, relieved sigh.

She needed to go back to the office. Her backpack with keys and credit card wallet was there. "Just one more drink first?" suggested Rick. "No," she said. "My head hurts and I want to go home."

A short while later, she arrived at the office. Felix's car, a red Jaguar about 10 years old, was parked in the alleyway - he only brought it in at the weekend.

The front door was ajar and Billie pushed it open. Inside she could hear the sound of an angry voice. It sounded like Sorrel. Billie stopped in the lobby, just inside the inner door for a moment, not liking to barge in.

Sorrel sounded as though she had been crying, her voice coming in angry sobs. She was saying: "I just can't believe what you're turning into, what we're both turning into. It's like, the way some of the kids we get in here act like they're modeling themselves on some wide boy, foot in the door reporter they've seen on the telly, well you are even worse. Who are you turning into?"

Felix's voice came back. He was shouting. "This is a bloody business Sorrel. It pays both our mortgages remember? We need to make a profit and we're barely getting paid at the moment."

Billie was caught between embarrassment and curiosity. If she moved back onto the street she might make a noise and make them think she had been listening.

Sorrel's tearful voice answered Felix: "I know, I know. But is there anything you won't do for money?"

"Maybe. But the deal's fallen though anyway."

"Oh, thank God for that."

"But it's lost us bloody eight grand and that's eight grand we can't do without, and frankly that is eight grand more than that kid is worth."

"I'm just starting to realise how much you've changed Felix. You're not the man I used to love. I gave up thinking that there was a future for that part of our relationship a long time ago when I realised you weren't going to leave Christine. I thought we could salvage the rest. But I'm starting to doubt that now."

"If that's the way you feel, Sorrel, maybe you should think about looking for another job. I've been thinking for some time that you just aren't cutting it, frankly. You know, life's more than just some sodding cocktail party where all you have to do is wander around being nice to people and handing round the canapés. You've got to care. You've really got to really care to make it in this business. I used to think you understood that."

"Oh Felix, I do care. You're the one who doesn't even know what that means any more."

Hearing footsteps, Billie moved in behind the open front door and someone rushed out of the office and went swiftly by, Sorrel from the footsteps. Billie waited. There was silence from inside the office. After a couple of minutes, she stepped out from behind the open door and banged it shut. Then she walked into the office, trying to make as much noise as possible.

"Wotcher, Felix," she said. "The door was open."

Felix looked up from his terminal. "Oh it's you," he said. "Sorrel must have left it open. Did you happen to see her?" He shook his head. "Where have you been, anyway?"

"In the slammer."

"Oh yeah?"

"They talked to me a bit and then shoved me in a cell, saying they were going to come back but they seemed to forget about me. Nothing happened, they didn't come back, then they let me out."

"I'm not surprised considering what's happened. Don't tell me you haven't heard, Ace? Even from your position right inside the HO of the police team that's leading the murder inquiry? I was hoping you were going to come back here with loads of insider information to file."

"I haven't. I might have been inside but not that kind of inside."

"Carlo Fernandez has gone missing. He went home, seems to have got in his car and taken off. His dad alerted the cops that he'd disappeared, then an hour or so later they realised that his private plane has gone from an airstrip in Sussex. Here, turn it up."

Felix handed her the remote control to the office telly which was tuned to a 24 hour news channel. Bennett's face had appeared on it.

"And take down what he says in shorthand would you? We should file those quotes to the papers we're covering for."

# CHAPTER EIGHT

B ennet was saying: "The evidence seems to point to the fact that Carlo Fernandez has definitely absconded."

"Did you get that, Felix? He's got away."

"OK ace. Can you get round to the house?"

"Whose house?"

"Bloody Carlo and Xavier's house. Where d'you think?"

"Oh what? You want me to doorstep Xavier? What d'you want me to ask him, is he upset?"

Felix looked over at her. "I know how you feel and I know how that sounds. But come on, it's got to be done. It's a huge story. We still don't know for certain what happened to Belle and we are in a sense part of the operation that will probably find the killer whoever he is. I'm not expecting you to come back with an exclusive chat but you must see we've got to go. In a sense if you're there it means there will be fewer reporters on the doorstep, not more."

"I suppose." Billie was trying to find an opportunity to raise her fear that Barmy may have stitched her up earlier.

"Look Felix, earlier on, Barmy took some pics of me and stuff. I don't know what he was planning to do with them…"

"For your press card I expect."

"That's what he said but I…"

"Don't worry about it Billie. They're not going to end up splashed over the papers tomorrow. I assure you."

"Yeah?"

"I'll talk to him about it if you like."

"Thanks."

Too far past tirednesss to argue, Billie got up, shoved a newspaper into her back pack and headed out of the door. "I'll call you when I'm there."

Feeling tired and glum, but a bit better thanks to the migraine relief pills she had had in her bag, she climbed the hill to the Fernandez' mansion once again, vaguely wondering why she always seemed to be the one working late shifts especially at the weekend. Where were all the old pros? Could it be because she was new and had not yet computed that the pay was unbelievably shit? She wished she had managed to wriggle out of it... After all, Antony had made a big effort canceling the wedding meetings and now she was so busy she had hardly seen him.

She pulled her back pack off one shoulder and fished her mobile phone out. This time, Antony answered. His voice sounded sharp and worried.

"Thank God. I've been really worried about you this time. Where have you been?"

Billie explained about the questioning, saying that she looked so like the efit someone who saw her that morning might have become confused about the timing and that the police had asked her in for questioning, then shoved her in a cell and forgotten about her.

"But that's terrible. That's like something that happens in Chile or somewhere. That doesn't happen in England surely."

"I suppose it was only for a couple of hours. Perhaps I should have made more of a fuss, insisted on calling a lawyer or something."

"I should say so. I was worried sick when you didn't call. I thought we were going out this evening. We were going to see a film weren't we?"

"Darling, I'm really sorry." Billie had forgotten this arrangement. "You must have heard what's happened now, Carlo's done a runner and I'm rushing off to cover the house."

"Oh hell, why?"

"I'm on a watching brief really. I'll make it up to you I promise. Tomorrow I'll do whatever you want."

Antony sighed. "Are you standing me up?"

"No, it's not like that, I'm at work."

"Work, work, work. That's all I hear about these days. I know it's important to you because you've just started a new job. I can understand that. But can I just point out that I earn three times what you do and despite the fact that I too started a new job quite recently, a, I do not go on about it all the time and b, I almost never work at weekends."

"Point taken. I won't do this to you again. I promise."

"That had better be true, Billie. Goodbye." He rang off.

Feeling even more glum, she approached the top of the hill where she could see a pack of photographers already assembled and a few reporters sitting in their cars.

Billie recognised a couple of faces. "All right?" she asked and was pleased to achieve the acknowledgement of a half smile and a nod before going to sit on a wall.

Gary, the photographer she had met up here before came to sit next to her.

"That was you wasn't it, with the bucket over your head earlier on? You looked a proper tit. What was that in aid of?"

"I just didn't want my picture on the news."

"Well it was great footage. Shame it got pulled. You were superseded by developments. Why did the cops pull you in anyway?"

Billie explained about the efit and the worry that someone who saw her at the scene might have got confused.

"That has happened before. A mate of mine got fingered to the police over a crime, it turned out the only thing he had to do with it was that his picture byline was over the story. Bad news mate. Sorry about the scrum earlier. Nothing personal, you know that."

"Yes, I do. But thanks for the apology."

"Looks like this story's nearly over."

"What do you mean?"

"It's obvious, innit? The stepson was having an affair with Rebelle. She threatens to tell the old man, he knows he'll get chucked out without a euro to rub together, panics, kills her, the net closes, he does a runner."

"D'you think?"

"Oh yeah, definite. It's in the bag, I reckon. The cops think so too. They're not looking for anyone else now. Scaling down already. Job for Interpol now."

"Hmm. Maybe. But why would she threaten to tell?"

"Who knows. But anyway, he did it, that's obvious."

Gary moved away towards the other snappers who were standing in a group on the pavement talking animatedly. Already, Billie knew better than to try to involve herself in their conversation so she sat alone on the wall. On impulse, she fished out her phone and called Antony.

"Hi darling. What are you up to?"

"Thinking dark thoughts about you. And organising a few things."

"Why don't you come up here? That would be really nice. There's nothing going on so we could just sit in your car and have fish and chips."

"Fish and chips? What about your bridal diet?"

"Oh, sorry. I forgot."

"I'll bring supper."

"Great. It's a date."

Forty minutes later, Antony arrived in his BMW, dressed suitably in a Goretex jacket, fleece gloves and walking boots. He had brought a delicious picnic.

"I love you," Billie said, sinking into the comfortable leather front seat of the warm car. Antony grinned and handed her a bacon and avocado sandwich.

"What do you want to drink? I brought your detox wheat germ juice."

Billie took a slurp and made a face, holding the liquid in her mouth and pretending she was going to chuck it up out the window,

"Swallow, swallow," Antony said. "Remember you want to be as lovely as possible for those wedding pics. But," he relented. "I did bring some beer too"

"I think I'll have beer."

They sat in the car for a bit, chatting, mainly about the murder. Billie explained more fully what had happened in the afternoon, to Antony's indignation, and they discussed the possible motive Carlo could have had for killing his stepmother.

Most of the other journalists and photographers drifted away. There were only one or two left when, an hour or so later the phone rang. It was Felix. "The Screws has dropped," he said. "The cops have taken Xavier to a safe house somewhere. He's not going back home. They've basically come out and said they're not looking for anyone else. They think Carlo topped her. You may as well go home."

"What about the Ian Ford stuff? Is that in the Screws?"

"Yeah a one page sobber inside, *Sad childhood of Rebelle's secret son*. Bollocks. Could have written it without even meeting the bloke. She was a sad, vulnerable selfish cow who was always chasing record deals and shoved money at the kid instead of spending time with him. She sent him to boarding school and bought him a racehorse but he had to spend the holidays with his gran. And she never mentioned him in interviews. Pass me the hanky. Anyway, two pages of that but three lines about some poor bloody Africans whose whole village was washed away by a storm. That's newspapers."

"And did my undercover wife-swapping ring make?'

"Don't think so. No hang on, here it is, page 47, down page, 15 pars. Looks like you've ruined someone's career there while furthering your own. First scalp. Oh hey, you got a byline. By Rick Wilding and Billie Wilson. Is he a Screws scribe?"

"I think so."

"Nice of him to give you a byline."

"I'll get off then. I wouldn't mind a rest. It's been some week."

"Sure. Why don't you take Monday off too? See you Tuesday."

"Cheers." Billie turned to Antony. "Home please, driver."

Arriving back into the lobby of Antony's block of flats, they saw someone sitting in the shadows of the stairwell, head against the wall fast asleep.

"This is outrageous," Antony said. "We can't have tramps coming in and out of the flats. They could cause all sorts of problems. I wonder how he got past the CCTV? Call the police."

"Hang on a minute," Billie said, remembering the horrible feeling of being shut in a cell. "If he's homeless perhaps we could give him a few quid and send him off to a night shelter." She went over to the figure to shake him awake.

"Angela! What are you doing here?"

"Is this a friend of yours?" Antony asked.

"Well, in a manner of speaking. It's the reporter I met up in Scotland." Billie shook Angela's shoulder and she opened one eye, winced and shut it again. "It can't be morning yet."

"Angela. It's me, Billie. Did you come to see me?"

Angela nodded.

"Stand up and I'll help you up to the flat."

Angela got to her feet unsteadily and leaned on Billie's arm as they walked up the stairs to the flat. Billie mouthed the word "Sorry" over her head to Antony who was not looking happy. "I did say she could stay," she hissed.

Antony shrugged. "OK, I'll go and make up the sofa bed. But why does she look like a tramp?"

"Perhaps she's undercover or something. Maybe she's been mugged." Billie said. Angela did look terrible. She had her big parka on over an outsize floral blouse and trouser combination which might conceivably been reasonably smart when she put them on that morning but now they were crumpled and there was a cut on her cheek and mud on her coat and in her hair.

When they got into the flat, Antony started to pull out the sofa bed and put on bed linen. He waved away Billie's offer of help and she took Angela into the kitchen and sat her at the breakfast bar which ran along one side, under a window with a view out across the lights of north London.

She got Angela a mug of tea and put it down in front of her. "This is a fabulous flat," Angela said. "It's really nicely done up as well. You must get a big salary at the agency." "Not exactly. I share it with my fiancé," Billie explained, nodding proudly at Antony. Looking through the doorway they could see his handsome face in profile under the glow of a lamp as he bent over the bed.

Angela sighed. "Gosh you're lucky, he's lovely. I noticed your ring when you were up in the Highlands. It's so pretty."

Finished, Antony came through to the kitchen. "Hi," he said. "Welcome to London. It looks like you've had a bit of an adventure. What happened?"

Long and involved, the story came out. Although able to talk semi-normally, Angela was seriously drunk and her sentences meandered off into nonsense. But in essence, she had arrived at Kings Cross, met up with an old school friend she had been planning to stay with and a couple of her mates. After perhaps too long in the pub they had found themselves in a nightclub called, according to Angela "Robbery". On a trip from the crowded dance floor to the bar, having completely run out of cash, she had asked for a glass of water and been refused on the grounds that there was nothing so simple as water available and if she wanted water she could bloody well pay £4 for a bouteille d'eau. She refused and tipped a bowl of nuts over on the bar. Immediately, she was surrounded by a large group of bouncers who escorted her from the premises, pausing only to flip her into a particularly muddy puddle.

After freezing outside for an hour, Angela concluded that her friends had not noticed her abrupt departure, so she trudged back to Kings Cross, managed to get some money from her overdrawn account by writing a cheque at an all night bureau de change, retrieved her back pack from a left luggage locker, fished out her contacts book, and found Billie's address and phone number. After calling and finding no-one in she decided, not wanting to sleep in a draughty Kings Cross call box, to hope that Billie was just out on a Saturday night event but would be returning later. She gave in to the persuasions of an African mini cab driver who smelled of dope but was prepared to take her to Highgate for a tenner. Two hours later and after a tour of central London which included a splendid view of the Houses of Parliament and a soundtrack of loud African a capella singing, she arrived at the flats and, after a small argument with the driver about what was the appropriate fare, sat down on the stairway to wait.

"It's not my fault if he hasn't a clue where Highgate is. Or where anything is. Mind you, the whole thing wasn't his fault. I blame the Channel Tunnel, " Angela said, returning to the original dispute in the nightclub. She was wandering into a forest of confusing ideas about the effect of European integration on the London nightclub scene when Billie interrupted to ask what had brought her down to the capital.

"Is it Ian Ford?"

"Yes it is in fact. The paper were really excited about it, well, at least they agreed to pay my train fare. And to give me unpaid leave to go. But if I get anything which they publish, they will pay me usual rates. Which are, to be honest, not generous"

"But it'll all be in *The Screws* today."

"Not all. It's true there is a bit in *The Screws* but not all, by any means. We want stuff about his time in our bit, and Rebelle coming up there and stuff, we want the real Ian Ford, not that load of crud that is in the paper today. I bought a copy at Kings Cross after I got chucked out. I couldn't believe it. It was a couple hundred words about how the only thing she ever did for him was to buy him a fantastic race horse when he wanted to be a jockey, and send him to one of the best schools in the country. And for that they paid thousands and spent a week with him in a hotel room. You couldn't make it up. Well you could and that's kind of what makes it so tragic."

"So where is he now?"

"I don't know. But he's not at Bogmillo, he's not with Grandma, he's not with *The Screws* mob any more now the story has appeared.

So I figure he's in London. That's where all his mates from his posh English school work, in the city and stuff."

"London's a big place. How are you going to find him?"

"I'll find him. Trust me, the pony club's net spreads far and wide."

The next morning, which was Sunday, the three of them went for a late breakfast to a cafe on Highgate hill. It was a beautiful morning, sunny though chilly and they wanted to sit outside with a stack of papers.

"It's way too cold to eat outside," Antony argued, so they took their bundle of tabloids in to the steamy heat of the cafe. The coffee maker hissed comfortably in the background as Angela waded through a plateful of bacon, eggs, fried bread and beans with toast on the side. Antony ordered an Americano and a croissant and Billie, conscious of an impending dress fitting, cupped cold hands round her mug of latte and made patterns in the froth with a teaspoon.

She couldn't get over the sight of her own name at the top of a story in a newspaper. She read it several times and then laid the paper down and glanced quickly at it, her name leaping out with a shock of recognition. She read the story too, wanting to be proud of it. But though she thought of phoning Marina she decided not in the end.

Antony was more interested, as was Angela, and they both giggled with horrified, yet gratifying amusement when she told the story of her first undercover job, omitting of course that she had got a little carried away.

Once that was thoroughly digested, they moved on to the Rebelle murder. Every front page and a lot more inside were devoted to Carlo's sensational disappearance. There were acres of pictures, lots of him peeping though the door of the mansion when he had opened the door to Billie that night. That stream of comments was reprised in great detail as was everything he had said at the press conference on Saturday. There were quotes from puzzled friends and acquaintances, saying that he had always seemed an easy-going type, unlikely to do anything rash.

Antony read out a piece from the Sunday Graphic by a magazine journalist who had once interviewed Carlo: *"It is a piece of folk wisdom that a young man with plenty of money must be in need of a wife and there was certainly no shortage of candidates for the post as far as Carlo Fernandez was concerned. Handsome, charming and the heir to the family fortune, he was usually seen with a pretty woman on his arm.*

*"Actress Jane Bailey, model Susan Farron, royal connection Laura Carew, were all among the bevy of beauties who were pictured with Carlo. But each new romance seemed to be a short-lived affair and the photographers who dog celebrities had hardly figured out how to spell the name of the latest conquest before she vanished from his side.*

*"There was no hint of sorrow behind the ready smile. At 27, Carlo was too young to settle down and seemed to enjoy his life as a bachelor about town. A polo-player and amateur musician, he had plenty to occupy him despite the fact that as far as anyone could see, the work he did for his father's international investment business was limited to reading the stock prices in the FT each morning at his club in Soho.*

*"Despite his reputation for indolence when it came to turning the wheels of commerce, he was a big wheel on the party circuit, one of those enthusiastic souls who would turn up to the opening of a clamshell T-mobile. Most of the international glitterati who flit constantly on the Ny-Lon route between New York and the UK capital knew him, many would have called him friend.*

*"And yet the new tragedy to devastate the house of Fernandez seems to have taken everyone by surprise. There was endless speculation last night about what could have caused Carlo to disappear with most coming to the inescapable conclusion that he must have something to hide. Rumours were rife. Was there a crime of passion?*

*"Until the horrific murder of his father's wife, Rebelle, the singing star, Carlo Fernandez seemed to lead a charmed life. It now appears that the truth was darker than we knew, that behind the*

*scenes some dreadful mystery lurked which ended her life and caused him to flee his."*

"Hmm. Basically, that says absolutely nothing, except that he liked to have his picture taken with posh girls." Billie said. "It's the same in all of them, a lot of sound and fury signifying nothing."

"Macbeth?" asked Angela.

"The Scottish play, yes. Are you planning to eat your bacon?"

"Not really. I'm feeling a bit rough all of a sudden."

Antony looked at her suspiciously, smoothing his white cashmere jumper. "You're not going to be sick are you?"

Angela shook her head, looking green. "I'll be all right in a minute. Listen, are you sure it's all right with you guys if I stay another night? My gymkhana pal Laura is bound to surface later on and I could easily move over to her place."

"Why don't you?" Billie said. Antony kicked her under the table.

"Thanks, I will. I sort of feel like I need to get started. I'm beginning to feel a bit stressed out about finding Ian."

"What's your first move?"

"Well that's it, I don't really know. Any suggestions?"

Billie shook her head.

"I thought I might go down to his old school tomorrow and nose around there. It's in Ascot."

"I'll come with you if you like, I'm off tomorrow." Billie said. After a moment's thought, she added. "I've got a contact who might be able to help you, a journalist who does shifts at the News of the Week, the person I did that wife-swapping job with. They might be able to find out something about where he went."

"That would be fantastic."

"I'll call." Billie went outside and walked up and down the pavement holding her phone, and scrolling through the contacts book for Rick's mobile number which she had entered sitting in the Screws office while she wrote up the story.

The first call got the answer phone. She tried again and he picked up after the fifth ring.

"Hello, who's there?" He sounded woozy and cross.

"Sorry Rick, did I wake you up?"

"Billie, hi." He was smiling now. "No, not really. I just couldn't find me dick."

"Your what."

"My mobile. Moby, Moby dick. Get with the programme, the old Cockney rhyming slang, innit. God is it twelve o'clock already? That's unbelievable."

"Did you make that up?"

"What little old me? No, no the monkeys use a lot of it."

"I'm sorry to bother you on a Sunday, Rick."

"I don't mind really. It's fine."

"It's just that I was wondering if you could help a friend of mine. That girl I met in Scotland,the one who helped me after Beattie stitched me up. she's come down to London and she's trying to find Ian Ford. The story was in the Screws this week and they've had him in some secret hideaway all week, so I wondered, with you shifting there if you could find out anything about that. Are you going in tomorrow?"

"No, I wasn't planning to. Sunday papers are shut on a Monday. But don't worry I can probably find out some stuff. I've got a pass after all. I'll head in this afternoon, I'll tell security that I left my wallet there yesterday and I'll root around a bit."

"Are you sure? That sounds a bit drastic." Billie wasn't sure what she had been expecting him to do, maybe call someone. But not to sneak into the office and break into the system.

"Sure, I'm sure. I really feel like I owe you one after getting you into all that trouble, getting you locked in a cell and forgotten about for hours. I felt terrible. I've got a couple of things to do first but I'll do it later today. Meet me in the Jolly Whelk Seller at nine and I'll tell you what I can."

"I'll bring Angela. Where is that?"

"It's near *The Screws* office."

"Packet of jellied eels mate? Only £7.99." A large man dressed in a striped apron and holding a basket full of paper wrapped packets of this disgusting sounding delicacy was more or less barring the entrance to the Jolly Whelk Seller.

"Oh, OK," Billie said grudgingly and handed over a tenner. The man handed her a small packet and moved aside. Angela and Antony filed after her into the empty bar and found a table in a dark corner as far as possible from the speakers which were blaring out cockney favourites. "Woll out the bawel, we'll have a bawel of laughs," a man's voice was shouting.

It was a cockney theme pub, decorated with posters advertising turn of the century music hall shows. In one corner stood a piano, with a cardboard cut out of a laughing man in a cap sitting at it.

""How interesting, " Antony said. "Is this the kind of place you come to with your work mates?"

"Mm." Billie looked around, wondering if Rick and Antony would get on. She had told Antony that Angela and she had to meet a colleague to get information in an offhand sort of way that was meant to communicate he would not be interested.

"I'd love to come along," he said. "I'm totally fascinated by this now."

Angela was pleased. "Yes, do come Antony. I'll feel much safer with you around to look after us." She smirked up at him worshipfully.

Antony drove to the bar, Angela sitting in the front while Billie squeezed into the narrow back seat.

Once there, Angela went to the bar and bought pints of lager for herself and Antony and a white wine spritzer for Billie. After setting them down, she looked at her watch. "It's twenty past. D'you think he's coming?"

Just then, Rick appeared, in his floppy coat, carrying a plastic bag.

"Wotcher," he said, sounding breathless and looked round. Billie introduced them. "This is Angela, and my boyfriend Antony."

"Soon to be husband."

"Really?"

"Yes we're getting married in a few weeks."

"Cor blimey, strike a light. I didn't know. Congratulations. Or whatever." He looked at Billie.

"Didn't she mention it? I expect she likes to get a break from it at work. You can imagine how involved in it we all are just now. Sometimes we feel like it's taken over our whole life, don't we darling?"

"'Uh-huh. So dish the dirt Rick. What did you find out?"

Rick looked pleased with himself, fished in the bag and pulled out a wad of paper. "Da-na," he sang, and put it down on the table. "Beattie's expenses. They were in a folder on the news desk secretary's desk so I whipped them. The only thing is, I'll need to remember and put them back or else he won't get paid and that would make him very, very annoyed."

"I can imagine," Angela said.

Rick filed through the wad of paper he was holding and put one down on the table. "Lots of stuff here, lots of lunches, dinners, hotel rooms. He has a nice life.

"Look: April 30, lunch for two in Maison D'Etre, that's that one with four Michelin stars in the west end. £600! And you should see the wine list. And here, a piece of paper where he's written £500 cash advance for illegal drugs, and just " See ML undercover". Nice job, huh?

"Here's the ones that concern us. Item one, print out of a Ryanair receipt, three returns to Nimes, from Prestwick in Scotland via London, very reasonably priced. Item two, hotel bill. Les Trois Pines, Nice. They were there until Friday, no doubt busting their pans putting together the story we all read yesterday. It appears from this as if all three returned to Stansted yesterday morning.

"Oh, and item four, a receipt signed by Ian Ford confirming payment of £1,000, cash."

"I was expecting him to have got more money for his story than that,"Antony said.

"Yeah, I know. He may have been promised a bit more when the story appeared but he probably won't get it. It didn't make that much.

Beattie's a sharp negotiator but generally people get a lot less than you think for their stories. Much, much less than they usually claim in print. and much, much less than people say."

"It seems like quite a lot to me," Angela said. "That's like a couple of month's wages."

"In a way," Billie said. "But it's not a lot for selling the story about his Mum to a tabloid for cash? Is he that hard up?'

"Yeah, there is that," Angela said. "I would have thought she must have had him on an allowance. But anyway, he manages the horse sanctuary and I would think he would get a decent wage. His grandmother and her husband own it and they're not short. And what can he spend his money on up there?"

They all looked at each other.

"Are you thinking what I'm thinking?" Rick took a packet of Silk Cut out of his pocket and lit one.

"I don't know," Antony said, frowning at the thin line of smoke coming from between Rick's fingers. "He likes eating out?"

Angela snorted. "Even if he did, there's not much choice in Bogmillo. If he drove 30 miles to Golden Eagle House every day and had the chef's special, he could spend it. But not on the occasional ham salad roll at the pub. There's one reason I can think of for needing a grand in cash that badly and that's drugs."

"Some tabloid hack comes up and offers you some dirty notes for spilling the beans about your Mum who's just been killed. What do you say?" she asked, looking round the table. Antony shrugged. "Exactly, you tell them no comment. He's got to be weird." Angela said.

"Whatever your relationship was like, whatever you felt about the way she brought you up, you would say no wouldn't you?" Billie said.

"Unless, maybe you were completely desperate for money or you had some kind of mental health problem which meant you couldn't deal with it. or…" Angela stopped and looked around for answers.

"You were just evil," Antony was looking through the pile of papers.

"Who wants a drink?" Rick stood up, ready to go to the bar.

"Sorry, let me get you one," Billie got up too. "And thanks a lot for going to all that trouble. You got some good stuff."

"I did, but I'm afraid it doesn't tell you where he is now. Mine's a pint then, cheers."

"A mineral water for me thanks, darling." Antony looked up from the papers to give Billie a long look.

When she returned from the bar, Angela was talking about her next move to find Ian. "I thought I might go to his school tomorrow. He's only nineteen, he was there until last year so I might be able to find out something about where he might go from them. D'you think?"

"It's worth a try," Rick was saying. "Phone up and say you're doing a feature for The Post on the top 100 public schools in Britain. They'll eat you up."

"Won't they check?"

"Quite likely not. Say you're a freelance doing it for Sherry Frankie, because she's hardly ever in the office and she never returns calls."

"I'm starving. Shall we grab something to eat when we've finished these?" Billie suggested. Angela and Rick were keen and Antony did not oppose the idea so a short while later, Rick and Billie squeezed into the narrow back seats of Antony's two door coupe and they headed for a Chinese restaurant Rick recommended in Soho which was open late.

# CHAPTER NINE

They found a small entrance to an underground car park, handed over the keys and watched the car slowly slide down out of sight into the depths before walking round to Lin Ho's, three brightly lit glass-fronted storeys popular with media types.

Too popular it soon transpired. Half-way though his plate of Singapore noodles, Billie heard a "Wotcher binhead," and looked up to see Barmy and a group of Worldwide staff at a nearby table.

She lifted a hand in answer and gave a false smile, feeling too sore about her recent stitch-up to go over and talk to them. The Worldwide staff had spotted Rick and pointed at him, accusing Billie of consorting with the enemy. Hearing loud laughter Billie looked over again and saw that Barmy had stuck a wastepaper bin over his head and was miming a paranoid escape from cameras.

She tried to continue eating her dinner in peace but it was no good. A few minutes later, Antony looked up from his boiled rice and asked "Why is that man looking at you and braying like a donkey, Billie? Do you know him?"

They looked over as Barmy leered at Billie and let out a particularly effusive bray. Rick picked up the hard, crusty roll which was sitting on his side plate, took aim and fired it at Barmy, who had now removed the bin from his head. It hit him hard and suddenly on the temple, cutting him off in mid bray.

"Good shot, sir." Angela grabbed a pair of rolls set out at plates on the adjoining empty table and lobbed them at Barmy's table. Billie joined in too, collecting rolls from other tables as ammunition, but Antony sat still, frowning.

"Oh oh," Rick said looking over at the other table. "Watch out, monkey see, monkey do." A split second later, they were hit by a hail of rolls. Rick lifted up the tablecloth. "Would you like to take cover, madam?" he asked Billie.

"Billie, get your coat, we must leave immediately." As Antony spoke, the throwing stopped as the restaurant manager came rushing towards them.

"You stop throwing bread. You throw bread we throw you - in jail," he shouted.

"But it was them." Rick said, innocently, pointing at the other table. "They started it. We was provoked. We was merely acting in self-defence, officer."

Antony got up and brushed some crumbs off his jacket. "Don't worry," he said. "We are leaving right away. I'll pay the bill at the till."

Billie jumped up to follow him, shrugging at the others." Do you want to stay Angela? You may as well finish your meal."

"I'll come back now. If you don't mind. Will you be OK, Rick?"

"Sure," Rick smiled. "Every man for himself. I'll go over and make my peace with the enemy." Picking up a napkin, he tied it to a fork and waving it like a white flag walked over to the other table where they saw him talking and laughing with Barmy and the others.

Angela and Billie followed Antony in silence to the car. They drove home in silence and it wasn't until they were alone in the bedroom that Antony spoke.

"I think that was one of the single most embarrassing experiences of my life. I don't want to cramp your style Billie but what do you think that kind of publicity could do to my chances of being a serious candidate at the next election? You know that's what I'm working towards darling. I don't want to throw all that away and I can't overstress the importance of PR - that stands for public relations not puerile and rude for your information."

In upset silence,. Billie took off her clothes and stood in her pants and bra, looking for a nightie in her drawer. Antony put a hand on her bare back.

"The age difference between us has never been an issue for me before. But it was tonight. I felt like an uncle taking his spoilt, badly behaved niece to the zoo. That's not how I want to feel when I'm out with my future wife. We get on so well when we're on our own, but these people you've started to hang around with, well they're just not my cup of tea."

Billie found the one she was looking for, which buttoned up to the neck, went into the bathroom where she cleaned her teeth vigorously and got into bed, in silence.

"Don't sulk now Billie. You must admit, I have a point." Antony got into bed beside her.

"It's not my fault," Billie said, turning towards him. "That picture editor is horrible. He stitched me up and I hate him. I didn't mean all that to happen, you should know that. It just…"

"I know." Antony took her into his arms and stroked her hair. "Never mind. It was that awful Rick as well, he was the main instigator."

Billie had decided, at Rick's suggestion, to pose as a Post photographer and next morning collected a small pile of cameras, Antony's digital, her own little sure shot and an old manual Canon she had used years before.

A persuasive phone call from Angela met little resistance and an interview with the head was arranged for the afternoon so they headed off into a cold, wet morning to take the train to Ascot, with a bag of hastily put together sandwiches and a pile of newspapers.

Carlo had not been found but the papers were full of speculation about his disappearance, possible whereabouts and motives for killing Rebelle. Although there were many theories, no-one seemed to have come across anything concrete.

The papers had got hold of an old picture of him standing in front of his single engine plane. Other pictures showed the front of the house in Richmond with curtains closed. Xavier was not speaking to the press but the papers reported that he had told police Carlo took the plane for a couple of hours, to take his mind off his grief. Xavier became concerned only when Carlo had not returned by nightfall as he was an inexperienced night-time flyer and the plane only carried enough fuel for a few hours.

The cops came in for a lot of criticism for not having grounded the plane first off, allowing Carlo to abscond like that.

There was one picture of Carlo and Rebelle together which most of the papers had got hold of. It showed him helping her out of the back of a car as they arrived at a celebrity party, leaning down to her as she placed her hand in his. Both faces were turned towards the camera, bright, false smiles in the harsh glare of the flash bulbs. One paper had the one word headline "Why?" Others had played on her songs, one asked: "Were these two secret lovers?"

A psychic said Carlo was in Algeria. A medium said his plane had gone down over the Channel, he was definitely dead and his troubled spirit was asking from beyond the grave for forgiveness. A fashion expert had analysed the outfits he and Rebelle wore in the weeks before her killing and diagnosed that they had both been in a state of deep anxiety and indecision. A retired police detective said that the case followed a classic pattern of a crime of passion. But there was very little in the way of actual information.

They left the papers on the train when they got off at the nearest station to the school. In a nearby telephone box, they found some mini cab numbers and ordered a car which arrived within minutes.

After a half hour drive through picturesque villages interspersed with enormous newly built homes set in their own grounds, the saloon car rolled up a gravel drive and stopped in front of a modern looking building, concrete, steel and glass with a triangular shaped entrance.

"This looks more like an avant garde theatre than a public school," Angela said as they walked in and introduced themselves to a middle-aged woman sitting at a desk behind a glass panel, marked "School Office".

"Welcome." She gave them a friendly smile. "Sit down for a minute," and she gestured to a group of armchairs in the spacious lobby.

After a short wait, she ushered them along a carpeted corridor to the head's office. Fixed to the wall outside was something that looked like a small traffic light with the green light flashing and the secretary pushed the door open.

The head was seated in one of three chairs next to a small glass coffee table under a window which looked out onto a wide sweep of lawn.

"Take a seat," he said. "Could you bring us some tea and biscuits, Sheila?"

Angela sat down. Billie indicated her camera bag. "Would it be possible for me to wander around a bit and look for a good place to take pictures?"

"I'll ask Sheila to take you round. But please don't try to photograph any children without permission. There are some sixth formers who are willing to be photographed but they won't be available until the end of this lesson. Sheila will take you to meet them in the library."

Angela set up her small, journalist's tape reorder and took out a notebook and pen.

"Fire away" said the head.

"Er...um...do you have any well-known former pupils?"

The head looked surprised and, Billie thought, suspicious.

"I am not of course prepared to discuss individual pupils. I was under the impression you wanted to talk about the school."

"Oh I do, of course I do. So why should we include this school in a list of the top 100 in Britain?"

The headmaster took a deep breath and headed off at a canter through a selection of facts, figures and sales talk.

Sheila returned promptly carrying a tray with big willow pattern china teacups on saucers and a plate of shortbread biscuits. "Here you are, Philip," she said.

The head interrupted his flow to ask her to take Billie for a look around and then to the library to photograph his study group.

It had started to drizzle and Sheila picked up a scarf at her office to drape over her head before taking Billie outside to look at the building.

"It's very modern isn't it? I was expecting something a bit more Hogwarts."

Sheila laughed. "I wouldn't fancy all those draughty corridors and ghosts thank you very much. This place is only about ten years old. It's much more convenient and comfortable than you might expect. All the upper school have their own rooms with en suite shower facilities for instance. Not all public schools are cold baths in the morning and run round the grounds ten times before bed you know. Where did you go to school?"

"A big comprehensive, in Brighton. It was OK. Didn't have much in the way of comfort though."

They trudged through the wet grass to the sports centre, Sheila chatting all the way, mostly about the sports centre, which she said was the school's pride and joy, enthusiastically pointing out its 25 metre pool and a climbing wall. Outside, the playing field had banks of floodlights at either end, which she showed off, reliving the heroic battle Philip had fought with the governors to get it built to the highest specifications and the work they had all put into fund raising. "But it was worth every penny. There's such a lot of competition in the public school sector today that you have to have that little bit extra. Howells has its own ethos but it still has to compete. That's why we always try to make ourselves available for interview. Aren't you going to take some pictures?"

"Yes, of course." Billie got one of the cameras and started to try and look professional with it, shooting off half a dozen frames of the empty swimming pool. "It's a shame I can't have any pupils in the shot."

Sheila said she would take her to the library to look for models and they walked back across the grass and through a central courtyard, in through another glass door along a corridor and into a long low room, which looked a little like an open plan office although lined with books, Sheila hardly pausing for breath all the way in her anecdotes about the school, its character and history.

Like the rest of the place, it was carpeted and quiet, a world away from the din Billie remembered from East Sussex High. Looking back, it was the noise that identified it in her mind, the pandemonium of booted feet on bare floors, scraping chairs, young voices yelling, laughing, and singing, the screeching of violins from the music room, teachers speaking, loud and stern. This was so quiet it was weird.

The study group had not arrived so they sat down to wait.

"Howells was mentioned in the papers the other week, wasn't it? Ian Ford, Rebelle's kid came here, didn't he?" Billie said.

"That's right. He's a very nice boy, Ian. I remember him well, he left just a year or two ago."

"Terrible shame about his mother."

"Isn't it, and now Carlo. Poor, poor lad."

"Oh did he know Carlo? I didn't think they were related."

"They weren't. Ian was Rebelle's son and Carlo was her husband's boy. But they both came to school here although at different times. Carlo came back to visit Ian. They were quite close I think. Both into horses, you see. Ian wanted to be a jockey but he was too tall, Still he had his horse stabled near here and he rode in some point to points and steeplechases. Carlo used to come and watch. And they both played polo."

"I thought it was meant to have been a secret that Rebelle was Ian's mother."

Sheila laughed. "I'm sorry but that's the papers for you. The family were pretty discreet but it wasn't exactly a secret. The staff knew. I don't know if Ian told any of the other pupils but perhaps not. To be honest, he wasn't here a lot, especially the last year or two. He was at the stables most of the time, looking after his own horse and training. He used to exercise the other horses too. He often used to stay the night there. I used to wonder if he had a stable girl for a girlfriend."

"Was he allowed to? Wasn't there a curfew or something?"

"It's a boarding school, not a prison. At Howells, we believe when you are talking about young men and women of seventeen and eighteen you have to give them a bit of freedom. If you deny them independence now you may find they are immature later. It's part of our philosophy. So long as they let us know where they are, it's OK.

"Ian didn't have very many classes because he wasn't very academic . I think the only reason he stayed on for Sixth was that he didn't know what to do next. He was only doing two A levels, in art and music but he did work hard at those. When he was here he was generally in the art room or the music room. He didn't actually have many close friends, he was a quiet boy."

Outside the glass door of the library, Billie could see a group of figures coming towards them, probably the sixth formers she was going to have to photograph. She fired one last question at Sheila. "Where's the stable?"

"The stable? It's just along the road from here. Next turning on the left. Dobey's Racing Stable. Why do you ask? Oh here are your young people now," she said, as a grown-up looking girl in hipster jeans and a pink long-sleeved T shirt with red hair tucked behind her ears and holding a pile of books, leant on the library door to hold it open for half a dozen others.

The next hour was stressful for Billie as she tried to convince a sceptical looking bunch of teenagers that she was a professional photographer. After shifting nervously under their steady gaze, she came up with the idea of asking them to walk back and forwards through, or stand as if chatting, in the courtyard as she took pictures from an upper window.

At the end of their study period the sixth formers disappeared off to a lesson and she was taken back to the reception area where Angela was waiting, sitting in an armchair leafing through the prospectus. She looked up. "This place is very, very expensive."

"Yes but feel the quality."

"Is that included? I might consider it, if so," Angela was looking out at a tall handsome boy who was passing the window, his jacket hung over his shoulder and a scarf loosely wound round his neck.

"Let's go," Billie said.

"Shall we call a cab?"

"We can do that from outside. I've got me dick."

"Your what, I'm sorry?"

"Mobile, moby dick, dick"

"That'll be some of your Mockney rhyming slang, me old Pearly Queen." Angela pulled her bag onto her shoulder and waved over at Sheila, who was on the phone.

They walked towards the end of the drive. "D'you get anything, then?" Billie asked.

Angela shook her head. "Not a thing, not a sodding thing. It's a wasted trip I'm afraid."

"Maybe not. I got some stuff from the secretary. She is the original amazing, talking woman. All I had to do was mention Ian's name and she was off. Couldn't shut her up."

"Spit it out then. What' d she tell you?"

"Carlo was here too although not at the same time. But he and Ian were mates apparently. Both into horses. Ian hung around the whole time at a stable near here and probably had a girlfriend there."

"That's more like it. Where's that?"

"Just along the road. Next stop the stable, then."

Angela bit her lip. "Hang on, let's not rush in. I think we need to plan our strategy a bit more carefully. If we roll up there saying we're journos and asking about Ian, what are they going to say?"

"What people always seem to say. Fuck off and die."

"Exactly. We'll need to play it a bit more cleverly than that."

They walked in silence for a minute.

"How about this?" Angela said. "I say something like, I'm an old friend of Carlo's. Just before he went off he gave me some stuff to look after for him and he wanted me to give something to Ian and this was where he thought I might find him. What d'you think?"

"Hm. Not sure." Billie thought back to her journalism course. One night they had heard John Pilger speak and Billie had taken away a leaflet and form for joining the NUJ. OK, she had never actually posted it but she remembered the basics. "The PCC, the Press Complaints Commission to you, code of conduct says that subterfuge is only acceptable in the public interest."

"Well," Angela said patiently, "That's OK then because this is in the public interest."

"How?"

"Well if the public aren't interested, why are they buying all this bilge about the Rebelle murder that doesn't even say anything? It seems to me that the public are really interested."

"Yes but that's not what it means."

"What?"

"The public interest means...it's, oh forget it."

"OK."

"But if you're going undercover, I think it'll be a lot more convincing if you turn up on your own. Don't you?"

"I guess you might be right."

"Well I've got all these cameras. If you were doing a favour for an old friend, why would you bring a monkey with you?"

"I don't know but I certainly wouldn't bring a photographer."

"The other thing is, what if, million to one chance, he strolls out of the bedroom and says OK then, here I am, give Carlo's stuff to me. What then?"

"OK, I say...Give up, what do I say?"

"I'd cut out the bit about something to give him. I'd just say, you are a friend of Carlo's wanting to get hold of Ian. Hopefully they give you a number or something. Then when we speak to Ian alone, fess up, say, look mate we're journalists but we don't think Carlo killed your Mum and we want you to help to clear his name."

"Don't we? Why don't we think he killed her? I mean on the face of it, it's pretty much sewn up."

Carlo's face, pale and vulnerable in the streetlights as he opened the door of his father's home, came into Billie's mind. "We don't know. Someone else could have killed her and him as well. Anything could have happened."

"Yeah, but he's probably done a Lord Lucan and is living under a different name in Cuba."

"Who knows?"

Billie felt anyway that she didn't have the stomach for lying to Ian's girlfriend, if Angela found her. It didn't seem worth it under the circumstances. She had a mental picture of the pack of hacks gathered round DCI Bennet at the murder scene. It reminded her of the buzzards circling a rabbit squished by a car she had seen in the Highlands.

Feeling incredibly jaded for someone who had been only a couple of weeks in the job, she explained where the stable was and then walked along the side of the road towards town where she had seen a bus stop, taking Angela's notebooks and her cameras. A timetable stuck to the pole showed that a bus was due in 15 minutes but it didn't look too promising. No one else was waiting and a cold wind blew through the shelter. A few minutes later, it started to rain and large drops hammered noisily on the plastic roof. Billie thought about getting another cab but didn't really want to spend £20 with no prospect of getting it back on expenses. Eventually, half an hour later, the lighted window of a bus loomed through the dusk.

Billie had arranged to meet Angela in the pub next to the station so she bought a half pint and a bowl of thick, gloopy lentil soup and a roll and sat by the fire drying damp shoes on the fender, quite happily for an hour or so before starting to get anxious.

Going outside, she wandered up and down outside the station and bought an evening paper, then returned to the pub, got another half pint and read the paper right through. There was still no sign of Angela. Billie wished Angela had a mobile.

What should she do? The options were, to go back to London without her, which under the circumstances Billie felt was impossible, to go and look for her at the stable, or to call the police. She looked in her wallet. £15. Not enough for a cab back to the stable.

After some thought, she picked up her mobile and called Rick.

"Wotcher, me old mucker," he said, cheerfully. "Are you hard at work at the coal-face of truth?"

"Not exactly. I'm sitting in a pub in Ascot, drinking beer and worrying."

"Don't worry, be happy."

She explained Angela's long absence.

"So you've lost baby face? She'll be OK. Probably waiting for a bus like you did."

"That's probably true. I just wanted some advice really. I feel like I can't go back to London without her."

"I'll come down. We can drive along and case the joint. I've got a pool car and I can be there in half an hour. I'm on a doorstep in Kingston. We'll drive along there and say something like, we've broken down and can they help push the car. I'll think of something."

"Won't you get into trouble if you go AWOL?"

"No. It's some Z list celeb who's supposed to be having an affair with a weather girl who lives in this house. But it's only me here so if I go away for a bit, they could come out and frolic naked in the garden and the news desk would never know. But they're not idiots. He's hardly going to come here if I'm sitting outside. I'm so bored I was thinking of going home anyway and just leaning out of the window with the phone when they call me."

"Why lean out of the window?"

"Traffic noise. Sounds like you're outside."

"D'you do that a lot?"

"Not really. It's pretty risky. Some of them do. Your lot had a photographer who got sent to Baghdad. He never went, pocketed the air fare and switched on a tape of Mosque music whenever the newsdesk called him on the satellite phone."

"How did they find out?"

"No photographs. They sacked him eventually but they never got the air fare and expenses back. Anyway, we'll speak when I get there."

"Angela might be back by then."

"Never mind, I'll have a drink with you and head back here after, if she is."

Half an hour later, as Billie stood outside the station a black Astra pulled up and she got in, relieved to see Rick's smiling face. The car moved off and she directed Rick towards the stables.

"Thanks for coming down."

"Not at all, I'm always game, me. It's nice of you to bother about her."

"She's just a kid. I couldn't just head off to London without her."

"I know. An eagle-eyed young reporter, fresh to the big city. Makes you want to pack her up in a box and send her home before it's too late."

"What d'you mean?"

"At the moment she's this cute, funny enthusiastic kid but if it all pans out the way she wants and she ends up making it as a reporter, that'll all change. Give her a few years and she'll be another dead eyed lady scribe with sharp nails and steel stilettos.

"You get involved in a lot of bad shit when you are a tabloid news reporter: rapes, murders, buggeries and break ups and that's the nice stuff. There are bombs and plane crashes and train crashes as well. Death knocks and doorsteps. And it's a really macho culture. Nobody ever talks about how it feels."

"You really sound like you've had enough."

"I am feeling a bit jaded at the moment. I did jack it in once before, I went to work as a volunteer at a camp for disabled children but then I came back. I mean, it can be a laugh as well. Of course. Is this the turn off?"

He headed up a gentle hill along a single lane track for about a mile before he came to the stable yard. Rick pulled over onto the grass verge and switched his headlights off. They sat for a moment in silence.

"Excuse me, before we do anything else, there's something I've been meaning to do for a while. Gently he lifted a loose strand of hair behind her ear. She smiled at him and he stroked her cheek.

Billie pulled away, her heart pounding. "Rick, no…it's like…I'm with someone already, you know that."

"Yeah. Sorry, I forgot."

He moved away and they sat in silence, aware of their nearness to each other. After a moment, Rick spoke. "Come on then. Can't exactly say we happened to be passing. What d'you reckon? Shall we be hearty hikers on our way home after a big walk? A spot of light drizzle wouldn't put us off."

"Light drizzle?" She looked out at the heavy, dark sky. "Of course it wouldn't. We love the outdoors."

# CHAPTER TEN

A luminous dome rising into the sky indicated where Ascot lay below them. Even out so far from London, beyond the suburbs, light-pollution turned the sky to a muddy orange and few stars were visible. Billie could pick out only the Pole star and Orion.

As they approached the brick-built archway which led to the stables and farmhouse, a series of security lights clicked on and they saw the red dots and square lenses of CCTV cameras placed above the entrance. The house, a long, two-storey building with a fenced-off garden lay beyond it, the windows all in darkness.

There was no sign of human life anywhere. Turning left, they walked through another arch into a big white painted square of loose boxes. The doors were closed but behind them, hooves clicked and they heard whinnying. A dog barked somewhere. They could just make out the shadows of more horses in a field beyond the stables, and a mare came walking silently over to watch them, her flanks shining black in the electric light.

"This is weird," Billie said. "You would think there would be someone about."

"Yeah, it's almost as if everyone has been kidnapped by aliens. That would be a scoop and no mistake."

Standing quietly in the yard, looking around they heard, faintly but unmistakably, laughter.

"I think it came from there." Rick pointed to a pair of big barn doors opposite. They walked over and tapped one of them. It swung open, revealing a tack room, palely lit by a glow that was seeping from under a small door, reached by a wooden ladder, close to the top of the wall. Music was audible. Billie recognised Coldplay.

"Hello?" she called.

There was no answer. The walls of the room were hung with saddles, hats, bridles, stirrups and other riding equipment. In the centre was a long table on which was piled some boxes of what looked like cleaning stuff, special brushes, big tins of polish and cans of spray.

"Hello," she called again, more loudly.

She went to the bottom of the ladder and was starting to climb up when the door opened inwards and a face peered out. It was Angela.

"Oh hi," she said, "I thought I heard someone," and she turned away, speaking to someone inside the room. "Lucy, Sue, it's my sister. I called her earlier and asked her if she might be able to swing by and pick me up." She looked out again and saw Rick. "And she's brought her boyfriend. Come up then, guys. Join the party."

The loft room was obviously a store room, lined with cardboard boxes, but the centre had been turned into a den, a couple of beanbags and some upturned wooden crates surrounding a coffee table. On it lay some JOB grant rizlas, a packet of Marlboro Lights and an open Tupperware container full of dried leaves, and the room was heavy with the powerful stink of Skunk.

The music they had heard was coming from a portable CD player which sat on the floor near an electric socket at the back of the room, CD covers strewn on the floor around it. Two young women were lounging on the floor, one lying, propped upon an elbow reading the notes from a CD cover, her chestnut hair pushed behind her ears. The other, long dark blonde hair loose over a brown hand-knitted jumper, was sitting cross-legged near Angela. Her eyes were wide and her face flushed, and she giggled loudly as they came into the room.

Angela was using the lid flap of a cardboard box placed in her lap as a flat surface on which to roll an enormous spliff.

"Thanks for coming to get me. Soo kind. But hey, why the long faces?" Both girls giggled even more loudly.

"This is Lucy," Angela pointed to the recumbent blonde, "and Sue", she indicated the brunette. "Don't get up girls. They'll excuse our terrible stable manners," she said. It wasn't particularly funny but all three of them were off, giggling hysterically. Angela had to lie down and hold her tummy, she was laughing so hard. After a minute or two they started to calm down, but Angela said again "This dopesmoking is making me hoarse," and that set them off once more.

Rick and Billie smiled at each other, sharing the left-out feeling of being sober in a room of stoned people, and they sat down on a couple of crates.

Angela recovered enough to say, "This is my sister Billie."

"Hi Billie? Wow, what a cool name. What's it short for? Billie Jean?"

This was an excuse for them to launch into a chorus of the Michael Jackson song.

Angela finished rolling the joint, took a few deep, inhaled puffs and passed it along. Billie took it and looked at it critically.

"You roll a mean joint, little sister," she said.

"You forget that I have lived in the Highlands, which must be Britain's most stoned region." She made her hand into a glove puppet speaking Gaelic: "Camera hatstand rizla callum clacher homegrown. Listen guys. I've got a riddle for you. A guy rides into town on June third, stays a week then rides out again on June third. How is that possible?"

"The clocks have all stopped?" suggested Lucy.

"No."

"He's fallen through a loose point in the space time continuum?" Rick offered.

"No."


Billie took a couple of tokes. She had smoked a bit at university and at home. Marina smoked dope most days but Billie did not really like it, finding it made her passive and paranoid. After a token inhalation, she passed it to Rick. He looked embarrassed and shook his head, so she got up to pass the joint and the ashtray to Lucy.

"He fell off his horse, got concussion and thinks he stayed a week?" Lucy said.

"No"

"Tell us!" clamoured Lucy and Sue but Angela refused.

Lucy looked around with blank eyes. "Who are these guys?" she asked. "Do we know them?"

Sue nodded solemnly. "Lucy, these people are cool. Angela says they're OK and I've known Angela for" she shrugged, "five years?"

Angela nodded. "It must be about that. I really remember you when I came and saw Ian here. We watched his horse, Brown Betty isn't it, racing somewhere, I can't remember where now but you were definitely there. The horse came fifth."

"That must have been one of her good days." There was a long pause. Billie was trying to work out how Angela might know this girl but her brain wouldn't stick to the subject, it was like wading through brown sauce. The thought made her want to laugh and so she did. That set the others giggling. Eventually, they lapsed into a long silence. Billie broke it.

"It's pretty quiet round here, isn't it? It took us a while to find you."

"Yeah, Ray's away. He's gone to the races."

"Can you believe he's left this bunch in charge?" Angela giggled and the girls joined in.

"When the cat's away." Sue said.

"The mice will get really, really stoned," Lucy added. "Not that we don't when he's here too. To be frank, we probably get out of it less when he's gone. He's a crazy guy. You must know that. So's your friend Ian. So was Carlo."

"Carlo was the wildest," Lucy rolled her eyes. "What a crazy dude. Was there a drug he wouldn't take? Whenever Man Ray came up with some new compound in his little experimental lab, we knew that there was one person who would take it whatever." She laughed.

"God, he was too much. Ray makes up these chemical cocktails. God knows what was in them. He had one called the Sundowner

Downer Downer. The first day he brought it up from the lab, no-one could touch it except Carlo. He took two and he was paralysed for thirty-six hours."

"Paralysed?"

"Literally, he couldn't stand up. He could hardly move his lips. Ray gave him a Bouncing Bomb, that's a mixture of speed and ritalin and that got him up. After that, he adjusted the SDD dosage. There was a box of the old SDDs left and one night when the cops busted us he and Carlo took them up onto the hills and buried them somewhere. They must still be there. Bluebeard's treasure."

"What abut Ian?" Angela asked. "He's usually game, didn't he take them?"

Sue shook her head. "Ian's a bit more cautious. He might take them second. But not first. That takes a lot of nerve. I was always half-expecting Carlo to turn into a toad or donkey or something after he took one."

"Sometimes he thought he had," Lucy said.

"Yah, but it was usually OK. I mean he'd done all that mainstream stuff, from crack to smack. there really wasn't anything he hadn't taken. He could afford it, you see. But mainly he liked the adventure of trying something different."

"Weird bastard really. D'you think he killed her?"

"Maybe. Scarey isn't it. " The girls fell silent. Lucy passed the joint to Sue and she inhaled deeply.

"Where do you think he's gone?"

"Oh God, it could have been anywhere. But that night, the night he was supposed to have gone off in the plane, Ray went away didn't he?"

"Yes," Sue nodded vigorously. "He came up to my bedroom in the middle of the night and woke me up and told me he was going away for a couple of days, and then he jumped in his car and drove off."

"Maybe he went to meet Carlo," Rick said.

"He could have."

"Then he came back. He didn't say anything about it. Like nothing like 'Hey, I wonder where me old mate Carlo's gone.' Nothing."

"Weird."

Nobody said anything for what seemed a very long time.

"Hey girl," Billie said eventually. "You know you asked us to drop by and pick you up? Can we get going. Rick and I are keen to get home and change our wet socks. Bit of a damp day for a country ramble, wasn't it darling?"

"Rather darling. I am ready for some scoff though. I daresay I could eat a horse," Rick said. "Not one of ours, I hope," Sue said. "Tell us the answer."

"No, work it out. It's easy."

"The horse is called June third?" Rick asked.

"Well done," Angela stood up and zipped up her jacket. "Girls, it's been a blast. See you Saturday if I can."

Lucy and Sue got up, Lucy draped an arm around her and pecked her on the check. "Ciao," she said. Sue flipped a languid hand in farewell and they slid down the ladder.

"See you Saturday?" Billie asked. An electric security light blasted on, dazzling them with its sudden brightness.

"Yeah, Brown Betty's racing in Brighton. They think Ian will be there. He usually shows up when she's racing apparently. What's the point of owning a racehorse if you don't get the buzz, I suppose. Fucking good story isn't it?"

"Carlo and Ian involved with secret illegal drugs factory?" Rick asked. "It's dynamite, or it could be in the right hands. But it's not runnable at the moment. You need to get more. We don't have tapes, we don't know those girls' names, we don't have anything that would stand up in court and no paper in its right mind would run those kind of allegations against a wealthy race trainer unless they had proof. Proper proof that would sink a libel suit. You could sell it as a tip but you wouldn't get much for it. If you've got the time, it might be worth worrying away at it trying to get some more."

"Uh-huh, Needs more work, then."Angela walked across the yard and unbolted the top half of one of the loosebox doors. "This is the lady." A brown muzzle appeared over the door, looking around at the sharply lit yard. Angela stroked her. "She's lovely, isn't she?"

"What was all that stuff about knowing Sue for five years?" Rick asked.

" She's a stoner. I said I remembered her from coming here then, bit of a gamble but it paid off. She sort of looked a bit puzzled and then said oh yeah, sure. My guess is that it's all a bit of a blur for her."

Angela pulled a hand out of her pocket and put it up to the horse's mouth. Roughly, Rick seized her elbow and pulled it down.

"Ow! What're you doing?"

"What are *you* doing?" He held her palm straight out. There was a white capsule in it.

"It's only a tic tac," Angela said. "I found it in my pocket and I thought she would like it."

"Leave her alone, Rick," Billie said.

Rick popped the pill in his mouth and chewed. "So it is. I'm sorry. But you don't go around feeding things to other people's racehorses a few days before a race. It isn't done."

"I guess not."

"Well to be honest, you shouldn't be able to. This place is pretty lax on the old security. CCTV and lighting is one thing but you need people to make it work."

"Well there's Lucy and Sue."

"Exactly."Angela stroked Brown Betty again, shut the loosebox door and bolted it.

They walked to the car.

"I hope we didn't cramp your style. We were a bit concerned about you that's all, you know, woman alone at night" Billie said.

"You landed on your feet all right. I wouldn't mind taking over and trying to stand that story up." Rick said.

Billie raised her eyes at him.

"They were cute. Especially Lucy. I like a girl with nice knits - it's the country boy in me. But on a purely professional basis. It would be safer for me than Angela hanging out here."

"Thanks for the concern, but I'm not a woman, I'm a journalist," Angela said.

"Are you planning to go to the race?"

"Of course. It's my best chance of finding Ian. I don't know what I can do until then really, I might come back down here and hang about a bit, trying to stand that up."

Rick drove off. After a few minutes, he said: "Can I drop you at the train station? To be honest, you'll be quicker going back from there than from the house I'm door stepping. It's in the outermost suburbs of west London."

"Fine." He pulled up in the lay by outside the station and they jumped out.

Billie leaned back in through the door. "Listen, Rick, you are a sweetheart. I really appreciate your help. I owe you one, eh?"

He nodded. "See you on the doorstep."

Billie slammed the passenger door and he drove off.

"Do you think he's in love with me?" Billie asked Angela.

"What, Rick? Probably. It's not fair. I wish he was in love with me. He's cute."

Billie frowned. "I don't think you're his type."

"I wish I knew who was my type. Are you in love with him?"

"Me? No. I like him though. We really get on. We click, you know, but just as friends."

"Well, that's cool. Just as long as you keep it that way. I wouldn't like to see Ant get hurt."

On the way back to London, Billie's phone rang. It was Sorrel.

"Hi, Billie. What are you up to? Are you busy?"

"Hi, er," she said, racking her brains for a killer excuse as to why she couldn't do a late shift or an early shift or whatever she was going to ask. Billie was about to say she had toothache and was on her way to the emergency dentist when she registered that she wasn't asking her to work.

"Because I was just wondering if it would be at all possible for you to meet me for a drink."

"What, tonight?"

"If you can. It's kind of urgent."

Billie looked at her watch. It was almost nine o'clock and Antony would be home from work waiting.

"Well it's a bit late, to be honest. I'm just heading home to see my boyfriend and get my dinner. I haven't eaten properly today. Can't I see you at work tomorrow?"

"No. I won't be at work tomorrow." She sounded tense.

Billy sighed and mentally pictured Antony emptying lasagne into the rubbish bin.

"OK. I'm on a train just heading into Victoria. Where do you want to meet?"

"Let's go somewhere with food. D'you know Lin Ho's in Chinatown?"

"Yes. Does it have to be there?"

"Don't you like it?"

"Bit too busy. How about the one next door? There's a little restaurant next door I noticed called the Golden Dragon. See you there in thirty minutes."

"Thanks."

Billie put the phone back in her pocket and looked over at Angela. "I'm going to have to meet someone before I go home. Are you staying at ours tonight?"

"No. I'll just grab my stuff and go over to my friend's house. Get out of your hair for a few days. Thanks a lot for being so good to me. I hope I haven't got you into trouble with Himself for being late back."

"Not at all, it'll be fine." Billie called home and got the answer phone and left a message explaining that something work-related had come up and she would be later than expected. She tried Antony's mobile but it was switched off so she left another contrite message. Oh-oh, Billie thought. It didn't look good. He must be pissed off. It was unlike him not to be immediately contactable.

Usually he even took his mobile into the bathroom, leaving it in the special mobile-phone holder he had fixed to the side of the bath.

"Here are my keys," Billie handed them to Angela. "When you've grabbed your stuff just pop them under the plant pot by the door for me. Obviously, ring the bell first to check if he's there before you use them."

"Cheers." Angela shoved the keys into her pocket and went back to making notes in her reporter's pad.

A few minutes later, the train rolled into the station and they jumped out and ran down the steps to the tube station, parting company at the ticket machine.

"I'm totally brassic, I'm going to bunk it, " Angela said. Holding a rolled up newspaper in front of her to block the laser operated turnstile's closing mechanism, she slipped through behind a slim man in a suit. Walking over to the escalator for the Piccadilly Line northbound, Billie saw Angela disappearing down the high flight of steps that led to the Victoria line, jumping down three at a time, hand on the banister.

Billie was starving by the time she got to the Golden Dragon. Sorrel wasn't there but she ordered a plate of Singapore noodles and a bottle of beer anyway.

A few minutes later, Sorrel arrived, looking incredibly tall and slim in a knee-length, belted beige coat and suede knee boots. "Thanks," she said and sat down opposite, smiling.

"You sounded a bit screwed up on the phone," Billie said. "Is everything OK?"

"Not really. Have you ordered?" She shrugged off her coat, hung it on the back of her chair and turned to speak to a passing waiter. "May I order? Just a plate of Chinese greens and boiled rice and a pot of jasmine tea please."

"Look I'm sorry to drag you away from your dinner like this. I hope you have an understanding boyfriend. But it is important. The reason that I won't be in tomorrow is that Felix and I are no longer running the agency together. I have resigned."

"That was sudden."

"Yes."

"And you won't be going back in at all?"

"No. I went in this evening and cleared my desk. That's it."

"That's a shame." Billie was wondering why Sorrel had chosen her to tell about it. After all she had only been there for a fortnight. She must have been working with some of the others for years. "Perhaps we can organise a leaving do for you. Drinks in the pub round the corner or something."

"Maybe. But that's not what I called you about, Billie. I'm going to set up on my own and I need an assistant."

"Right."

"I'm hoping to persuade you to join me."

"Wow, that's very-" Billie gathered her thoughts. "That's very flattering. Why me? I've only been there for five minutes."

"Well." Sorrel locked her hands together and pulled them apart. She had long, thin fingers and her wrists, escaping from the tight sleeves of a tight pullover, were surprisingly large and bony. "Lots of reasons. One, I think you're very talented. As you say, you've been with us for a very short time but you really have a nose for news. You pick things up quickly, you're honest and you work hard. Two, you're a woman and that suits me. I want to work in a less macho atmosphere I think.

"On a more personal note, I like you, you're easy to talk to. That's important.

"And, lastly, you are kind of the reason that Felix and I are parting company."

"Am I? How?" A forkful of noodles Billie was carrying to her mouth returned to the plate.

"He stitched you up basically, and I walked out over it. Among other things. You know when you got taken in for questioning? He sent Barmy round to take your picture and get a few personal details. Somehow Barmy managed to get a snatch of you and your boyfriend."

"Yes, I remember." Snatch was just about right, Billie thought, visualising the picture of her standing next to Antony in her white bikini.

"Well, between them they sold the package to the Screws for about eight grand. I was appalled. You are a member of staff for God's sake. For me it just marked how far we had gone on the road to becoming the worst kind of gutter press. I thought it was beyond the line." She paused. "I can see you're upset."

"I'm furious. I had a suspicion that I was being stitched up but Felix said..."

"Well events, as often happens, overtook and the story was spiked, so all they got was an eight hundred pound kill fee. But it's still there, ready to be brought out again if you ever get your 15 minutes of fame."

"That is outrageous," Billie said. "My boyfriend would go mad."

"Really? You see, I felt you wouldn't want to go back there once you knew the truth."

"No." Billie felt as though she were being adroitly manoeuvered into a corner.

"But I don't want to force you to work for me. If you want to you can pretend we never had this conversation, or you could go and work for someone else."

"Sure."

"But let me put what I'm offering you on the table. I was a photographer although I became office-based at Worldwide and did mostly admin. I'm quite experienced. The agency would do words and pictures but we would both need to do both - I can teach you pictures."

"Yeah?"

"Don't worry about it, it's a doddle."

"If you say so."

"Yes. I worked for a couple of papers and then went freelance and I got some valuable shots. I can offer you training and I will also cut you in on the pictures. I'm prepared to pay you 25 % of what I make after tax. And that can be substantial. When I was freelance, on one picture of Camilla Parker-Bowles screwing up her face while on horseback I made £20,000. Well? What d'you think."

"So it's like paparazzi kind of pictures?"

"You could put it like that. Mostly it will be. There might be some scope for stand alones, shifts and so on but I'm not really interested in that. Paparazzi is where you make the money."

"It seems ironic that you walked out over snatched pictures of me and my boyfriend just to do the same to other people."

"I suppose it is. But I do have limits, things I'm not comfortable with. That felt really wrong to me. I'm not sure why.

"But if you want to have that debate then I guess I'd say, for me the people I chase are fair game. I don't do friends, I don't do colleagues and I don't really do ordinary people at all. I do the top brass. They are fantastically rich and powerful and the price they pay for a life of idle wealth is that they are hunted just as they hunt other creatures. But there's no malice in it. For me, it's not personal. It's just like any other blood sport."

"Hm. That's interesting. Now you are making it sound like part of the class war instead of just a way to make lots of money."

"Do I? Perhaps it's a hangover from my leftie past. I was a Marxist at university you know, a card-carrying revolutionary. But I'm not trying to make any ridiculous moral claims for what I do. It is what it is. It can be boring, it can be fun. But I don't stitch up my staff. What d'you say. Are you going to take the job?"

Billie played for time. " Thanks for telling me what you did about Worldwide. On a personal level that is just unbelievable."

"I know. I just think they've lost any sense of perspective. They probably think if they offered to cut you in on the dosh that would make it OK. Felix even tried to sell it to me as doing you a favour, defending your reputation. But we both know that is bollocks."

"Yeah, donkey sized bollocks." Billie chewed on her last mouthful of noodles thoughtfully and washed it down with the end of her beer. "So if I were to take the job, when would it start and what would we do?"

"Tomorrow. If you phone up and tell Felix you're coming to work for me he won't want you to do any notice. He's going to be hopping mad when he gets into work tomorrow. Look." Sorrel brought out two large black books and propped them on the side plate next to her place.

Billie had been at Worldwide long enough to recognise the holy books. They were the contacts book and the diary. She picked the address book up reverently and flicked through the pages. Each was densely covered with names, addresses and phone numbers of well-known people ranging from forgotten weather girls and rent-a-quote psychologists to some of the wealthiest and most influential people in the world. "Attorney General, mobile phone, home number, address, Abba, home telephone numbers, Dame Jane Astor, actress, Jack Andrew, chief constable of the Met. Wow, they will be mad. Won't he try to get them back?"

"I don't think so. He's got quite a few of the numbers on disc because he's been updating the list. I do have some claim to it because I'm walking away from a business I helped to set up. This is all I'm taking, nothing except my salary in money terms. Felix's not going to get a lawyer. He's too mean to want to pay their fees and I can't afford to. But he'll be lost without them for a while at least."

She opened the diary and flicked through. "You see, Thursday is a year's anniversary since Davina Jones and Chris Barr held a press conference to say they were splitting up. He's not around, he's probably in LA filming. But she's in something at the West End so she's here. We could tail her, watch her coming out of her house. If we get a picture of her doing just about anything, buying a bottle of wine, coming out of a dress shop with a carrier, meeting a friend or better still, a man, we can sell that-a year to the day that her marriage break up was announced, Davina Jones has found new happiness with X, cheers herself up with some retail therapy, prepares for a consolation dinner. We mention the show she's in and everyone's happy. Get the picture?"

"Yes."

"That's the bread and butter stuff. The front page shots take longer. Years sometimes. But they're worth it. Well, what d'you say?"

A mobile phone started to ring in Sorrel's bag. She pulled it out and looked at the number display. "Excuse me, I'll just take this outside." She put it to her ear and started to talk as she went to stand outside on the pavement. Billie could see her through the restaurant's plate glass window, phone tucked into her shoulder as she shivered and hugged herself in her thin pullover, her face earnest. It was obviously Felix she was talking to. This could be a messy situation, Billie thought.

It was a shame in a way about what had happened. Bilie felt she had been working incredibly hard at the agency but felt angry that she had had so little value to them. Luckily Sorrel had opened up another avenue. Billie liked her and what was more, thought she could probably trust her. Whether it would work out for them both freelancing was harder to say. But what the hell. Billie thought she would get a kick out of phoning Felix and saying she was leaving. There was no way she could do anything else now anyway.

She ordered another big bottle of beer and two glasses, pouring some out for Sorrel. When she came inside, a little blue around the edges, Billie lifted her glass.

"You're on," Billie said. "Here's to us and to the new agency. Bottoms up."

# CHAPTER ELEVEN

When Billie got home Antony was asleep, or pretending to be, and he got up early, before it was completely light. She listened to him getting dressed in the semi-dark room, which was lit only by the orange light coming in from the city outside.

"Put the light on if you like," she said. "It won't bother me."

"It's OK. It's early. I want to be in work by 7.30am. I've got a big report to write and I need some thinking time." He sounded civil but cold.

Billie tried again. "Come and give me a cuddle."

He gave her a perfunctory peck on the cheek, grabbed his jacket from the hanger on the back of the bedroom door and left. Billie turned over and tried to get back to sleep.

For a while she lay awake, feeling miserable but must have fallen asleep again because the next thing she was aware of was the electronic doorbell screeching on the clock next to the bed. Shit, it read 10.05. Oh, shit. Sorrel, who lived in Kentish Town, had said she would come and pick Billie up by car at 10 am and take her to the first job. Billie leaped out of bed and hauled on her jeans, T shirt and fleece before rushing to open the door.

Sorrel was standing there, one leather-gloved finger poised to ring the bell again.

"Good," she said. "You are up. I was beginning to wonder."

"Sorry. I was on the telephone. But yes, ready to go. Just let me grab a couple of things." Billie left her on the doorstep and rushed into the flat again, dragged a comb through her hair and picked up her bag, mobile phone and jacket. Keys, keys. She slammed the door behind her and followed Sorrel down to her car, a blue Audi.

"Have you had breakfast?" Sorrel asked.

"No," Billie said. "Wouldn't mind a snack."

"OK." She stopped outside a cafe. "Grab me a black coffee with two sugars, please. I can't park here. I'll go around the block."

Billie came out a few minutes later balancing two large coffees, a cold bacon and mustard sandwich wrapped in greaseproof paper and a couple of pieces of fruit and waited for Sorrel on the curbside for several minutes.

"Sorry," she said. "Got caught in the one-way system. Cheers." She took the coffee and placed it into the driver's cupholder. "Good you've got plenty of provisions. But first rule of the snapperazzi, don't drink too much fluid. You don't want to have to go to the loo at the crucial moment."

Billie stopped munching on her sandwich and nodded to show she was paying attention.

"I'm going to take you back to my flat now. I'm going to show you how to use the equipment. You won't have any problems with it. Basically most of it these days is point and shoot. Tabloid editors don't want art. They're not interested in composition. All they want is a nice, clear shot of whoever and sod the background, unless it's relevant."

Sorrel lived in a loft style apartment, one large room with a nice view of rooftops and in the distance, the park. There was a sleeping platform under the ceiling and the ground floor was a living room with two large, black leather sofas and a glass coffee table. A kitchen area was divided off by a breakfast bar.

On the coffee table was a pile of photographic equipment. She went through it, naming each item lovingly and showing how the bits fitted together, handing each over and pointing out how it worked and what its function was. There were three basic Canon cameras, an assortment of lenses and flashes, a tripod, a sure shot for emergencies and other gadgets like a light meter and lights for interior shots. She selected pieces from the pile and stowed them carefully into a camera bag like the ones most of the photographers carried, a large, rectangular bag with one reinforced shoulder strap and dozens of small pockets. As she packed it, carefully loading each piece into its special compartment and then carried it down to the car, placing it into the boot with an obvious sense of anticipation, she aroused a faint memory of Billie's grandfather packing to go on a fishing trip.

"OK done," she said. "Here endeth the first lesson. First thesis on photography, photographers have interpreted the world, the point however is to get a nice clear shot of it. Did you get all that?"

Billie nodded, looking down at the notebook where she had jotted down a few of her explanations in shorthand.

"Still a scribe at heart, I see. Good for you," Sorrel said, getting into the car. "Come on then, we best be off."

"Are we going to that actress's house?"

"Actually we're not. Bit of a baptism of fire for you today, I'm afraid. We're going to Heathrow."

On the way, Sorrel explained that she had heard on breakfast radio that Xavier Fernandez had been with a police escort on a secret trip to visit the family house in Argentina to search for news of his son and was that morning arriving back in the UK. "He's huge. It's going to be a real scramble. We'll try and get him coming out the arrivals gate but they may let him leave by another exit. If he gets away without shots and there's a chase, I've hired a motorbike."

"I've never driven a motorbike."

"Don't worry. I have. Most of them will hire couriers and ride pillion, that's the usual strategy but as I can do it, I thought we'd save ourselves the expense. I'll give you the sure shot and you can go on the back."

"Wow."

"Yeah, it'll be a gas if it happens. Don't worry, I'm not expecting a masterpiece. It's your first day after all, but we can give it a bash."

Sorrel had called an old friend on the Sun newsdesk who had told her the singer was expected in at 3 or 4 o'clock at terminal three but that was all the information they had.

But as soon as they walked into the terminal building they knew they were in the right place. A group of bored-looking men with camera bags was surveying the arrivals board. Billie recognised a few faces and Sorrel lifted a hand in greeting but then they wandered off.

"There's no point in hanging with the pack. If he walks straight out and everyone gets a shot of him, no-one's going to pay for ours."

Again waiting was the name of the game. Sorrel was constantly on her mobile. Billie lolled on a bench flicking through the papers... Bored, she looked up and saw Rick coming up the escalator, his hands in his pockets and a pen stuck behind his ear.

"Hi," he said. "Don't Worldwide have any other reporters? You get all the best jobs. Like me, I'm getting the teas in for the monkeys."

"Actually, I'm not working for Worldwide any more. I've left, I've gone freelance and I'm going to do photographs. I'm working with Sorrel Amhurst."

"Oh yeah? Is that that middle-aged lady who worked for Worldwide?"

"She's not middle-aged, she's in her 30s."

"Well that's middle-aged. If you expect to live to 70, 35 must be the middle age."

Rick looked at his watch. "Best get these teas in. Come with me."

Billie followed him over to the tea counter and helped him fill a tray with polystyrene beakers. Rick didn't seem his usual self, he was quiet and an aura of gloom hung about him.

"Cheer up," Billie said. "It may have already happened."

He looked at her with scorn. "You're taking this photography lark pretty seriously aren't you. Do you get a book of daft remarks with the camera?"

"Cor blimey. You did get out of bed on the wrong side this morning, didn't you Mister," Billie said in RADA Cockney.

Rick smiled. "OK I am a bit pissed off. The Post aren't giving me any more shifts. I screwed up on the weather girl. Someone else got the story, the bloke's wife showed up with all his stuff and dumped it all over the lawn. Someone else got a tip and got the story but I should have been there."

"Shit, I'm sorry. It wasn't because you came to help me was it?"

Rick shrugged. "It could have been. But it doesn't really matter. It's me that's the problem. It's my attitude. I just don't care any more. I've kind of lost the edge, it doesn't seem to mean anything. I'm leaving Global."

"You can't! I'll be lost without you. "

He smiled. "That's nice of you to say. But I've got to now, anyway. Something came over me when I was in the office on my own at the weekend and I wrote lots of bollocks in the diary."

"What sort of stuff?"

"Just you know, things like, sex discrim Woburn Place, boss inspecting secretaries' knickers. That was one. They'll go mad for that, get loads of orders. It's going to be bad. So I'm moving on."

"What'll I do without you?"

"You'll be fine. You've got a real talent. You're better than me already and you've only been doing it a couple of weeks. You're going to be good, I can tell."

"But what are you going to do? Maybe you could join this new agency that Sorrel is starting."

Rick looked serious. "I'm going to do something else. I haven't decided. I'm either going to train as a doctor or teach English as a foreign language. I want to do something to help people for a change but I also really want to travel. I'm sick of this country."

"Wow. That's exciting."

"Anyway, I'm having a leaving party on Friday, at my flat. I hope you'll come."

"Sure."

"Hey, your boss is looking for you."

Sorrel was standing by the phones, looking around. Billie walked with Rick and the tray towards her.

"Sorrel, this is my friend Rick. He works for Global."

"Oh." Sorrel raised her eyebrows. "Hi, Rick." Then she smiled. "I thought your staff and ours were supposed to be deadly rivals?"

"Oh we are, professionally. But personally we get along quite well."

"Isn't that nice. But as I'm sure Bilie's told you, we're setting up another agency in a slightly different line so we don't need to be rivals now."

"Yeah," he said. "But actually I'm leaving anyway. Excuse me, I better take these teas down before they get cold."

Two more hours of hanging around, looking for information, scouting the airport for extra exits passed before anything happened. Information arrived, they didn't know from where, that the quarry had also visited his home in Sicily and was almost certainly on the 3 pm flight from Palermo. As the board showed that it had landed, the pack by the arrivals gate became increasingly edgy, with some scattering trying to find hidden exits. Some newspapers had several staff present and they operated as a team, watching different gates. As time passed, it started to become apparent that Fernandez had been smuggled out of a side exit. Finally, at 3.30 a young reporter came running in, shouting that Xavier had left in a limo with outriders.

There was a scramble for the exits. Outside a group of motorbike couriers were waiting and photographers began to climb on the backs of the bikes. Sorrel's bike was parked on a yellow line, near the exit. She stripped off her coat and shoved it into a pannier on the bike, at the same time taking out two black helmets. Under her coat, she was clad head to foot in a leather catsuit. "You've got to have the gear," she said, handing Billie a helmet and a sure shot camera which she hung around her neck.

"Now, remember lean *with* me," Sorrel shouted back, as both astride the powerful bike, they roared after the others.

Billie had never been on a motorbike before. At the age of 19 she had lobbied hard for one but Marina, who saw them as a macho, dangerous and polluting form of transport had argued her out of any interest in them.

Now, hurtling along the motorway well above the speed limit, Billie hung on and closed her eyes.

When she opened them she found they were in a group of motorbikes chasing a large Mercedes. Behind the Merc were two big men on police motorbikes who appeared to be blocking anyone who tried to get closer to it- the outriders.

As the convoy got into the London traffic, their attempt to block the riders became more and more difficult as the pace slowed down. But the Mercedes driver was adept at dodging the followers and made several dramatic last minute turns down side streets, Sorrel and the others clinging to his tail.

At one point they rode down a narrow street and the Mercedes slowed. The two outriders wheeled round and stopped horizontally across the street, blocking the way.

"Get ready," Sorrel cried and Billie felt her take one hand off the handlebars and unzip the top of her leather catsuit.

The outrider on their side looked towards her - did a double take at the bare-breasted woman roaring by - and she whipped up on the pavement and passed him, accelerating back onto the road. "Watch the lady," he shouted back towards the car.

Billie lifted the sure shot to her eye, Sorrel slowed down and as they passed the Mercedes she snapped the shutter, hoping she had captured the heavy lidded face of Xavier Fernandez leering out of the window at them.

They kept going, the Mercedes following at top speed.

"They want the film," shouted Sorrel, into the air stream whipping by and took them off fast and furious through side streets until she was sure she had lost them. Then she pulled over and zipped her leathers back up.

"Did you get it?"Billie nodded. "I think so."

"Good girl," she said, and held her hand out for the camera. "Thanks. Now you may as well run along. I need to get this developed and see how much I can get for it." She pulled her coat and handbag out of the pannier and put them on. She dropped the helmets in and locked it. "They won't recognise me like this. I'm going to leave the bike here for the moment and drop it off and pick up the car later. I'll call you."

"Please do," Billie said, anxious to know if she had got the shot.

Sorrel called as she was lounging on the sofa at home that afternoon watching Countdown and drinking fruit tea.

"You got it," she said.

"Yahoo!" Billie shouted.

"And I think it's the only shot of him arriving back in the UK. Everyone is going to want it so it's worth something. I reckon you've earned yourself a couple of grand this week. And it's only Tuesday."

The week had started with a bang and it ended with a bong, in a manner of speaking. Sorrel was excited by the story of the drugs factory at the racing stable and Billie spent the next couple of days sitting in a tree which overlooked the farmhouse where Ray Harris lived. The oak tree was on the hill behind the house and accessible if you crawled along a ditch from a quiet country lane nearby. Cars came and went, four wheel drives, jeeps and horse boxes but nothing of any note. Nobody pulled up in a convertible wearing shades.

Sorrel did a cutting search and a library search and found out a bit about Ray Harris, who was in his 40s and an Australian by birth, mostly from the gossip columns were he was referred to as a race trainer but there was little information to be had. She also had the business to run in terms of selling, invoicing and planning, and managed to sell the picture of Xavier Fernandez to two US magazines and one in Australia as well as to a UK tabloid and weekly magazine.

That took the pressure off as far as Billie was concerned, but Sorrel was keen to nail the next one.

"We've just got to be patient," she kept saying. "I know it doesn't feel like we're getting anywhere but we're building up a picture. What we are going to have to do now is go hang out in the pub they go to and get to know them."

HACKETTE

Billie was cold, bored and her fingers and knees were all chaffed from clinging to the branches. "But those girls have already seen me."

"So what?" But the girls didn't seem to go to the pub much and no opportunity arose before Friday, Billie's last day of watching before the weekend.

There was still no sign of Sorrel by the time the sun was setting through the branches on Friday and she amused herself by taking some pictures of the skyline.

While she was doing that, Ray came out of the farmhouse doorway below carrying something. Billie picked up the binoculars and stared down. Ray was dragging a large trunk. It was obviously heavy because after a few feet he had to stop and rest before pulling it again. He opened the back door of a jeep and with great difficulty turned the trunk onto its side and pushed it into the back. "Wonder what that is," Billie thought. "Probably a load of junk to the church jumble sale, knowing my luck." She snapped a couple of frames of Ray with the long range lens and then turned back to the sunset.

A few minutes later she became aware of Sorrel who was at the foot of the tree, looking up. "Oh no," she said. "Don't tell me you're turning into a photographer. You don't want to waste film on crap like that." Billie clambered down stiffly and almost limped along the muddy track to where she had left the car. She handed over a silver hip flask and Billie took a swig of what tasted like good brandy.

"Why shouldn't I turn into a photographer? Isn't that what you're training me to be?"

"Not exactly. Not an amateur landscape photographer who takes soppy sunset pictures."

"What's soppy about the sunset? It's beautiful."

"Yeah, but just put your camera down and look at it. Taking pictures is a way of not looking at it until later. But no picture you can ever take will be anywhere near as beautiful as an ordinary sunset. Actually, I wouldn't have hired you if you'd been a photographer. I don't want someone who thinks they're being creative, I just want someone to point and shoot."

165

"And you thought I was the kind of moron who could stick to doing that."

"Well. Not exactly." They were driving back to London by now. Sorrel leaned over and switched on a music station.

"Anyway," she said, changing the subject. "We've had a pretty good first week all in all. You've worked hard and done what you're told. Here." She pulled a brown envelope out of her jacket pocket and chucked it in Billie's direction. She caught it and opened it. Inside was a thick bundle of £100 notes.

"Wow. Fantastic. How much is here?"

"Two grand."

"Fuck." Billie took a huge gulp of air and felt a stitch develop in her side.

"I told you I'd be fair. I'll split what I earn with you, after costs."

"That is absolutely amazing," Billie couldn't stop grinning now. Her body was stiff and bruised and she had torn her trousers but it felt good. "I can't wait to tell Antony. I'll buy him dinner at somewhere really fuck-off. How about Fabrisio Garibaldi Smith's gaffe?"

"Excellent idea."

""What are you up to at the weekend?"

"Hm. Not much. I'll go down to my health club tonight. Sit in the jacuzzi and unwind and eat the Friday night buffet they put on for sad workaholics like me. Maybe I'll call a friend and go to the pictures but I doubt it. The thing I can get my head about London living even after all these years is that you have to book people so far ahead if you want to meet up."

"Hey you could always tag along with me and Antony if you like. We're going out for a meal and then onto a party, a leaving party actually. It's that reporter from Global we met at Heathrow, Rick," Billie offered, part of her hoping she would refuse.

"That's sweet of you but I don't want to be a gooseberry. You can't have seen Antony much this week anyway. You've been doing long hours. But another time we'll go for a pint after work, eh?"

"Sure."

Billie remembered that Ian's horse was running in a race the next day and mentioned it to Sorrel.

She was thrilled. "That's fantastic. It could be a great opportunity for a picture exclusive. Sounds like not many people have figured out that he's likely to be there, except for your friend Angela of course. Ian's story has been told but there have been developments. It could still be good, particularly if the horse wins or something. I think we should go."

"Yeah?"

Billie was doubtful. Antony had been pretty understanding about her setting up in business although it had been a tough week. But she had been hoping they could mend some bridges this weekend. Billie hit on a compromise.

"Can I bring Antony?"

"Sure, a day at the races might be a laugh."

Billie was happy at the thought of hard cash in their pockets. It seemed sad that she shouldn't share her happiness. She tried again.

"Honestly Sorrel, why don't you come along with us tonight? Antony's really keen to meet you. It'd be nice. We can have dinner and crack a bottle of champagne to celebrate our first earnings."

"Remember we don't know when there's more coming."

"Sure, that's true. We can't blow it all at once, but I think a little jollification is in order."

She looked away from the wheel for a moment.

"Well, that would be nice. If you're sure Antony won't mind."

"Of course not. See you there at 8pm. Let's push the boat out."

At home, Billie managed to secure a table for three at a suitably posh restaurant, showered and changed into a backless wine-red dress which Antony had bought for her birthday.

She had arranged to meet Antony straight from work but on the way to the tube station, called to explain that she had invited Sorrel too. "I think you'll get on," she said to Antony's slightly exasperated sigh.

He was philosophical. "It's OK really. I was looking forward to it just being the two of us, but I'd like to meet your new boss and size her up. Is she nice looking?"

"For a middle-aged lady."

Antony laughed. "How old is she? 35?"

Sorrel and Antony seemd to hit it off. They kicked around current affairs for a while, being careful not to express too firm a view. Sensing that Sorrel's Marxist leanings would not blend with Antony's middle England views, Billie tried to head off any confrontations. Eventually they retreated into celebrity gossip, the conversation becoming animated for the first time as they discussed the marriage break-up of the weather girl's lover, a radio DJ. The story that Rick had missed, about the man's wife tipping his clothes all over the lawn had been picked up by TV and the gossip magazines.

"Why did she do that?" Sorrel asked, rhetorically. "It was just so stupid. it's going to increase media interest in the story and put the family under more pressure."

"I know," Billie said, feeling angry at the woman for stitching Rick up. "How was anyone to know she was going to do that?"

"Maybe she was just angry," Antony suggested. "Or maybe she wanted to increase the media interest in the story. Perhaps she wanted to sell her angle or perhaps she's got something to publicize."

That's true actually," Sorrel said. "She's a Z list celeb, maybe she's just teasing the media dragon. Good luck to her if she is. Dangerous sport though."

"I know," Antony said. "I'm in PR remember."

After the main course, Billie suggested they move on to the party. "Bit early yet isn't it?" Antony said, looking at his watch. He ordered an espresso and Sorrel ordered an Irish coffee. Billie sighed, gave in and ordered trifle and a cappuccino, a combination which made the waiter look at her with scorn.

Eventually, they got the staggeringly large bill which Billie insisted on paying but which put a slight dent in the contents of the brown envelope and headed off to Rick's in Antony's car, Billie politely folded into the back seat and Sorrel in the front.

# Chapter Twelve

A ntony grumbled most of the way about the folly of driving across London "just for a crummy party".

It took a while to find it, but finally they did, a basement flat in a crumbling Victorian house with peeling paint and rotten windows. The steps down to the basement were slippy with fallen leaves that had not been cleared away and there was a strong smell of cat piss. Billie knew immediately it was not going to be Antony's kind of scene. However, he said nothing.

They rang the bell several times but no-one answered. Someone came down the steps behind them with a clinking plastic bag. "Push it, I expect it's open," he called.

Looking round, Billie saw it was Barmy.

"Wotcher," he called down. "Didn't expect to see you here. Is that you Sorrel, well hello Dolly." He grabbed her shoulders and kissed her cheek, Sorrel remaining stiff in his arms. He moved back and looked at her. "Hey Dolly, we're still friends aint we? No hard feelings. It's so good to have you back where you belong. I didn't mean to hurt you, I'm sorry that I made you cry."

"I know," Sorrel said. "In fact it wasn't you that did. Look, is there going to be anyone else here from Worldwide?"

"No, nobody worth mentioning. Just a couple of snappers. You can calm down. Felix won't be here. Hardly. You know his attitude to Global."

Sorrel's shoulders relaxed. "Yeah, true."

Barmy went on: "Photographers are allowed to fraternise, you can't stop them but the reporters don't usually...well apart from Billie Liar over there. She plays by her own rules."

Billie said nothing and pushed the door. It opened easily revealing a long corridor to the back of the house covered in ripped brown lino. They walked along it to the end where on one side of the hall, she could see into the kitchen where people were clustered round a long table where food was laid out and on the other was a living room where the music was coming from. A portable CD player had been wired up to a couple of large speakers which were blasting out what she recognised as Rebelle's first album.

No one was dancing. There was a large, knackered cloth covered sofa at the end of the room and Theo was sitting in the middle of it, holding an enormous spliff. Rick was sitting next to him and he had his arm round a girl with big blue eyes, fluffy blonde hair and a round, young face. Another girl, a plump brunette in a short, rose pink satin dress that was too tight for her was standing in front of the sofa trying to persuade them to get up and dance.

When Rick saw them, he jumped up and came over. He was wearing jeans and a sweat top and had had his hair cut. He looked young and serious and handsome.

"Thanks for coming. It's really good to see you." He pointed to the rose pink girl. "These are my colleagues, Julie, and"-he pointed to a youth in a ripped jacket leaning against the wall -"Pete. They both work for Global."

"Hi!" Julie called. Theo unwound his arm from the blonde and got up too. "Hi. Nice to see you. Been on Crimewatch again?" He laughed. "OK Julie, I'll dance with you." He grabbed Julie and started to salsa around the room with her.

"Can I get you a drink?" Rick asked.

"Hi," Antony said, half lifting a hand in greeting. "Mineral water for me please. I'm driving."

Billie trailed after Rick into the kitchen to help get the white wine for Sorrel and beer for himself.

"You look fantastic Billie. I'm afraid we don't have any mineral water. Will he drink tap?"

"Er... he'll have to I guess. Eau de toilet he calls it."

Barmy walked by and brayed in Billie's ear, then put his hand on her back just above her bum.

"Oy, gerrof."

"Sorry. Just trying to say, no hard feelings I hope, mate. Nothing's personal in this business."

"Sure," Billie smiled back at him. "There's no point in holding grudges."

I don't reckon there is," Rick said. "Thanks for coming."

"Wouldn't miss it. I can't believe you're leaving."

"Nor can I. Angela is here by the way," Rick said. "She phoned me about something so I invited her along. She showed up about half an hour ago with a bottle of malt whisky. There she is."

Angela was sitting at the end of the kitchen table next to a large bottle of Laphraoig. "Hi Scoop, how you doing? I hear you've changed jobs." She gestured to the chair next to her.

Rick perched on the table. Billie slipped off her jacket, stuck it on the back of a chair and sat down, beginning to talk about the Fernandez story again. The papers had been full of leads about Carlo. Scotland Yard detectives were reported to have flown to Sicily where he was supposed to be being hidden by the Mafia, someone had seen him crossing the Gobi desert on a camel, there was another report of him stopping to refuel the plane at a private airfield in Tangiers, there was endless speculation.

"D'you get anywhere with it this week?" she asked "Sadly no," Angela shrugged, "How about you?"

"Naw, I reckon we should muck in together on this one," Billie suggested, telling Angela about the agency, and forgetting about the drinks for Antony and Sorrel which stood on the table until Antony came in and removed them, raising his eyebrows slightly to show he was annoyed.

A while later Billie wandered back out of the crowded kitchen into the living room to look for him. He was sitting next to Sorrel on a small sofa, but they had fallen silent. The music was probably too loud for easy conversation. Theo and Julie were still dancing and the blonde, another Global reporter named Pippa, Billie had learned, had been joined on the other side of the room by an older man in a tight suit and a carelessly-knotted, brightly-coloured silk tie. Looking over, Billie realised with a shock it was Beattie.

She looked over at Rick who was hunting in the CD collection for some more music. He caught her eye and came over. "Is something the matter?"

Billie gestured towards Beattie. "What's he doing here? You didn't tell me he was coming!"

"Sorry. I didn't know it was a problem. Julie probably invited him. She met him on a job. I think he's taken a bit of a shine to her. Anyway, he comes round here sometimes to drag us out for a drink. He only lives across the park. He's all right really. Anyway, I thought you said you saw it all as a game?"

"Well yes, I might have, but…"

Beattie and Julie came and Beattie draped an arm around her shoulder. "Hello there, ye wee bezom," he said, affectionately. "You're looking awfie bonny the night. Nae hard feelings about that time in the Highlands, eh?" He guffawed at the memory. "That was a laugh, was it no. Huh you should have seen your face! Hey lassies, did I ever tell you about the time…"

Billie smiled, trying to look as if she thought the story was hilarious and then disentangled herself from Beattie and went over to the sofa where Antony was sitting.

Billie raised her voice over the music. "How you doing?"

"It's a pretty crap do in my opinion. I'm not really in the mood. Can we go soon? I'm knackered."

She perched on the arm next to him. "I can see it's not your scene sweetheart and I appreciate the effort that you've made to come along. But I'd quite like a chance to talk shop with some of the guys so why don't you just head home? Have an early night. I'll hang out here for a bit and get a cab home later?"

"I'd be quite keen to get a lift home too," Sorrel said. "These kinds of parties make me feel old. It's like being a student all over again." She lifted the cheap, vinegary white wine in its glass tumbler to her lips and made a face. "And it's such an effort talking over the music. You know what they say, if it's too loud, you're too old."

"OK." Antony said, getting up and stalking towards the door. Billie followed him. In the hall, she put her arms round him.

"Hey, you're not angry are you honey? You know I love you but I can see this is boring for you. But it's good for me to get to know these people. You know, if you want to go now, that's OK."

"I suppose I could wait a bit longer. How long do you want to stay?"

"A while, I don't know. But you go and give Sorrel a lift. You've had a busy week. Hey," she stroked his cheek and looked into his eyes. "You can trust me."

He smiled back. "Yes, I know. Although you do look gorgeous tonight."

" Why thank you sir. Don't worry, I'll fight em off. I'll see you later."

Sorrel came over carrying her bag. "Ready to go?"

Antony nodded and they left. Billie went back into the party, feeling the lightness of freedom in her step.

In the living room, Theo had collapsed on the sofa again. Julie leaning against him. There was a magazine on his knee with cigarette papers, cigarettes and a packet of grass and he was rolling an enormous spliff. Pippa and a drunk man were shuffling round the floor. The man was fondling her bum.

"All right?" Theo said as Billie sat down beside him.

"How d'you get away with that then, being a copper?" she asked.

"Simple. I'm not a copper. I'm a civilian."

"I know. But you work at Scotland Yard."

Theo lit the joint and shrugged his shoulders. "It's not a big deal though is it, smoking a bit of dope. Not these days. Who cares? So long as I don't hang out with the wrong crowd or have anything to do with, like the stuff that big bird's punting." He passed the joint, then

173

started to tickle Julie who looked as if she was falling asleep. She wriggled and giggled under the onslaught. "Now I've woken you up, let's dance," Theo said, pulling her to her feet.

She took the joint and had a perfunctory toke, wondering what Theo was on about. Was there some coke around? It was possible. Angela appeared at her side and took the joint gratefully, pulling on it hard. She seemed thinner than a week ago and more drawn and pale, her skin slightly clammy.

"Is there some coke going around?"

"Yeah, want some?"

Billie shook her head. She was a dabbler in the world of drugs and did not intend to venture out of the shallow end.

"Who is that bloke?" Angela gestured at Theo.

"That is the Scotland Yard Press Officer mate."

"That's a bit dodgy isn't it?"

"He's not a copper."

"Hm. I don't know if I believe that. I wonder if he's on some kind of undercover job."

"Why on earth would he?"

"Just to keep tabs on the press. I mean these people might not matter much at the moment but in a few years some of them might."

"Pretty big might. Sounds a bit of a conspiracy theory to me. You want to steer clear of those," Billie said. "Let's go and get some more of your malt whisky." They headed for the kitchen again where they sat comfortably seeing off the whisky.

After a while, conscious that she was starting to have trouble keeping track of the conversation or making sense, Billie got up to go to the loo. Hunting for it, she opened a bedroom door. Rick and Pete were standing over an oval mirror laid on the top of a table. There was some white powder on it and Pete was holding a rolled up note which he shoved quickly in his pocket as Billie entered.

It was a small room with a single bed above which hung a naked light bulb. A pile of clothes was heaped untidily onto a chair and books were stacked along the wall in piles, highlighting the absence of a bookcase.

"Oh sorry," Billie said and went to shut the door. "No," Pete said. "Come in. I was just leaving ."

"Oh. OK." Billie went into the room and sat down. Pete left, winking at Rick as he shut the door.

"Well," Billie said, sitting on the bed. Rick came and sat next to her and rested a hand on her knee.

He lifted a hand to her face and turned it towards him. "You know," he said "I really, really like you. I think I fell for you that time we snogged. Ever since then I can't stop thinking about you. "

"What can I do to help you?" Billie looked over at him. Their eyes met. It seemed the most natural thing in the world to move her mouth towards his. They kissed.

Afterwards, they slept in each other's arms. Billie woke up first. Grey pre-dawn light filled the room. Her mouth tasted of whisky, tobacco and cannabis. Rick was lying under the covers, facing away from her. She touched his arm and he woke up and turned over, rolling straight into her arms.

"Jesus," Billie said. "I don't know what came over me last night. I've got to go now," she said. "You understand don't you."

Rick nodded. He smiled. "See you, Princess,"

Going into the kitchen for a glass of water, she found Angela, asleep at the kitchen table, her head resting on her arm, next to the empty whisky bottle.

Billie shook her awake.

"Good morning, Angela."

"Oh is it? Fuck." Angela gagged on her own breath. "Yeeuch. What, where, and most of all why?"

"It's Saturday morning. Are you going to the races?"

"Of course."

"Want a lift? I'm going with Antony and my new boss. Tag along."

"Cheers."

They left the flat in silence and walked to the tube. It had just opened and they caught the first train across town back home.

As she put her key in the lock, Antony came to the door, looking tired and strained.

"Thank goodness," he said. "I was worried. I tried your mobile but it was switched off."

"God, sorry. Angela and I made a bit of a night of it, kind of slept where we fell and caught the first tube. Sorry to worry you," Billie hugged him, her heart pounding.

He sighed. "Well, thank goodness you're OK." Billie looked at him, feeling terrible. She was aware that Angela would not meet her eyes.

Angela coughed. "Sorry to interrupt. Mind if I go into the kitchen and grab some food? I'm starving."

"Sure."

When Sorrel arrived, they arranged to go in two cars for greater flexibility. Antony and Billie were planning to drop by for lunch with Marina and Lotty and so they set off for Brighton in Antony's car.

Conversation in the car was stilted at first. Antony turned on the radio and they listened to some music for a while. But he was restless and kept changing the channel.

Finally, he turned it off altogether and said.

"Billie, I need to know. Did anything happen at that party last night. Did you get off with someone?"

Billie sighed and looked over at him. "I don't want to lie to you, Antony. It kind of did. I snogged someone. I was really drunk on whisky and I don't know what got into me."

She looked over at his profile. It was set in a straight line. "I'm really sorry. It doesn't mean I don't love you. I've never done it before."

"Did you use a condom?"

"A condom? It didn't go that far...Oh all right then, yes I did."

"Why did you do it?"

"You know what, I think I was feeling a bit, you know. Trapped."

"Oh, come on."

. "No don't. I really want to marry you. I do, it's just, as it gets closer, I'm getting nervous. But I'm happy with you. I really am."

"I was happy with you too. When I asked you to marry me it was because I thought I'd found a woman I could spend the rest of my life. You were everything I ever wanted Billie. I would have done anything for you."

"I'm sorry. I'm so sorry." Billie was sobbing by this time, tears running down her cheeks and her nose was running. She fumbled in her bag for a tissue and Antony hauled one out of his pocket and passed it to her.

# CHAPTER THIRTEEN

I t was almost noon when they arrived at the narrow Georgian town house the two women shared, at the less fashionable end of the sea front, in Hove. The nearest parking place was five minutes away and they had to brace themselves against an ice cold sea breeze that was whipping its way through the streets. It was a grey day and Hove looked shabby and run down, the white paint on the houses peeling and dirty. Each house had a tiny front garden, just room for a dustbin and a patch of garden but most seemed infested with weeds and the bitter wind had blown the grass into thinly spaced spikes. They walked in silence, Billie's hair lashing into her red eyes. She couldn't recall a time when she had felt so grim.

Her relationship with Antony was the one stable, secure part of her life. How could she have jeopardised that for a one-night stand at a party with a guy she hardly knew. She felt confused and angry with herself. Whenever she caught sight of Antony's white, drawn face she felt a stab at her heart.

Lottie came to the door, a plump, middle-aged woman with grey hair swept back behind an Alice band, wearing a blue striped apron over a purple tracksuit "Arabella! Marina's so pleased you've come," she said, flinging her arms around Billie. "She may not show it but she's really thrilled that you've made the effort. I made her get up at dawn this morning and we drove out to the downs and gathered great armfuls of young nettles for soup because I know how much

178

you adore it. It's just the right time of year for nettles," she ushered them through the living room into the large, sunny kitchen. Passing the foot of the stairs she paused to yell up: "They're here."

A long table, covered with a floral patterned oil cloth was laid for lunch and a pan of bright green fluid was simmering on the stove.

"Lovely, such a vibrant hue, isn't it? Such a fresh, spring taste they have I always think," Lotty went over to stir the soup.

The most comfortable seat was a fixed bench which ran along under the window, covered with a yellow, flowered cushion seat. Lying right in the middle of it was a large cat the colour of bitter marmalade.

"Off Irigary," Billie said, prodding the animal's portly rear and he let out a miaow of protest before heaving himself down and stalking towards the back door, tail high.

Lotty clucked "Oh dear," and came rushing towards the seat with something in her hand. "Don't sit there just for the moment would you mind?" she said, placing something where the cat's body had been.

"OK," Billie said, turning two hardback chairs round from the kitchen table to face into the room for herself and Antony .

"What's all this about then?"

"It's crystals." Lotty looked faintly embarrassed. "Your mother thinks it's rubbish but I'm quite convinced it's helping. You see, the idea is that animals are much more sensitive to psychic power than we are. So Irigary tends to sit where there are em, vibrations, for instance near a lay line, or in a spot that has a good north/south alignment. So wherever the cat likes to sit, that's where we put the crystals and they pick up on the vibrations and create like an energy field and then you can use them to, you know, cure diseases etcetera."

"Hm," Antony said. "Don't you think the cat likes to sit there because it's warm when the sun comes in the window?"

"I suppose he does but then that's valid too because the sun gives out really intense vibrations."

"Right. I suppose you can't argue with that."

There was a silence, as Lotty turned back towards the work surface. She got some tomatoes out of the fridge and began chopping them rapidly and chucking them into a salad bowl. Billie got up to help. "Let me do that," she said politely.

"Oh how engaging. Thank you." Lotty bustled off, putting bread and butter and napkins on the table. "Are you quite well, my dear?" she said, looking at Billie more closely.

"It's very windy out. Some sand blew into my eyes."

Marina wandered into the room holding a newspaper folded at the crossword. "Sorry," she said. "I was on the phone." She kissed Billie's cheek and nodded at Antony before going to sit on the bench, picking up the crystal and putting it on the window sill. Lotty said nothing.

"So," she said. "How's the defence of democracy going?"

"Not bad," Billie was noncommittal. "I think we should eat though Mar, because Antony and I are going to the races this afternoon. We want to be there fairly sharp."

"It's all ready, " Lotty said, decanting the soup into a large pottery tureen with matching ladle "Let's sit in then."

"Mm, delicious," Antony said, after his first mouthful of soup. "How do you make it?"

"It couldn't be simpler. You simply gather in, or should I say, harvest, the nettles, wearing gloves of course, isn't that right Marina? She had some idea that if you grasped the nettle firmly you wouldn't get stung, didn't you darling?"

"I'm sure I read that somewhere. Not true, I'm afraid." Marina drew in her breath and shook her hand, indicating pain. "Well, I won't make that mistake twice."

"Then you just soften up some spring onions in butter without letting them brown and a touch of garlic, add some stock, wilt the nettles and swish the whole thing up in the whizzomatic. There is something wonderfully recondite about found food. We love it. It's one of our things, isn't it, darling?"

Marina nodded. "What have you two been up to? More wedding fever?"

"Not really," Antony said. "We put it on the back burner for the moment."

"Really?"

Lotty cut in: "Marina told me that you were worried about the top table and the composition of that and I just want you to know that I'm not at all offended that you are sitting me somewhere else. Not at all. After all I'm not actually Arabella's parent although I do like to think of myself as a kind of extra mother. Maybe I only got to know her in the difficult teenage period but I think we have managed to build a really rather special relationship over the years." She smiled at Billie.

"Thanks," Antony said. "We haven't done the seating plan yet because ... well we were waiting to find out about Billie's Dad, but he can't come."

Lotty gasped. "He can't? What a selfish bastard that man is." She shook her head and shot a sympathetic glance at Marina.

"Where did you get hold of him?" Marina asked.

"He's working at a big hospital in Chicago. I usually get a birthday card and a Christmas card, with a 20 dollar note in it. I emailed him a month or so ago. What he actually said," Billie looked at her plate. "Was that he would try to come to the next one."

Marina choked on a piece of bread. Lotty clucked and slapped her on the back.

"I know Mr Polewault is a bit of a joker but I thought that was a bit off. So did Mum," Antony said. "Unsupportive."

Billie broke off a bit of crusty roll and buttered it. "It's a bit insensitive. But I do understand his point of view. I mean he's got young kids and about two weeks holiday a year. He can't afford to bring them all over and he can't just take off because his wife works too. He's a bit cynical about weddings anyway, after all, he's had three. He invited us to go and visit him over there and I actually think that would be really nice, we'd be able to see him properly."

"Anyone ready for main? "Lotty jumped up from the table. "It's a yummy seaweed omelette."

"How fab," Antony said, standing on Billie's toe.

"Eow!" she said.

"I can see you're keen too, Arabella. How refreshing. I'll just whip it up then." Turning to the stove, Lotty began to mix up a pre-prepared egg mixture with a vigorous fork. Billie asked Marina a question about her work and she told a couple of amusing stories about departmental politics.

As Lotty placed brown triangles of omelette specked with dark green seaweed in front of them, Billie responded with the tale of her stitch up by Barmy and Felix, the distance of a week or so having softened her anger. The picture of her emerging from the office, wastepaper bin over his head, stumbling on the arm of a police officer had Marina and Lotty wailing with laughter, but there was an element of concern once that subsided.

"Well, I'm glad you've left," Marina said.

"'Me too." Billie looked at her watch. "And speaking of changing jobs, I'm supposed to be meeting my new boss in five minutes. Lovely omelette, Lotty."

"Cheers."

In the car, Billie turned to Antony and stroked his arm.

"You didn't say anything."

"I didn't want to give her the satisfaction."

"What d'you mean?"

"Oh, come on. Your mother would be thrilled to hear we had split up. You know she would."

"We haven't split up and I don't think so."

"Oh, come on. She hates me. D'you think I don't know that?"

"Let's not argue about my mother. Who cares what she thinks? She's not marrying you. I am-please. I'm crazy about you, you know that." Billie's phone began to ring and she took it out of her pocket, looking at the screen. Rick's number flashed up. She switched it off.

"Is that him?"

"No, it's Sorrel, probably wanting to know where we are."

"I can't face seeing them. I'll drop you off. I'm going to head back to London. I need some time alone - to think."

Billie nodded. They drove along to the race track in silence, Antony dropping her at the gates where racegoers were filing in through the turnstiles.

She leant over and kissed him. "I love you," he said.

Sorrel and Angela were sitting in the car waiting near the gate. Sorrel had binoculars and a camera slung round her neck and was reading "The Racing Times". A weak sun had come out and they had rolled down the convertible top. Angela was sitting in the back wearing sunglasses and lying back as if asleep.

"Hi," Sorrel said. "Nice lunch? Where's Antony?"

"Something came up. He went back home."

"Oh really? I hope you didn't have a row." Billie shrugged and saw Angela twitch slightly. "Let's get going."

Over a beer in the bar they looked over the race programme.

"Here she is," Sorrel jabbed a long finger at the fourth race, "Brown Betty."

"I suppose if they are here, they will be in the owners' bar," Angela said.

Sorrel nodded. "I'll go and take a look."

"How will you get in there."

She frowned. "I'll say I'm with someone. Ray Harris, it'll have to be. It'll be easier alone. You hold the fort here. Keep a close eye out." She handed them her binoculars, fastened her raincoat and neatly folded the collar. "How do I look?"

"Very nice," Angela said.

"Smart," Billie added. "You could easily pass as a racehorse owner's arm candy."

She nodded and smiled. "Well, thanks."

It was a while later before she came back.

"Did you get in OK?"

"No trouble."

"Well, spill the beans."

"He is in there. He's with Ray, and he looks pretty nervous. Scared of his own shadow, he jumps at everything. Ray looks like a bit of a dodgy geezer. I tried to fall into conversation with them but they weren't having any. It's a bit like, Ian's under escort. I didn't manage to get a snap, it would have been too obvious. I'll try later when they are in the stand." She shivered. "He is a bit scarey that bloke."

But Ian and Ray did not appear to watch the race. The horse trailed home, sixth in a field of seven. Angela lost a ten pound bet which seemed to make her even more subdued and Billie, head thumping from last night's whisky, could hardly speak.

After the race was over they trailed around trying to find Brown Betty being loaded up into her trailer. Finally they spotted Lucy, Harris's stable girl, leading the horse away from the racecourse.

Angela walked over and slapped the horse's neck. Sorrel and Billie stood a few feet away as she chatted to Lucy.

Then she came back over. "Looks like we've missed them. Lucy said she thinks they headed off as soon as the race was over, she doesn't know where they've gone."

They drove back to London in silence. "Sorry that was such a wash out," Billie apologised as she got out of the car. She had got the keys back from Angela and let herself into the flat.

"Hi," she called hopefully but there was no answer. In the kitchen, a note in Antony's neat handwriting was propped up against the kettle saying that he had gone away for a few days and not to try to contact him. It was signed just "Antony", without the usual "Love and Kisses".

Billie's mobile rang and she fished it out of her pocket, hoping it might be Antony but Rick's number flashed up again. Not in the mood for a heavy conversation, she turned it off, ordered a curry and flopped down in front of the telly, cheered to find a double bill of Sex and the City repeats was just starting.

After that, she watched Newsnight and then a late film, fetching the duvet from the bed room half way through and falling asleep on the sofa, comforted by the companionship of the TV.

The phone woke her early next morning and she picked it up sleepily, wondering if it was going to be Antony. It was Sorrel.

"Rise and shine, cabin girl Wilson, the sun's above the yard arm."

"What are you talking about? It's Sunday."

"Yeah yeah, I know. Sorry about that me hearty but big big news is breaking this fine morning. Have you been listening to the radio?"

She looked at her watch. "I'm not really in the habit of turning the radio on before 7am on a Sunday morning, Sorrel."

"Yes, of course. I forget not everyone is an early riser like myself. Carlo's body's been found.'

"What!"

"Carlo's body's been found."

"Where?"

"A man spotted him floating in the Thames near Richmond. Looks like he never left the country at all. There's been some dirty work afoot."

"So it seems. What can we do about it?"

"I think we need to go to the scene and then back to the farm, to Ray's place. The story's wide open at the moment, I just feel we might get something today. You can get a day off next week in lieu."

Billie sighed. "Oh all right, captain. Just give me ten minutes to get my kit on."

"Good woman. Well said. I'll be round in 15."

A path led down from the summit of Richmond Hill through a steeply sloping park full of primroses, crocuses and snowdrops down to the riverbank. Here, the Thames ran wide and slow through a green field where a few flea-bitten cows were grazing. The area was still quiet so early on a Sunday morning, but some rowers were out, skimming along in a two-man scull and from the top of the hill they could see a crowd of people gathered below on the riverbank, TV cameras standing out.

Scrambling down, canvas photographer's bags on their shoulders, Sorrel and Billie joined the outskirts of the press scrum. There were already three TV crews and several dozen reporters and photographers, notebooks and cameras ready.

A senior officer in the uniform of the river police was standing in the centre, to the side of him was a Thames River Police launch with frogmen visible on the deck.

"The body was seen floating in the river last evening by a man walking his dogs. Police frogmen secured the body and it has now been identified as that of Carlo Fernandez. The cause of death has not yet been established but is thought he has been dead for some time. His father, Xavier Fernandez, who identified the body, is being questioned by police. Thames River Police frogmen are searching the water for clues."

Billie heard a voice in her ear and turned to see Rick, standing at her elbow in his brown coat. She was wearing no make-up and looked pale and drawn.

"Hi Billie. I thought you'd be here."

Hi, Rick," she said. "I thought you had left."

"I am leaving, but *The Post* offered me some more shifts and I'm covering this for them... How's things? Are you OK?"

"Yes. You?"

"Yeah. But I would like to talk to you. Can you meet me for a drink later? Please?"

"OK, I guess."

"Eight o'clock OK? I'll meet you upstairs in the Cambridge at Cambridge Circus."

They stood around by the riverbank for some time, watching the frogmen disappearing under the brown water. Sorrel shot off some film of the scene and the frogmen and Rick went to buy some rations, returning with welcome cups of hot tea, and croissants.

"There's no clue yet as to how he died?" Rick asked.

"No, no obvious cause of death, so he wasn't shot or stabbed. I really thought he'd left the country," Sorrel said. " But perhaps Xavier caught them at it, killed both of them and dumped Carlo in the river?"

"Maybe. That would be a pretty outrageous thing to do." Billie said.

"These Latins are very passionate you know."

"The English can be passionate too," Rick said.

"D'you think?" Sorrel asked. "It's not exactly what we're famous for. Marmite, buggery and parliamentary democracy are more what you associate with the English, I'd say."

"All, of course, invented by the Greeks. Well except for marmite. Look, they've found something." Billie pointed at the frogmen who had attached a harness from the launch to a large object which was being pulled from the river.

"What is that?" Sorrel said. "It's like an enormous tray."

"I think it's the lid of a trunk." Billie said. "Pass me the binoculars, would you?" Sorrel got them from her bag and passed them over. Billie adjusted them to her eyesight and looked at the object.

"Hm. I saw Ray Harris moving a trunk last Friday evening."

"Wow!" Rick said.

"Did you take a picture?" Sorrel asked.

"I think so. It should be in the sure shot, that film, I gave you on Friday."

"Are you going to tell the cops?" Rick asked.

Sorrel thought. "Yes. I'll develop the film and take it to the press bureau. You get back to the Harris place though now and watch it. Take my car, I'll get the tube back to the studio." She took the keys out of her pocket and handed them over.

An hour or so later, Billie was back up in her tree, looking down below at the stable yard. Lucy and Sue came trotting into the yard on horseback, each holding another two horses on a lead rein.

They dismounted and put the horses back in their looseboxes, then Lucy started up a hose and they began to wash and groom them one by one. There was no sign of Ray.

Her thoughts drifted towards Antony and the guilt she felt was like a clamp round her heart. She wondered where he was and what he was thinking. He had been so kind to her these last years and given her the stability she had longed for. Perhaps they would have to cancel the wedding. She could lose her home, the life they shared. An ache of anxiety knotted itself into her cold muscles and she felt a rush of certainty that what she wanted was to put it all back together the way it had been.

She was cold and stiff and utterly miserable when finally the side door of the farmhouse opened and someone came out. It was a slim youth with a slightly round-shouldered posture. Billie watched him anxiously through the binoculars. She had only seen press pictures and once glimpsed him through the window of a car but she had a feeling this was Ian Ford. She called Sorrel on her mobile to ask for a description.

"That sounds like Ian. It's funny but you usually know when it's the one you're waiting for. I don't know how. Go with your instincts, babe. If he leaves, why don't you follow him? Get a picture if you can."

Sure enough after standing chatting to the stable girls, Ian walked out through the archway to where the cars were parked and got into a bottle-green Fiat.

Billie slipped from the tree, ran to the car and leapt in, heart thumping and drove as fast as she could along the muddy farm track where it was hidden, bumping speedily down the lane after Ian, getting a sight of the Fiat just in time to glimpse it turning onto the road to London.

The traffic was heavy by mid-afternoon and it was not too difficult to keep Ian in sight. Billie was starving and needed the loo but didn't dare risk stopping at a service station so kept on Ian's tail along the M4 through west London and the Chiswick flyover, sitting in heavy traffic as they waited to get into Hammersmith and then along the Old Brompton Road. Just before Harrods, Ian turned left into a residential street. Billie followed. The Fiat made a couple more turns into a large Victorian square with a central garden, pulled up without warning and parked in a residents' bay. Billie carried on slowly and saw in the rear view mirror, Ian getting out of the car.

Pulling over and pretending to study an A to Z, she noticed that Ian didn't look in her direction as he walked round the square, ran up some steps to a large white front door, took some keys out of his pocket, opened it and walked in. She took a note of the number, 22.

Billie called Sorrel who sent her along to the local library to look up the address on the electoral roll, got directions from an old lady and found a small, almost empty library in a back street which was closing in 20 minutes. Inside, she persuaded the middle-aged librarian to let her have a quick look at the roll which was alphabetical by ward, saying that she had been born in the house and wanted to write to the current inhabitants to ask if she could look around. Luckily, she didn't ask why she didn't simply drop a note though the door but told her which ward the square was in and Billie found the address quickly. It was registered in the name of Rebelle Fernandez.

"Cool," Sorrel said. "Your picture came out by the way. It's a little bit out of focus but it looks similar. I'm going to take it to the cops now. They might want to speak to you, keep your mobile on. Why don't you go back and watch Ian's place for a bit?"

Billie found a meter space to leave the car and walked back to the square. In the corner was a pub, and standing on the pavement outside, nursing a pint was Angela. She looked guilty when she saw Billie.

"Hi?" she said. "Would you like a drink?"

"What are you doing here? I guess I can work that one out actually. How did you find it?"

"From Sue. I called her later and managed to get the address out of her. I was going to tell you. I just thought, you know, in the circs that you might not be working today. I thought you might have, you know, stuff to sort out with Antony. I wasn't trying to stitch you up. Honest."

"The hell you weren't."

"Just a little bit, then. I was going to tell you, I thought I'd be better on my own at first that's all. If it was just you I would have said but I didn't want Sorrel taking over."

"Hm. Actually, Antony's gone away for a few days."

"OK. How do you feel?"

"Confused. Upset."

Angela nodded as if she understood and they left the subject.

Ian didn't come out again that afternoon and no-one went in. Billie left Angela still waiting because she had to go and meet Rick. She was half an hour late but he was still there, sitting by the window with a pint in his hand looking out at the bright lights of the theatre opposite.

Looking round and spotting her, he smiled.

Billie got herself a half of lager top, and sat down.

"Hi," he said smiling. "I was beginning to think you weren't coming and I couldn't believe that."

"Well, here I am. What was so urgent?"

"That was amazing the other day. Wasn't it?"

"Yes, it was."

"I felt sad when you left."

"Me too. I'm sorry. I guess I shouldn't have let it happen, I mean, I'm the one who's engaged."

"Can we just get this straight? Are you still planning to marry that old bloke?"

"He's not old. He's 39."

"Well, how old are you?"

"25."

"Well then, that's old compared to you. When you were five, he was like 20. That's disgusting. You should stick with me, I'm more your age."

"I'm 25 now. And it's a well-known fact that women grow up a lot more quickly than men."

"And you're a living example of that are you I suppose?"

"Yes, I am."

"Bollocks."

"Anyway, I'm engaged to Antony. I love him. He is my one and only."

"Not quite."

"Well that was a mistake."

"It wasn't. We really click. There's something special between us. Don't you feel that?"

"Yes I do. There has been something and that's why last night happened. It shouldn't have happened but it's probably best that we get it out of our systems before I get married. Oh I don't know, I didn't really think it through, but I've definitely been attracted to you since we met."

"I'm glad you admit that much."

"Look, we were drunk, it was a party, we had sex, we shouldn't have. I'm not going to say it didn't mean anything because it did, it was beautiful. But it's not going to change my life."

" You need to give it a chance, our relationship."

"I can see why you feel that. But maybe it's just the heat of the moment. Antony and I have got something really good together. We live together. It's great, it works, it's a successful, healthy relationship."

"You could have that with me."

"Oh Rick. You're sweet, but no I couldn't. We couldn't like, get married. You're too young to be married. You're just a kid. You don't know who you are yet, you don't know where you're going. Maybe you're going to work with disabled people, maybe you're going to Japan."

"What's Antony got that I haven't? He seems like such a boring, old fart."

"Don't slag him off. That's not fair. He hasn't done anything, we have. He's a different person from you. I like living with him. I mean, look at where you live, it's a tip, a grotty, shared flat. Antony's sorted. He's got a good job, we live in a nice place. We cook for each other, we watch telly."

"What sort of a life is that to want at your age? It sounds so boring and middle-aged."

" Maybe it sounds boring to you but I never had boring and safe when I was growing up, Marina's lovelife was crazy, always new relationships, break ups, crises. Antony's what I need. We're happy with each other. It's safe. Are you really saying you could give me that? Because I don't think so."

"How do you know that's not what I want? How do you know I couldn't give you that? Maybe I don't know exactly where I'm going. But we could travel that path together. You're the same age as me. We could grow up together, we've got something. I couldn't be wrong about that, it's there, that magic spark and how often do you really find that in a life?"

"Maybe there is a spark, maybe there really is. But I'm already committed to someone that I feel connected to. We have a great life and I'd be mad to throw that away." Billie looked around the room, searching for inspiration. Then she reached into her bag and took out the book she was reading. It was a history of Arab women.

She turned it over to the author's picture. "See this book, Professor Jessica Taunenbaum is a lecturer at New York University, and the author of several books on the Middle East. She is an adviser to the UN on peacekeeping, a former radio journalist and a prize-winning poet. In her spare time she is a keen golfer. She lives with her husband and teenage daughter and an Afghan Hound called Michel Foucault, in upstate New York."

"That's the kind of life I want. I want to do big things in my life, to get somewhere, to make a difference. I want to be a foreign cor for a big paper, I want to make things happen. I want to be married and have a family too but I don't want that to be all. I'm practical, you're romantic that's the difference ."

"From what you're saying it sounds like you're more like Macbeth."

"I'm not as bad as that. But I want to come back from a busy successful day to someone else who's had a busy, successful day, have a glass of wine and a chat. I don't like drama. I don't want to come home and find that, I don't know, you've decided we're moving to Nepal or that your job is meaningless and we're going to stick our heads in the oven, and I sense that life with you might be a bit like that."

Rick paused. Then he said. "I think you should go now. But for the record, I think you're wrong. The kind of relationship you have with Antony, it isn't enough to get you through. I expect I'll remember what you've said to me for the rest of my life. And I wonder if some time down the line, you'll wonder if you were wrong to throw this away."

Billie decided to let Rick have the last word. There wasn't much else to say anyway. As she was leaving the room, she noticed he was looking out of the window, tense and still. On impulse, she went back, touched his arm and said. "You know I love you, don't you?"

"Yeah. I knew it wasn't a total flyer," he answered.

"What's a flyer?"

"It's like... a news story that doesn't stand up. You fucker." Billie picked up the book by Professor Jessica Taunenbaum that she had left on the table, put it back in her bag and walked away.

# CHAPTER FOURTEEN

H ome seemed quiet without Antony. There was a message on the answer phone from Sorrel saying she was to be present at a Scotland Yard press bureau at 10 am. Nothing from Antony.

Billie threw the foil curry trays in the bin, picked up her clothes from last night, tossed them into the bedroom and ordered a pizza with extra, extra jalopenos. She wondered where she would go if Antony chucked her out when he came back. The envelope from Sorrel had grown half empty in a stunningly short space of time. There was always space in Brighton but too much of Lotty would drive her insane.

Billie slept in front of the TV again, falling asleep midway thought the Ten o'clock news. The bed was too big without Antony.

Theo was in professional mode when she arrived the next morning, not as friendly as usual, taking her straight to DCI Bennet who thanked her for the information, had her identify the photograph and sign a statement saying she had taken it.

"I don't know if it's going to be admissible in court. You were trespassing and all that but we'll see. Obviously we're questioning this character, taking him in this morning. The boxes do seem similar but it doesn't prove anything of course. Anyway we'd appreciate you hanging fire on this at the moment. It may prejudice any future trial and you could be in serious trouble if you print it. I've spoken to your boss about that and we'll keep you posted. Thank you, good bye."

Afterwards. Sorrel and Billie went for a coffee, sitting at high stools facing out the window and drinking cappuccinos.

"What now, Cap'n?" Billie asked.

"It's a bummer in a way. We can't really do anything with that stuff at the moment. We're kind of stuck."

"See what happens. If they're taking him in today, we should know by the end of the week what's what. Keep watching Ian?"

"Well OK, a bit. But we can't afford to waste too much time on this. We need to branch out. I've heard that Celia Carson, the supermodel, is in the Kensington Private Hospital with anorexia. That's not far away from Ian's, why don't we do a bit at each. We can make some money with a photo either of Carson herself or her family and celebrity friends coming to visit her. Keep taking the tabloids, you have to know those faces."

The week passed slowly. Billie spent all her time standing or sitting patiently waiting for people to come and go, at Ian's flat or the hospital, while Sorrel mostly watched the hospital.

On Tuesday the newspapers said that Ray Harris was helping police with their inquiries, on Wednesday that he was released without charge.

Sorrel said she'd find out what was going on with that. On Wednesday, she got a snap of Carson's pretty younger sister bringing flowers which she was busy selling around the world and which brought in a few grand but there wasn't much from Ian's place.

Angela was watching it too, and confirmed that he seemed to spend pretty much the whole time holed up in the flat, leaving occasionally to do some shopping at the deli down the road.

On Friday night, Billie picked up a ready meal from the Kensington deli on the way home. Putting her key in the door, she was startled to hear Antony's voice calling "Hello" as she went through the door.

"You're back," she said. Antony had cleared up and was sitting in the kitchen, at the breakfast bar, looking out at the city lights with a photo album open in front of him.

"Yes I am. You certainly seem to have taken to the heavy carbs while I was gone."

"I was depressed."

"Me too. I missed you when I was gone. We've been good together haven't we?"

"Yes."

Antony pointed to the pictures in the album. "Do you remember that holiday in Ibiza? Wasn't it a laugh? Look at that picture, that's just after we met."

Billie nodded. "I remember that day. There I was wondering if I really had to go and hear the visiting lecturer on PR…"

"And you came in late, I remember you standing in the doorway, with your hair just washed and the sun streaming through it. I was like -Oh-oh…"

"So you asked me if I wanted a week's work experience for a top PR agency. And I'd seen what you looked like by then, so I was, just, yes please…"

"And then when I was trying to get you on your own to ask you out, you thought I wanted to tell you off for putting out olives with pips at the classic software drinks do because the marketing director broke a tooth…"

"But that wasn't it at all, you just fancied me." They laughed together.

"So I've decided to forgive you… I talked to Frank, you know. I just think it made a lot of sense what you said about feeling trapped in the run up to the wedding. It's a big commitment. And I was impressed that you told me. A lot of people wouldn't have had the guts. In a funny kind of way it means I can trust you more."

"I see."

"And Frank said something to me a long time ago about men getting scared. He said watch out you don't get too scared to cross that bridge. Women have biological clocks, it's like a deadline, do it now or else. But men don't have that and if they get to a certain stage without crossing the Rubicon they might find they just can't. But obviously fear can hit you at any age. Everyone's entitled to get scared and everyone's entitled to one mistake. Just don't do it again."

"I won't. I'll try not to. It wasn't premeditated, it just, you know, happened."

"Yes. I know. Because the other thing I didn't say, is that something similar happened to me."

"It did?"

"Yeah. With Sorrel. After you packed us off together, she asked me up for a coffeee. Well she just wanted a shoulder to cry on really, her love life hasn't gone to plan. But well, one thing lead to another..."

"You what! With my boss. You bastard. And what a conniving cow...Wait till I. Have you seen her since?"

"A couple of times."

"What!" Fury rising through her, Billie went to the living room to sit down. "I need some time," she said. She didn't immediately realise that Antony was laughing.

"Calm down Billie. It's not true."

It took Billie a few minutes to register what Antony was saying.

"So you're jealous. That's ironic. I just made that up to let you know how it feels actually."

"God it hurts. I'm sorry."

"It does, doesn't it. Could you have forgiven me?"

"Yes, of course."

Billie put her arms around Antony's neck and pulled him towards her.

The next day, Saturday, she was working. Sorrel had persuaded her to stick at it on Saturday as it had been a fairly thin week. She said she felt in her bones that something might break and that Saturdays were good for celeb pictures as they were thin news days.

Ian came out of the flat morosely at lunchtime, not seeming to look about him much. It was a sunny afternoon and Angela and Billie were standing outside the pub. He walked in their direction, looked at Angela and stopped.

"Hi," Angela said, smiling so broadly that her ears wiggled.

"Hi," Ian said. "Do I know you from somewhere? You look kind of familiar."

Angela stuck out a hand to shake his. "Em…maybe Ray's place. Ray Harris, the racehorse trainer? Do you have a horse stabled with him? I used to hang out there a bit and I feel like I've seen you there."

"Probably. Yes I do have a horse. Brown Betty."

"She's a beauty. Wasn't she running at Brighton last week? How'd she do?"

"Not too well really, I'm a bit disappointed with her from this season really."

"That's a shame. Fancy a pint? This is my mate, Billie."

"OK Don't mind if I do. I'm not going anywhere."

They went into the pub and sat down, Angela ordered a round of halves of bitter with whisky chasers, what she called "A wee haw and haw". She mucked about a bit and soon had Ian relaxed and laughing.

One drink became three and then four. Afterwards, he asked the girls up to his flat for a smoke and they accepted.

Following Ian, they climbed to the top of a shared stairwell and went into the top flat, a converted attic with big skylights letting in the light. The main room was a spacious living room with double doors onto a roof terrace, furnished with two bay trees in terracotta pots and a trellis with a climbing plant Billie thought was bougainvillaea. The room was sparsely but tastefully finished, a huge, silk rug across the blonde sanded floors, a music centre with a bookcase full of CDs, a heavy brass standard lamp, one low leather sofa and two matching footstools.

"Put some music on," Ian invited. "I'll put a number together," and he sat on the sofa and started rolling an enormous spliff.

"Cheers," Billie said, walking over to the CD collection. "Nice flat this."

"It was my mother's. It was her bolt hole, where she came when she wanted to be on her own. She died recently and she wanted me to have it."

"I'm sorry."

"I know. it's terrible. She was murdered."

"No, that's awful. What was her name?"

"Rebelle actually."

"Wow," Angela said. "I loved her stuff, she was amazing."

"I know"

"I didn't know she had a son."

"Well, she kind of kept it quiet early on in her career and then it got to be a habit. We preferred it that way."

"Listen, hadn't you a stepbrother..."

"Yes, he's dead too."

"God, poor you. What a nightmare you've been having."

"How did your stepbrother die? Have you any idea?"

"Yes, yes I know how he died."

There was a pause. Then Angela said, softly dropping the question into the silence like a fisherman dropping a baited line into a still pool, "How did he die?"

"I think it was an accident, he o'd'd on some bad drugs. Or like, a combination of drugs. He was a bit of a nutter, to be honest. He took a lot of shit, all together and all the time. It was only a question of time."

"How did he end up in the Thames?"

"I don't know. Someone didn't want the police calling round I guess."

"So, it had nothing to do with your Mum?"

"I guess not. I don't know. People have got all kinds of theories."

He lit up the joint and took a deep breath, holding it in for almost a minute before exhaling. He took another toke and passed the joint to Angela, who had come over and was sitting on one of the footstools.

"What's yours?"

"Well, like a couple of weeks before she died, she went out to lunch with this journalist... I don't know who he was or how he persuaded her to go, must have said he had something on us. It seemed he told her that, well, Carlo was in deep with drugs. He'd become a bit of a crackhead by then, but, he's dead now so there's no harm in saying, he was a nutter and he would take anything. I think this dude more or less accused her of being involved in the whole drugs thing."

"And was she?"

"Not really. She took a bit of this and a bit of that, she was quite wild in the old days, but she'd calmed down a lot. I don't think she was selling anything which was what this Rick accused her of. She was furious, really upset and shaking.

"She called me and Carlo and we came here, she wanted us to lie low for a bit. I was OK, not really involved on the scene as I only smoke a bit of blow and a few other things sometimes, I told her it was bollocks as far as I was concerned and went away home to Scotland.

"The next, I heard, she'd been killed."

"What d'you think happened?"

"Well, I don't know. I've been, you know, asking about and I've got my theories. Maybe she and Carlo were up to something. I don't know but I think Carlo was in trouble. I think he'd been looking after drug money for someone, like cleaning it up, getting it into the stock market. He punted it on the wrong shares and lost it. Maybe. I don't really know, but I think she was taken instead of him.

"I know he blamed himself. he wanted to tell me but I was too angry with him, I couldn't take it. I told him to get lost and not to contact me again. Now I'll never know for certain."

"That's really sad," Angela said.

"I know. I can't believe he's gone now too. I'm cracking up about it."

"Maybe you ought to tell someone, tell the cops."

"Yeah, I have."

"I wonder why the journalist never ran that story, about your stepbrother and the drugs."

"I don't know. Maybe he didn't have enough to go on. Mum said she just denied it."

"So you think, whoever killed her, it was like a revenge killing?"

"I don't know. Maybe she was dropping off drugs for Carlo or picking up money, or maybe it was to do with the money he owed these guys. It was to do with him, I know. She was quite impulsive, you know. She was very generous too and I think whatever trouble Carlo was in, she like thought it was her problem. She thought, she worried that she hadn't been a good mother, hadn't given us enough of her time, particularly me when I was younger. She was always apologising, she was desperate to make up for it. Anyway she was paranoid about this reporter being on our tail because the last thing she wanted was to embarrass Xavier or implicate him in this kind of scandal. She told Carlo to stay in the flat and what he was trying to tell me the time we met, after she died was that he had some important deal to make and she went instead and never came back. That's it."

"That's just really tragic."

Ian shrugged. "Hey man, life goes on. Let's change the subject. What's it like then, riding in a steeplechase? I've always fancied it but I haven't done it yet?"

Some time later, Angela and Billie ran down the stairs and out into the night air. They ran towards the tube and stopped.

"It's fucking dynamite!"

"Did you get him taped?" Angela brought a small journalist's tape recorder out of her bag.

"Sure did. You?"

Billie pulled a similar machine with a tiny mike covered in black foam, out of her jacket. "Yup. me too."

"Joint bylines then?"

"You bet. I better call Sorrel though."

"OK,"

Sorrel picked them up at the tube station and drove straight to the offices of the Post newspaper. "Let's not delay."

The editor ushered her in, friendly and a little bored. As they played him the tape, he seemed if anything, a little more bored.

Over his head, Sorrel winked at them and started to toss large numbers around.

A junior reporter was given the tapes to transcribe, someone else was sent to fetch coffee.

They were interrupted, mid negotiation by a rap on the door. A middle-aged man with glasses and a balding head, his shirt sleeves rolled up, came in.

"What's the matter, Mark? Something break? You know Sorrel Amhurst don't you? She's brought us some interesting copy."

"Thought I ought to show you this." Mark held up the front page of *The News of The Week*. "We just got a fax of their first edition," he said and held it up.

The front page headline was "Drug Secret of Pop Star's Last Hours."

"Well, oh well," the editor said, scanning down the story. "Looks like they've been working on this a while. I wonder what's brought it out now. Did they know you guys were onto it?"

Sorrel shook her head.

"You can't libel the dead?" Mark suggested. "Best defence really."

"True. Yes, this is all about Carlo...Ned Beatson, eh... He's a smooth operator. Additional reporting, Rick Wilding. Mm. Never heard of him."

"He used to work here."

"Oh did he? Pity he got away."

"Mm. You sacked him actually."

"Oh yes, I remember now. I didn't like his ties."

The editor turned to Sorrel. "Well, Sorrel. Thanks for thinking of us and all that. But I think we'll have to lift the stuff we need from here now." He nodded, dismissing them and they got up to leave.

"Shit," Angela said as they left the building.

"Shit, shit, shit," Billie added, kicking a stone and groaning as it hurt her toe.

"That's newspapers. I know it hurts...but always remember it's just the lining for tomorrow's cat litter tray when all's said and done," Sorrel said.

"Thanks for those kind words but they don't help. It's a bummer being stitched up, and by that old has-been of all people," Angela said.

"And Rick. How did he get in on the act?"

Sorrel opened her car. " We should have suspected. It was a bit of a coincidence him always turning up at the Fernandez jobs supposedly shifting. He's obviously been covering this undercover for *The Screws*. Get in, guys. Let's go to Victoria and get a copy of the paper."

The bus station outside Victoria station was busy with people waiting for the night services. A man was selling first editions of the Sunday papers on a long trestle table near the entrance and Sorrel bought three copies of the News of the Week and handed them out.

"Pages four, five, six and seven," she read. "They have been working on this for a while. Let's go and read them in that cafe."

They walked over to where she pointed, an all night cafe by the bus stands and grabbed the only empty table. The waitress came over and they ordered tea and bacon sandwiches.

Billie skipped the banner headline and turned to the inside story.

*How I Discovered Secret Life of Murdered Pop Star by NOW reporter Ned Beatson (additional reporting Rick Wilding) Carlo Fernandez was well known among the glitterati as a party animal and as a show biz reporter, I had come across him many times showing all the signs of someone high on drugs. I might have put him down as just another rich kid experimenting if it hadn't been for one chance meeting.*

*Several months ago, I came across him in very suspicious circumstances while working on a top secret assignment following the explosion of crack cocaine in London. Visiting a drug dealer's flat on the notorious sink estate of Ramsfield Towers in Hackney, posing as a dissolute and degraded crack fiend, I was surprised to find myself in company with this scion of the upper classes.*

*What could one of the richest and most fortunate young men in Britain find to bring him to this Godforsaken spot, I wondered as we passed each other on the urine -soaked stairwell? He glanced at me and for a moment, I was afraid he would recognise me and expose me to the dangerous gang I was attempting to infiltrate. But thankfully, he passed by without penetrating my disguise.*

*That meeting alerted me to Carlo Fernandez's fall into the depths of addiction and I began to investigate him more seriously.*

*It took a relatively short time to establish that he was in the drug world up to his septum. Fernandez was not only a regular crack user but an experimenter with all kinds of mind bending substances and it appeared that he was not only buying - but supplying too, marketing a range of designer drugs to the using fraternity.*

*After following the young man for some time, I came to believe that his family, the financier Xavier Fernandez and his stepmother, slain singing star Rebelle, were unaware of how far he had sunk.*

*Rebelle was perhaps the one he was closest to, as he had fallen out with his hardworking immigrant father over his lackadaisical approach to the family firm. The paper decided that she ought to be informed before we took the story any further.*

*I arranged to meet Rebelle in her favourite restaurant, the Maison d'Etre in London's Belgravia, where I confronted her with our suspicion of what her stepson was involved in.*

*Rebelle was obviously overcome with emotion. Hiding her lovely eyes behind sunglasses, she could not touch her food, only toying with a rocket leaf salad.*

*Of course, she denied everything on his behalf, but I could see she was intensely moved by what I had to say.*

*The next day Carlo disappeared from his usual haunts and it was impossible to find out what had become of him. His family had obviously spirited him away to some hideout where they could tackle his drug habit.*

*I now believe that Rebelle, who hated family rows, had concealed the truth from her husband. She had taken upon herself the whole burden of trying to sort out Carlo's problem.*

*On the night before she died, Rebelle did a foolish thing but a brave thing, a thing prompted by the purest mother love. She took a large sum of cash and went out to the address that Carlo had given her to try to "score" some crack for the young man she saw as her adopted son who was going through the agonies of withdrawal.*

*It was on that terrible mission that she met her fate. We do not know - we may never know - exactly what became of Rebelle. But her clothes, her car, her well-known face would have alerted criminals to the fact that she was easy prey who might yield rich pickings.*

*The police have established that a large sum of money was taken from her cashpoint machine that night. The most likely theory is that one pitiless desperado, or perhaps a group of ruthless thugs, forced her at knifepoint to take the money. We don't know quite what happened. Next, perhaps she tried to escape - she had courage and spirits enough for anything. There are some signs that she struggled with her attacker or attackers but she was stabbed, many times over. Whoever committed this foul and bloody deed then probably drove her in her own car to dump her body in a quiet residential cul de sac before running off.*

*The next morning, Britain, and indeed the world was aghast to hear that her lifeless body had been found in Canterbury Gardens, Hackney, stabbed through the heart.*

*It was a horrible crime and police have high hopes of catching the perpetrator or perpetrators. Anyone who saw her car or saw Rebelle that night at Ransfield Towers may have a vital clue to who was responsible for her death.*

*After that night, Carlo, half mad with grief, was a broken man. Unable to confess to his father what had happened he took refuge in drugs and, by accident or design, lost his own life, making Rebelle's brave sacrifice a pointless waste. The so-called friends he was with, in a fit of cowardice, afraid of being implicated, appear to have callously thrown his body into the Thames where it was spotted by a passer by last week. Police are still looking for a trace of his private plane, which they now believe he landed somewhere in these shores.*

*Here ends a tragic morality tale for our times. Let every young man and woman be told it, so that they may be warned of the pitfalls which await those seduced into the perilous world of drug addiction.*

*Note: The News of the Week has passed all relevant material to the police.*

"God, it's really sad" Angela wiped an eye.

"Is that what happened though?" Billie asked.

"In a manner of speaking, perhaps. Jerks the old heart strings."
Sorrel took a bite out of her bacon roll.

"Well, at least they've done a good job on it. Anyway, time to hit
the hay. Tomorrow, a new horizon, a new story. Maybe we could buy
up those stable girls. Anyone need a lift?"

"No thanks," Angela said. "I'm going to head off." Billie looked
at her. Something seemed to be on Angela's mind.

"No thanks," she echoed.

Sorrel looked hard at them and then shrugged and headed off.

"Thanks," said Angela. "I mean I like her but she is such a journo.
I don't quite trust her."

"Yes. Well, what is it. Spit it out!"

"I am just a bit worried about Ian. When he sees this he's going to
be really upset."

"Yes, but it's not our problem is it?"

"I guess not. But I feel a bit concerned that's all"

"Well, maybe we can go see him tomorrow or something. Come
and crash at mine," Billie invited.

But by the time they got round to going there, it was already too
late. It was Angela who turned on the 24 hour TV news at Antony's
flat the next morning.

The smartly-dressed woman on the desk was saying: "And let's
go straight to our reporter at the scene, Charlene, what's happening?"

A beautiful young woman with dangly earrings and a bright scarf
was standing in front of what Billie recognized as the *News of The
Week* building. Next to her was Rick.

"Hi, Fran. I'm here at the scene where News of the Week reporter
Ned Beatson was shot early this morning. With me this morning is a
colleague Rick Wilding.

"Rick. What happened?"

Rick looked dishevelled, his hair was flopping over one eye and
he had no tie on.

"We're just trying to piece it together at the moment. A couple of
friends and I were in the bar here last night. It's our local and we often

had a jar here. Towards the end of the evening, Ned got a call on his mobile. He went outside to take it and then when he came in he said he had to go to meet someone."

"Did he say who?"

"No. But we didn't really expect him to. He was a *News of the Week* investigative reporter and he played his cards pretty close to his chest – I mean plays...

"He had a big story in today's paper which was just hitting the streets last night. I suspected it was something to do with that...Anyway he had just left the scene, I mean the pub, when we heard a crack, like the sound of a car backfiring.

"I heard a shout and I went outside. Ned was lying on the ground groaning and a man was running away...We called an ambulance and he was taken away quite quickly. That's about all."

"Did you get a description of the man running away?"

"Yes, he was slim, tall, late teens, twenties...that's all."

"This must have been a terrible shock for you and all Ned's colleagues. What kind of a man is Ned?"

"Well, he's, well he's a very committed newsman..."

"It's Ian," Angela said.

"You reckon?"

"I'm sure of it. He must have got Beatson's number that time he sold the story. He must have been trying to find out who it was who put his mother through all that."

On the television, a reporter was talking outside a hospital.

"It appears that Ned Beatson who is 48 and has been an investigative reporter for *News of the Week* for 15 years is in a critical but stable condition in the hospital behind me where dedicated staff are doing their best to save his life. We are getting news through that a man has been arrested in connection with this incident. He cannot be named for legal reasons..."

# CHAPTER FIFTEEN

Now they were up in the plane, Billie didn't feel quite so nervous about the wedding. Of late, a strange feeling she couldn't identify had been gnawing at her insides. She had put it down to wedding nerves, but in the night, she often woke, seeing a pair of brown eyes that were not Antony's and remembering what their owner had said to her in the café the last time she saw him.

"It isn't enough to get you through," he'd said and the phrase hung about her like an aroma.

But for now, she was too busy worrying about whether her parachute had been packed correctly and whether she could remember the safety drill.

The door was open. That was unnerving enough, watching the rectangle of bare sky. She couldn't hear anything over the noise of the plane and the whoosh of the air outside but Antony caught her eye and gave her a big smile and thumbs up. He looked thrilled at the prospect of jumping out of a plane, something he claimed was one of the biggest hits ever.

All Billie felt was terror. But at least that was over-riding the anxiety she had felt previously.

Now, Antony was at her side. He was shouting something into her ear. "What?"

"Don't worry, you've got three parachutes - if you count the dress." Then he pushed her out. Screaming, she pulled the chord and was aware that miraculously, the parachute had opened. Looking back up towards the plane she saw Antony falling towards her, his parachute unfurling too.

A sense of blissful relief and she was floating down through a vast sky, into a cloud and down through its misty vapour.

Below the cloud, she could see the magnificent castle set in rolling greenery, and the field that was used as a car park, bright with scores of squares of coloured metal in front of the castle, the hats of the women standing out. Some of them had seen her, a strange sight no doubt with the white, voluminous skirts of her wedding dress blowing up around her. Thank goodness she had had the foresight to wear matching knickers. Some guests began running, towards where they thought she might land.

At the front of the running group, she could pick out her brother Oscar, moving easily in his white tunic and sandals and Angela's round figure in pink silk.

She had barely registered that the order of magnification had multiplied so rapidly that she couldn't take it in and the ground smashed into her body.

Christ. She felt an agonising pain in her ankle. She lay looking up at blue sky that seemed a million miles away. A few feet away, she could see Antony landing on his feet, just like the illustration from the training video.

Angela jumped up and down and clapped her hands. "Antony," she screeched. "You did that so fantastically. You look like everyone's favourite film star."

Antony's face came into her field of vision. She smiled. "Billie, are you OK?" he asked.

"A bit winded." She gritted her teeth and tried to stand but her ankle was badly hurt. Oscar and Antony helped her to her feet and she tried to lean on Antony's shoulders and walk, painfully, towards the terrace where most of the guests were gathered, waving towards them, cameras and glasses in hands. But it was no good.

"Put...me...down," she managed to say. "I must sit down."

She could see the Moomins, looking anxious in shades of purple. Marina, who was wearing a lilac trouser suit, flat shoes and no hat, walked down the stairs from the terrace and came towards her.

"Billie, I've called an ambulance," she said crisply. "What have you done to your ankle? Is it broken?"

She felt Antony's shoulders stiffen. "Don't flap. Just a bit of an awkward landing," she said, through gritted teeth. "But we won't let it spoil the day."

"Don't be ridiculous. You're in agony. There's the ambulance now." Sure enough, it had driven into the car park. For some reason Billie felt only relief at disappearing from her own wedding.

Marina was giving orders. "Oscar and Antony, you make a chair seat for her and carry her to the ambulance. I better go with her. Antony, you stay with your guests."

"Oh Antony," Angela breathed. "How awful for you. I'll help you as much as I can."

Billie was soon sitting in the ambulance heading for the local hospital."

"Don't try to talk dear," Marina said. "I can see it's hurting you. We'll soon get some help."

"Wedding or no, there's a two-hour wait to see the doctor," the receptionist told them with a hint of relish. The next couple of hours were spent with Marina pushing Billie in wheelchair from waiting room to waiting room, first to get an X ray and then to have it read. On the way she managed to get a couple of paracetamol for the pain.

Over time it did begin to subside and Billie was relieved when the junior doctor told her that he believed she had only sprained her ankle as there was no sign of an actual break.

"Well, that's a relief," Marina said when Billie emerged from the consulting room. Outside, a porter in a brown coat was waiting for her.

"This is Billie," Marina told him, standing up to push the wheelchair.

"She's to go down the corridor to the specialist," the porter said. "Sorry, adult patient only. You wait here, Mum, please."

"OK. You'll feel better soon darling." Marina sat down and picked up the two year old copy of *Hampshire Field* she had been reading.

The porter pushed Billie along a series of corridors.

"It's a very long way to the specialist isn't it?" she commented.

"Sorry, it is a bit."

He ushered her through a hanging plastic draught excluder into an ambulance bay and up a ramp into the ambulance. "Sorry madam, just as a security precaution I have to take a picture of you now." he pulled a Canon sureshot out of his pocket and fired off a couple of pictures of her.

As he shut the door behind her, Billie was saying: "You didn't say I was going in an ambulance..." The ambulance was already revving up.

"Goodness, what a state the NHS is in," Billie thought to herself. "You hear stories like this but you don't quite believe them. I wonder where I'm going? They ought to have told Marina to come with me..."

"Driver!" she called, looking through the window into the cab. The driver turned round and with a shock she saw it was Rick.

"Rick!" she screeched. "What's happening! Where are you taking me?"

"I'm rescuing you" he said calmly.

"You what? Why!"

"Because you can't be allowed to marry him. ."

"But he loves me..."

"Frankly this isn't about him. It's about us. Last time we met, you made me really angry. I was furious with you for weeks. I even stalked you. I knew you were in Ian's that time - so I tipped Beattie off that you had a handle on his story."

"Well it didn't do him much good."

"No. But he's all right now, more or less. Out of hospital."

"It's Ian I feel sorry for."

"Oh come on. A couple of years in rehab are probably what he needs after all those pills he's popped. It'll save Xavier the cost of a year at the Priory. Stop changing the subject. Look I thought about leaving you alone. But then I started to remember that you had told me that you love me."

"Love you, you byline thief!"

"This isn't just about you making the wrong choice, it's about me too. I don't know when I would ever meet someone I care about as much as you. I don't believe there's another girl for me round the corner. I think you only get at the most a couple of chances in life to find the sort of thing we've got. I need to talk to you, I want you to think about what you're doing."

"How did you find me?"

"I knew you were getting married today. I was so screwed up about it I didn't know what to do but I decided to go into work."

"You're still at Global?"

"Yes, I weathered the storm. The ambulance press office told us about your accident. It's a great story you know - skydiving bride breaks ankle. The guy who was doing the wedding video's made an absolute fortune already. He's practically hysterical with joy. The news crews want it for the funny.

"There are TV cameras outside the hospital now waiting for you."

"Anyway I seized the chance to come down here. I wasn't quite sure what I was going to do but I thought maybe there was a chance of finding you and making you see sense. I think your mother will be relieved. She thinks you're making a mistake."

"How do you know what she thinks?"

"I saw her in the waiting room. You never told me that Marina Wilson was your mother. I think she's great. I took her course on feminine sexuality at Uni."

"Really?"

"I got a merit.

"Well done. Did you discuss this 'rescue' with her?"

"Em, no. Although she may have guessed that I had come to try and persuade you to change your mind. The snapper came in and brought you out for a pic and then I seized the moment. I had found this unwanted ambulance lying about."

"You could go to jail for stealing an ambulance."

"I'm not. It's borrowed. I'll take it back."

"What about me. What about if I want you to take me back to Antony?"

The ambulance pulled over and Rick climbed into the back.

"Do you?"

Billie opened her arms to him. "Actually, no, I don't."

For a while, nothing else mattered.

Until that is, the door of the ambulance jerked open and a familiar figure holding a flashing camera got a shot of the skydiving, runaway bride snogging a bogus porter in the back of a hijacked NHS ambulance.

Lovely," Barmy said. "Hold that pose."

# ACKNOWLEDGEMENTS

Thanks to kind James Hale, my agent who died before I completed this. Thanks also to Susan Kemp, Tom Bancroft, Maisie Hennessey and Euan Ferguson for reading it and giving me feedback. Thanks also to Alistair Sim, Kate Tregaskis, Fiona Parker and Mary Jane Bennett for proof reading.Thanks to Douglas Dunn and John Burnside my creative writing tutors at St Andrews University where I began this for their encouragement. Thanks particularly to my mother Sandra Kemp and my husband Rob Bruce for their support, mainly in helping me to find time for this.

In loving memory of Arnold Kemp, my father.

Thanks to Kate George for the cover design and to Joni di Placido who modelled for it.

Printed in the United States
55209LVS00002B/136-174